Chapter 1

Jake Stilton, former detective first grade of the Las Vegas PD, recent resident of Liar's Gulch, Wyoming, and perpetually errant son of disgraced senator, Aloysius Stilton, stared down the horse who refused to move.

Not one single inch.

Not for kind words.

Not for more deliberate commands.

And not for sugar cubes.

If he wasn't so irritated he might have laughed at how much of a kindred spirit he was attempting to familiarize himself with the ranch, their roomy training paddock and the rehabilitation program they'd created here in their small corner of the world.

"He doesn't like you."

The words were spoken with that uniquely distinct ennui only a fifteen-year-old could utter, and he turned to stare at Olivia, his friend Trace Withrow's recently adopted daughter and, much to his endless surprise, one of Jake's most favorite humans to walk the earth.

"Not many do."

"Yeah, but he really doesn't like you. Want me to try?"

Jake nodded, well aware he was going to regret giving

up his leadership with the horse on these necessary training exercises. "Give it a shot."

He kept a close eye on Olivia, ready and willing to move in to help her if things got out of control, but equally willing to give her the room to try.

She was lanky, the tails of her flannel shirt flapping in the whippy fall wind. He'd been here since early spring and despite not having experienced a full year of seasons, had expected this cooler weather far more than the hot summer they'd just finished. His exceptionally well-trained K-9, Hogan, was enjoying the cooler weather as well.

Even now, his German shepherd had his head on his paws on the far side of the paddock, watching the entire exchange with a mix of what looked like canine amusement and extreme boredom, the breeze blowing the tips of his ears where they pointed toward the sky.

Olivia fished a few sugar cubes out of her pocket, placing them in her flat palm as she extended her hand. "You're safe here."

The large quarter horse didn't move, but Jake saw the distinct quiver of his lips as he stared down at Olivia and the proffered treat.

"I wasn't safe before I came here, but I am now," Olivia continued on, no sign of that ennui in evidence. "You are, too."

A hard clench at the truth of her words squeezed his chest, the reality of her life before continuing to haunt her no matter how well she was adjusting to her new one.

Don't pretend you can't relate.

That inward taunt was swift and immediate, a reminder they'd all come here to heal in one way or another.

Him.

The kid.

"You want to talk about it?"

"Don't you want to finish breakfast?" Caroline asked.

"I've got a hearty constitution. You won't spoil my appetite," Jake insisted.

"Your father was involved in a lot more than the trafficking ring that brought him down."

"I can't say that comes as a shock. But there was a thorough investigation after the trafficking ring came down. What's changed? Nothing else came to light during his trial."

"More has. Your father's been operating under the protection of a cabal of several wealthy donors who wanted a puppet in Washington."

"Clearly they're not getting what they paid for."

"That's the problem, Jake. They're not. And your father's crimes with a local lowlife put their years of investment at risk."

"What does this have to do with me?"

"They want payment, Jake. They'll do anything to get it."

"That's my father's problem."

"If what I believe is true, it's yours, too. They want revenge and you're at the top of the list."

Dear Reader,

Welcome back to Liar's Gulch, Wyoming. The Withrow ranch has been busy, its inhabitants settling into their new lives now that Trace and Garner Withrow have both married their loves.

No one's happier for the lot of them than Jake Stilton, the third member of their ragtag band of justice seekers. The former Las Vegas PD detective and K-9 expert has been in Wyoming for a little over six months, finally healing from the trauma of his father's political disgrace and the subsequent blowback that fell onto Jake in Vegas.

He's focused on the horses and, when needed, supporting Trace and Garner with the occasional mission to help someone who needs it. Little does he expect the next person who needs help will be himself.

But when the woman he left behind in Vegas, Assistant District Attorney Caroline Esterson, arrives unannounced, Jake's pulled straight back into everything he thought he left. Only someone's very interested in cleaning up the mess made by Jake's father...and removing anyone who might know anything.

Caroline's struggled to get over Jake, but when she learns he's in danger she has to warn him. Because the person cleaning up loose ends doesn't care how much distance Jake's put between his new life and his old one. They just want him gone.

I hope you enjoy the passion and the danger. My thanks for coming on this adventure with me!

Best,

Addison Fox

RENEGADE K-9 RECKONING

ADDISON FOX

ROMANTIC SUSPENSE

Harlequin® ROMANTIC SUSPENSE™

Recycling programs for this product may not exist in your area.

ISBN-13: 978-1-335-47196-3

Renegade K-9 Reckoning

Harlequin Enterprises ULC
22 Adelaide St. West, 41st Floor
Toronto, Ontario M5H 4E3, Canada
www.Harlequin.com

HarperCollins Publishers
Macken House, 39/40 Mayor Street Upper,
Dublin 1, D01 C9W8, Ireland
www.HarperCollins.com

Printed in Lithuania

1 2 3 4 5 6 7 8 9 10 LIT 28 27 26 25

Addison Fox is a lifelong romance reader, addicted to happy-ever-afters. She loves writing about romance as much as reading it, from cowboys to cops to those committed to making the world a better place. Addison lives in Illinois with her family. You can find her at www.addisonfox.com or across a variety of social channels.

Books by Addison Fox

Harlequin Romantic Suspense

Wyoming Warriors

Renegade Reunion
Renegade Baby Protector
Renegade K-9 Reckoning

New York Harbor Patrol

Danger in the Depths
Peril in the Shallows
Threats in the Deep

The Coltons of New York

Under Colton's Watch

The Coltons of Owl Creek

Guarding Colton's Secrets

Visit the Author Profile page at Harlequin.com.

For Beth, Denise, Jen and Regina.

Seriously fun travel partners.
Extraordinary theme-park planners. Dearest friends.

Here's the One Where They All Get a Dedication.

His best friend, Garner, and Garner's brother, Trace.

And the families both were making now that women who'd been sad histories in their lives had come back in somewhat spectacular fashion.

It was a reminder that they'd all come to this place in the middle of nowhere determined to make a new start. For his friends, that start was full of hope and promise and renewal.

As for himself?

He counted himself lucky to be here and had grown content to leave it at that.

Since that one shifted a bit too close to both introspection and maudlin musings, Jake kept his focus on Olivia and off his past.

The kid still hadn't removed her hand, instead leaving it and her gentle words as a sort of outstretched welcome to the horse.

Which made it that much more of a triumph when that large chestnut-colored body took a few steps forward, his tongue delicately lapping up the treat.

The animal was what Jake had always considered the standard color of horses, with a deep-colored coat and black mane and tail. Since coming to Wyoming, he'd learned a whole host of other colors, from bay to roan to something Trace had referred to as cremello when they were looking at some stock a few weeks before.

That horse had found a home before they could bid on it, but they'd gotten this beauty standing before Olivia instead.

"You know, kid. He still doesn't have a name."

"If we leave it up to Jordan he'll be named Horsey Shark."

Jake couldn't hold back the commiserating smile with Olivia. Garner's toddler daughter, Jordan, was obsessed with an online video that seemed to run on a loop inside the house. One that had earwormed its way into all their heads.

When he'd found himself humming it while feeding Hogan the day before, he'd recognized just how far gone he was.

"I don't think she's old enough to get a vote," he finally said, far more diplomatically than he felt on that subject.

"You think I do?" Olivia's eyes widened.

"I think so. You're the one who's getting him to respond to you. And you're the one who's been out here with him every day making him feel welcome. Seems only fair you name him."

"I've been thinking about Orlando."

"Like Florida?" Jake asked, somewhat surprised at the choice.

"No, um, from *As You Like It*. You know, Shakespeare. Nic, I mean Mom, and I were watching one of those movies from when she was a kid and it was part of the story."

If shark songs had become a part of his daily existence, he'd diligently avoided the teen movie fest Nic had introduced Olivia to over the past few months. Mia, Garner's new wife, had gotten into the swing of things and after you added in Jordan's nanny, Astrid, and Bernice and Bennie, the couple who'd helped care for Jordan before they came to Wyoming, the TV had been overrun with love stories after dinner.

He, Trace, Garner and Bennie had revolted by working on the small guesthouse he was turning into his own digs on the property when Nic's seemingly endless supply of old DVDs came out.

"It's a good name."

Olivia turned toward the horse, her face settling into firm lines. "What do you think, Orlando?"

The horse's ears perked up, twitching when Olivia used the name once more.

And then he bent his head, allowing her to stroke the velvet softness of his nose.

Olivia's smile was nearly blinding as she took another step closer, patting Orlando on his neck and bonding in the moment. Jake marveled at the small step forward.

The subtle reminder that there were *always* pathways forward, even when they seemed impossible to find.

He nearly took his own step closer, determined to double down on that same gentle acceptance that seemed to be working, when he heard the distinct slam of a car door. He turned in the direction of the large parking area at the end of the driveway that abutted the paddock.

And stopped dead in his tracks when he saw the woman who stood beside the car, sunglasses shielding the eyes he knew were a blazing blue.

Caroline Esterson stared at the tall, lanky man across the roughly twenty yards that separated them and knew that subtle stillness as he stood and watched her was an act.

In all reality, he was a predator, even if he did have a petite teenager and a horse by his side instead of a lethal gun in hand. He still had the lethal-looking dog beside him at the ready, though.

A subtle shiver raced down her spine and she wasn't entirely sure if it was fear or gratitude for those attributes she could catalog so easily.

Not that she had a right to any of her opinions.

Or memories.

But she had them all the same.

It was one brief interlude. Then you two went back to hating each other.

She reminded herself of those twin facts often enough, she'd have thought it would have sunk in by now.

Since there was no place for standing there staring at each other—especially since she suspected that preternatural stillness was an act he'd perfected—she moved toward the paddock.

She wouldn't give him a bright, soothing smile, though.

Those she'd been saving for herself and the pep talks she forced herself to listen to each morning.

The dog, Hogan, that Jake was never without, stared up at her. His canine visage remained bored but his tail thumped on the ground, that subtle and unexpected show of support pushing her spine a bit straighter.

"Jake. Good morning."

"Caroline." He nodded his head before his gaze drifted to the girl behind him. "Do you think you can take Orlando back to his stall?"

"I—." The kid looked about to argue before she nodded. "Sure."

Jake directed a command and a hand signal at his hairy faithful companion, and the dog was up and trotting after the girl in a matter of seconds.

"That's a big horse."

"She can handle him. And if she can't, Hogan will let me know."

Something erupted low in her belly. While other circumstances might have suggested the stirrings of desire, Caroline opted to believe it was nerves and the sudden recognition that she had made it here.

To him.

Finally.

But it also meant now she had to do all the things she'd come to do.

With a skill she'd honed far too well in the courtroom, she procrastinated, keeping her gaze directed on the retreating form of the kid for a few beats longer.

"Why are you here?"

She was surprised he spoke first but her response—the fluent smart-ass they managed around each other—came winging out of her mouth. "To say hello?"

"Yeah. Right."

Although he didn't say it, Caroline heard the unspoken add on of *Strike One* as plain as day.

"I could ask you the same question."

Jake only stared at her, even as the obvious notes of *Strike Two* hummed between them.

"I don't answer to the Las Vegas DA's office any longer," he finally said, only after allowing the tension to unfurl between them several beats more.

Undeterred, she pressed on. "I have information you might be interested in."

"There's not a single thing I can think of that fits that bill—" He leaned forward ever so slightly, his complete sentence distinctly incomplete.

Caroline fought to stand perfectly still instead of squirm under that focus.

Well, that, and the subtle heat that drifted off his impressive chest.

"Counselor."

Despite the flat tone and not-so-subtle layer of mocking, his steel-blue gaze sparked with interest. Caroline saw it in the slight crinkle around his eyes and the subtle tilt of his eyebrows he hadn't managed to suppress.

Like Hogan's tail thump, she took it as a good sign. Especially since Detective Jake Stilton was known for having the best poker face in the Las Vegas PD.

Since it was a skill that had been honed by more than a few of his colleagues in Sin City, his mastery of that bland indifference stood out.

Jake's the best. You need to talk to someone, you go find him.

Her grizzled mentor had encouraged Caroline to seek Jake out for a trial she'd faced that hadn't only seemed full of holes but also actually had so many of them you could shine a light through each and every one.

Jake had been that light.

He hadn't wanted to get dragged into someone else's poorly handled case. He'd made that more than obvious, but he'd helped her all the same. It was a trait she admired the hell out of, even when the two of them could barely breathe the same air without wanting to kill each other.

Or destroy each other in far more interesting ways…

Once again, heat licked across her skin as those memories that were never too far from the surface electrified her nerve endings.

What they'd had was technically not a one-night stand since it had lasted a full weekend, but Caroline had wasted far too many brain cells reliving those heated moments together.

And with everything just fizzling after, she'd ruined any shot at repeating the experience.

Since he'd dismissed her problems, Caroline figured she'd use that to her advantage and see just how indifferent he really was. Shifting her attention toward the large barn the kid had gone to with the horse and Hogan, she said, "This is a nice place."

When he said nothing, she added, "It's a far cry from Las Vegas."

"Most everything is."

That large frame was still preternaturally still when she turned back to face him. A light breeze ruffled the ends of his hair he kept a bit too long, and those sharp eyes still remained immovable on her.

"Is she yours?"

"Who?" Confusion flashed—quick and immediate—in his eyes. "The horse?"

"That teenage girl who just walked off with a horse four times her size."

"She's my friend's daughter."

Relief slammed through her in waves so stark she nearly lost her breath. And had to admit to herself she'd braced far harder for him to say yes than she cared to admit. "She thinks you're pretty great."

"The feeling's mutual."

Jake took a few steps back. "Why don't you just come out with it. I'm not some jury you're trying to lead down a primrose path. And I may not know you well, but I know you well enough that you won't leave until you tell me what you came here for."

"Your father's in trouble."

The hard, bitter laugh wasn't a surprise, but the utter disdain that painted his features was. She'd have expected to see anger carve its way into that firm, stubble-lined jaw.

What she hadn't anticipated was the absolute sadness that seemed to settle over him like a blanket.

"What has good old Al done now?"

"Rumor is running high he got in with the wrong crowd."

"Running with the wrong crowd is my father's specialty. I'm sorry you came over seven hundred miles to tell me this. Especially because last time I checked, we still get phone service up here in the Wild West."

"Would you have taken my call?"

The question was deliberate and she'd bet Jake knew damn well why she'd asked.

It was why she'd gotten into her car and driven all night to get here.

It was also why she was willing to face her own sizable baggage to come up here and speak to him.

And even with that level of understanding and expectation, his quickly winged back "no," still cut her off at the knees.

Would you have taken my call?

Despite the fact that his resounding *no* still hung between them, Caroline's question slammed between Jake's ears like a pinball.

He'd have wanted to talk to her; that was for damn sure.

But would he have?

It pissed him off that he'd likely have caved then.

It pissed him off even more that he already felt the subtle clues that he was going to cave now.

Hadn't it always been that way?

The woman intrigued him beyond his better judgment and had since the first time they'd met, shooting hostile barbs at each other over a breakfast of steak and eggs at an off-Strip all-you-can-eat buffet.

Actually, the steak had been for him. She'd primly sipped black coffee and picked at a few scrambled eggs.

That first time she'd come to him she'd wanted his help with collecting evidence on a hotshot drug dealer who kept slipping through the system. Despite his own desire to get the man behind bars, he'd told her it was a fool's errand, the dealer's cadre of loyal foot soldiers ensuring he operated above the law.

Unable to resist the determination in that earnest blue

gaze, he'd helped anyway, finding the evidence she needed to make her case, capped off with Hogan's undeniable find of a cache of heroin stowed in a warehouse just shy of the Vegas-Henderson border.

Not that it would have mattered. The merger decades ago between the Las Vegas PD and the Clark County sheriff's office had ensured he could have crossed that boundary and still been well within his jurisdiction.

But she'd been right.

And that ridiculous streak of determination he was hard-pressed to say no to had come to him again six months later, detailing a prostitution ring that was actually a human trafficking organization. He'd helped there, too, wading in once he'd gotten nothing substantial in the way of help from the captain of the vice squad.

Only the joke had been on him in the end.

Because he'd gotten Caroline the evidence Vice chose to ignore, but he'd gotten a hell of a lot more.

The knowledge that his father was aiding and abetting the entire operation, rolling in profits in exchange for using his influence to eliminate suspicion on the perpetrators.

It was only then that he understood the world was far worse—and considerably more corrupt—than he'd ever imagined.

Hard-won wisdom, his grandmother would have called it.

All Jake had figured was he'd spent his career observing the worst in people, never actually realizing he felt so comfortable with the work because he'd come from the same.

And then Caroline had showed up.

Bright and fresh and standing outside the courtroom where his father had been indicted. She'd extended a hand and invited him to drinks at a watering hole about a mile away.

"I don't do lawyer bars," Jake had muttered, even as he took her hand.

"I don't, either."

"Then why are you taking me to one?"

He had no idea why he'd taken her hand. Even less why he was allowing her to walk him out of the courthouse. But her hand fit perfectly in his and her dark hair framed her face as she glanced back over her shoulder at him as they exited the building.

"I'm taking you to my favorite dive in Vegas. Even the poorest lawyer working on a first year's public defender's salary wouldn't be caught dead in this place."

"I guess that's all right."

"The wine is pure crap but they have surprisingly good beer. All on tap."

"I'm in."

Caroline hadn't said anything else—likely a record for the two of them—but she hadn't let go of his hand, either.

And in a matter of hours he was inviting her home, claiming he needed to get Hogan fed before they could continue their evening bar hopping and splitting the car service bills by each leg of the trip.

Only they hadn't called a car. And he'd barely gotten the dog outside and fed before he was dragging her up into his arms, positioning her on the counter as they tore each other's clothes off.

Bone-melting counter sex had morphed into a few deeply interesting hours on his couch before they'd ended up in his bedroom. Other than taking care of the dog and calling in takeout since the contents of his fridge were bachelor-cliché empty, they'd spent the entire weekend together.

When they took a car on Sunday back to the bar where they'd left hers on Friday, he'd considered asking her to dinner that week. By the time she drove him to the courthouse parking lot to pick up his car, the air between them was so thick a jackhammer couldn't have broken through.

Whatever happy bubble had descended over them through the weekend had somehow hardened into an ugly shell of reality by the time the courthouse came back into view. And whatever thoughts Jake had about asking her out or continuing whatever had exploded between them faded as he got out of her car to get into his.

It had felt like a switch flipping, one more example of how he wasn't truly cut out for relationships.

And in the year since, he'd only ever taken solace in the reality that he was right.

Whatever halcyon moments they'd shared inside the bubble couldn't keep the ugliness away.

Nor could it hide all that was to come.

His father's fall from grace.

The collective fish eye that kept casting his way from his colleagues as his father's trial progressed.

And the reality that he was ultimately under suspicion, too, no one entirely sure he wasn't tainted by Senator Stilton's crimes.

He'd cleared that hurdle and was already thinking about his next gig when Garner Withrow's call came out of the blue, inviting him to Liar's Gulch and the horse rescue he and his brother started.

With his natural love of animals, a ranch in the middle of nowhere that was as physically different from the Las Vegas Strip as a person could get felt like a good idea. But in the months since Jake had arrived, he could admit to himself it had been a very good idea.

The ranch was exactly as advertised—they did train as well as rehabilitate horses—but it also fronted a group of people committed to finding justice for others where needed. Garner's career in the Navy SEALs and Trace's in the CIA had made them perfect for taking on personal jobs that they got to choose themselves.

No big missions.

No government interference.

No risk that others were pulling the strings from behind the scenes.

Individual work that actually helped people.

Jake had only just arrived in Wyoming when they helped Trace's new wife, Nic, with finding and rescuing Olivia. He'd then supported his friend when Garner's old flame, Mia, showed back up with their daughter, Jordan, in tow. Her role as analyst on Garner's last mission gone horribly wrong had led her to keep the baby out of sight until she could figure out who was behind the death of three SEALs.

It had been satisfying to take down the tech mogul behind those deaths, Theo Stockton, with Garner and Mia. That mission had been oddly cathartic, too, especially since his old man had been a huge supporter of Stockton's company.

They'd taken on two other jobs since he'd been here. An older couple in Liar's Gulch were victims of a phishing scheme, and he'd used his police training to help reverse engineer the crime and lead the county sheriff, Dawson Kane, to the perpetrators who were working just over the Idaho border.

He'd also supported Nic when she'd quietly hunted down information on Olivia's mother. The woman had been responsible for putting her child in danger, and he'd gladly run down as much dirt on the woman as he could find. More than enough to ensure the court ruled in favor of Nic and Trace's adoption of the child who already wanted the life they offered her.

It was all a far cry from where he'd come, but his new life felt right. Solid.

And most of all, it *fit*.

Which was the lone point that finally sank in. This wasn't the life he'd known but it was a life he was building for himself, and she had no right to come in and screw it up.

"Why are you really here?"

"I told you. Your father got in with the wrong crowd."

"Old news."

Caroline stared at him, considering. That intense gaze was something he'd never been able to look away from, and it was humbling to realize that despite almost a year passing since he'd last seen her, he was helpless to look away now.

"Please tell me you're not so naive as to think your father's big disgrace was limited to some low-level players in Las Vegas?"

"I stopped worrying a while ago about whatever choices dear old Dad makes."

Her eyebrows shot up. "You don't care?"

"I said *worry*, but sure, we can go with *care* if that makes you feel better."

That subtle tension that had always characterized their interactions faded as Caroline moved closer. Jake didn't want to think about the way his body warmed or how he caught the light scent of her—a surprisingly arousing cross between strawberries and freshly sharpened pencils.

Nothing about that should be sexy, yet it was.

It made no sense.

It never had.

But rational or not, his body wasn't immune to her nearness.

"I'm here because it's bad, Jake."

With that same sinking sensation he'd had all those months ago sitting across from her in a noisy Las Vegas buffet, Jake recognized the truth.

He was going to help her again.

"Bad how?"

Chapter 2

Caroline recognized the gamble she was taking coming to Jake's turf. Entering his world was fraught with risk for both of them, and while the temptation to see him ran as high as it always had, she'd never wanted to come here.

Her plan—solid as it was—had been to keep him ignorant of all that was going on in his father's case. Jake had suffered enough at the exposure of his father's crimes and she refused to drag him back into things.

Especially because she feared his duty-and-honor streak would drag him down a path he'd never escape.

Her handy plan came to an abrupt halt when a man attacked her three nights ago as she headed for her car after work. Only then had she finally admitted to herself that what was going on had far more sinister tentacles than she'd first realized.

And that, maybe, it was possible she was in over her head.

The mounting evidence against Aloysius Stilton had been managed by a small team of prosecutors, working in tandem with the federal government. Caroline wasn't assigned to the work, but an anonymous tip had proved too tempting to ignore and she'd gone and tugged the lead anyway.

Only to find the corruption went back a lot further than she'd imagined.

"Can we go somewhere private to talk?"

Jake briefly glanced around the paddock, a wry smile on his face. "God's country isn't private enough for you?"

"I was thinking I could buy you lunch and walk you through it all. I saw a diner when I drove through town."

It smacked a bit too close to their very first meeting over breakfast, but Caroline persisted anyway. She'd always believed food bonded people.

Sex does, too, her conscience whispered.

Since that avenue wasn't up for discussion, no matter how much her body hummed to life each time she looked at him, Caroline deftly ignored those whispers.

Their lone weekend was a magical interlude in a personal life that was basically a sex desert.

Which was the real danger in coming here.

A prosecutor needed calm reason on their side, and every bit of hers flew straight away whenever she got within six feet of Jake Stilton.

But she needed his help. And if her suspicions were correct, he needed hers, too.

Even if her lunch invitation was still hanging wide-open right here in the middle of the paddock.

With a glance toward the barn, Jake nodded. "Let me go check on Olivia and put Hogan up and we can leave."

Without waiting for her to agree or disagree, he turned and headed for the barn, following the same direction child, horse and dog had headed off to earlier.

The urge to call out his lack of hospitality was strong, and Caroline almost called him back to ask for a glass of tepid tap water just to bait him, but held off at the last minute. The verbal sparring had always been part of their repertoire, but it had never included that desolate look in his eyes. One that tugged at places she kept deeply buried, refusing to look too closely at her feelings.

She avoided thinking about him as an act of self-preservation. Their weekend of amazing sex and even more amazing personal connection had ended as abruptly as it started, and she hated her role in that.

How quiet it had gotten between them as they took a taxi from his place to get her car left behind Friday night in the bar parking lot. The even more awkward quiet that had descended as she'd driven him to his at the courthouse.

It was like a demarcation, those car rides giving the space for reality to slam back in.

In the time since, she'd berated herself that maybe they should have just left in opposite directions and had a chance to salvage more time with each other. If they'd only done that, retreating to their respective corners after all that *connection*, perhaps they could have had a date later that week or made plans to meet up for lunch.

Or, ya know, just had more sex.

But reality had come back, and Jake had been forced to work through the embarrassment of his father's fall from grace as well as a review of his own work through Internal Affairs.

Caroline had kept tabs on all of it, working her sources and well-honed ability to exchange gossip as a means to finding out what was going on. *Quid pro quo* might be illegal as a business strategy but it worked incredibly well when it came to earning social capital.

The unbidden thoughts of their weekend together might be ruthlessly tamped down each time they filled her mind, but the need to understand what was happening to Jake professionally was non-negotiable as far as Caroline was concerned.

What she hadn't banked on all these months later was to see how he'd changed. The man who'd left Las Vegas six months ago was too thin, his blue eyes haunted as his powerful, whipcord body edged toward gaunt.

The man who'd stood before her in the fresh Wyoming air still carried that haunted look in his eyes—especially if you knew to look—but he'd put weight back on. His skin was tanned, with a healthy, fresh-faced look that was reassuring.

And far too enticing for her own good.

"Hello?"

The gentle voice pulled her out of her musings, and she turned to find an older woman with a kind, careworn face waving to her from the large parking area that spanned the distance between the paddock and the house. In deference to the cold, the woman had on a vivid red coat that perfectly complimented her dark skin. In a move Caroline saw as pure stylish genius, the older woman managed to telegraph warm grandmotherly vibes with hints of sassy talk-show hostess.

Although there wasn't a single hint of hostility, Caroline wasn't fooled that the kind visage hid anything but steel.

"Hello. I'm Caroline." She walked toward the woman, her hand extended in greeting. "I know Jake from when we worked together in Las Vegas."

The mention of Jake seemed to thaw the subtle ice, and a warm smile quickly appeared as the other woman shook her hand, matched by a twinkle in her deep brown eyes.

"I'm Bernice. And you're a long way from Vegas, sweetie."

"Don't I know it."

If Bernice was surprised by the tart response, she didn't show it. Instead, she gestured toward the car. "I'm heading for the market to pick up a few last things for dinner. I'll make sure there's enough for you to join us."

"Oh, I'm not—" Caroline broke off, not sure what to say. She had a room in the very small three-story hotel in town. Rumors were that it was haunted but she'd booked a few days anyway, not willing to risk having nowhere to go after arriving here.

For all her deep-seated need to believe Jake would talk to her, there was the equally large risk he'd have grunted a hello and sent her on her way.

Bernice waved a hand, undeterred. "You'll stay and enjoy my steak enchiladas with the family."

"That sounds delicious."

"They're one of my specialties. And since Olivia asked for it, well, that child pretty much gets whatever she asks for." Bernice gave a quick wink even as she beamed. "And since she's a growing teenager I can use that as an excuse to spoil her endlessly."

Although Caroline had made a mental note earlier to ask Jake more questions about the people he lived with, it was obvious they'd made a family. This woman's sheer delight in the teen from earlier in the paddock was the height of grandmotherly support and love.

"I'll look forward to it, then."

And she would. Home-cooked meals weren't part of her personal repertoire. She ate as a source of fuel and little else. Salads she grabbed at the office cafeteria were a mainstay, as was whatever takeout she managed to grab on the way home.

She was…a desert in more ways than one, Caroline admitted to herself. Somehow, the work she loved had become her life in a way that was all consuming. It had built for a long time, the increasing responsibilities coming from the proof that she could handle the work with deft skill.

All that responsibility had felt good at first. She'd never been short on a solid streak of self-assurance, and joining the DA's office had felt right. A path to use her skills for good and an ever-changing caseload that kept her mind active and busy.

Only lately, especially since Jake had left Las Vegas, all that pride felt misplaced and rather empty.

She was damn close to hung up on him—and she'd own that—but it wasn't the reason for the disillusionment.

The work was a treadmill that never seemed to produce different outcomes.

And now?

The question hovered in her mind as Jake came strolling from the paddock.

Now, she feared, the work had turned deadly.

Jake avoided ordering the steak and eggs—too on the nose for him—but he did dig into his Western omelet with relish. Caroline had the coffee he'd rarely seen her without and had stuck true to her two scrambled eggs.

He was oddly pleased to see she'd added bacon this time.

And damn it, why was he comparing this to their first meeting?

Or even *remembering* their first meeting.

They'd exchanged stilted pleasantries on the drive to the diner. He'd briefly considered driving separately into the small strip that was considered Main Street in Liar's Gulch, but was ultimately too curious about why she was there. And when he'd suggested they take his SUV, she hadn't said no.

The limited small talk they had shared was about mutual acquaintances and the cases she'd worked the past six months since he'd been gone.

He was pleased that they'd closed in the prosecution's favor on a bookie with a side drug business Jake had captured a few months before leaving town. One of her colleagues had also effectively prosecuted a money-laundering case one of Jake's first partners had captured after a long, two-year sting operation.

"So far as I can tell from our catchup on the ride over here, justice still turns and sometimes in the good guy's favor," he started in after swallowing a large bite of his omelet.

"Sometimes it does."

"And a lot of times it doesn't." He caught her gaze and the subtle acknowledgment that the time had come to tell him why she was here. "You want to talk about it?"

"Don't you want to finish breakfast?"

"I've got a hearty constitution. You won't spoil my appetite."

He wasn't sure why he grinned at that but something about the semi-snarky response felt right.

At least it did when it was with her.

He also didn't miss the subtle smile that tilted the corner of her lips.

Whatever they were with each other, *unaffected* wasn't it.

It was both the frustration of spending time with her and the odd electric charge he got when he was with her.

Relationships had never been his strong suit but he'd had serious girlfriends through the years. He'd progressed to sharing an apartment with one woman just after college and had briefly considered engagement to another about five years ago before dropping the idea.

He cared. More than cared, he'd realized. But he hadn't been in love.

Or in that place where he actually saw himself binding his life with another person.

And all that was before his father had disgraced himself and their family with his crimes.

"Your father was involved in a lot more than the trafficking ring that brought him down."

It wasn't a surprise. Or it shouldn't have been, Jake admitted to himself. But no matter how casual he acted about his father's crimes, nothing changed the fact that he also wanted to believe somewhere deep down inside, Al Stilton was a good guy.

"I can't say that comes as a shock. But there was a thorough investigation after the trafficking ring came down. What's changed?"

Caroline nodded as she pulled her coffee mug toward herself, warming her hands on the sides of the thick ceramic. His gaze caught on her long, slim fingers, remembering how he'd watched those same hands stroke their way across his chest in the early-morning light.

It was a jolt he didn't need.

A memory he'd ruthlessly eradicated.

Or thought he had.

In frustration over the fact those memories still lingered despite his every effort, his voice was harsher than he intended when he added, "Nothing else came to light during his trial."

"More has. Or it's known to a select group of people. Your father's been operating under the protection of a cabal of several wealthy donors who wanted a puppet in Washington."

He snorted at that. "Clearly, they're not getting what they paid for."

"That's the problem, Jake. They're not. And your father's crimes with a local lowlife put their years of investment at risk."

"What does this have to do with me?"

"They want payment, Jake. They'll do anything to get it."

"That's my father's problem."

"If what I believe is true, it's yours, too." Her gaze never wavered.

It never dipped to her coffee or shifted to look away before she spoke.

"They want revenge and you're at the top of the list."

Clearly, they're not getting what they paid for.

Jake had no idea, Caroline thought, just how close he'd hit the mark.

Even if that stubborn set of his jaw and distinct notes of dismissal in his tone suggested he didn't believe her.

"I've worked in law enforcement a long time. Vendettas work far better in Hollywood than the actual reality of hunting down other human beings."

"You're an asset. And you have more skills than the average person. They could use those skills."

Their waitress chose that moment to come over and refill their coffees. They waited until she moved off, those few beats giving Caroline a chance to marshal her points.

She knew them all, had practiced them endlessly.

Why did they feel so much different saying them to his face? Those sharp, blue eyes steady on her.

"In what world does anyone think I'd fall in line for that?"

"People do a lot of things when pressure's placed on them. Pressure that gives them no way out."

"That's not me."

"They've been involved for a long time. You have no idea what information they had or what strings they'll know how to pull."

Although his expression hadn't changed in any way, Caroline got the sense she was losing him. So she shifted her approach, framing her argument in a new way.

"Why do you think you moved all those years ago? Your father was a man with growing influence in your home state, but suddenly you and your family were uprooted and moved to Nevada."

"A fact he explained to his constituents over and over. He felt he could make an impact in government and moved because of it. He's not the first person to do it."

"Who funded it? Why?"

"Donors. Again, Caroline, it's the way of the world. It can feel sordid at times, and I'm not here to argue that it isn't. But those choices weren't inherently wrong."

"They were motivated by something that was. Deeply wrong. And even more deeply rooted."

He pushed his empty plate to the side, his expression devoid of anything.

It was that blank slate that worried her more than anything else.

Whatever else hovered between the two of them, it was never blank.

Or flat.

Or empty of emotion.

"I'm right about this, Jake."

He shook his head. It was subtle, but it was an obvious expression of his denial. "About what, exactly? Some rich guys are pissed my dad failed them with a spectacular fall from grace? They're somehow sitting around plotting a mass act of revenge, assuming they could get away with it and force me to take part in it?"

"They've already started."

"Started how? Dad's in jail with no hope of getting out any time soon."

"Your mother's assets have all been frozen. Your brother's home was broken into when he was out of town."

His demeanor didn't change, but she didn't miss the way his fingers flexed into the tabletop where his hands had lain flat.

"They made their choices to support him. To follow him and to stand behind him."

The words were harsh but the gravel underneath them—emotions that were rockier than he'd likely ever want to admit, even to himself—was clear.

It was the lone clue she might have a shot at getting him to listen to her. "Your whereabouts were traced. People know where you are, Jake."

"I didn't make my departure a secret."

"I'm quite sure you didn't share a forwarding address."

That gravel grew even rockier as he persisted in his pushback. "I can take care of myself. We can take care of ourselves here."

Although Caroline didn't doubt that, the ranch hadn't been all that locked down when she drove up, either. There was no question her arrival had been captured on cameras but it wasn't like she'd had to pass that many barriers to get in.

Was that because she wasn't viewed as a threat?

Or because they didn't know there was one lurking?

"These threats are real. I know it. I've made it my business to know it."

"Why?"

Because I care.

Because I can't let it go.

Because...

"I can't let go of the fact that something's wrong. That it has been wrong all along."

"This isn't your battle. It never was."

She might not have been expecting a heap of gratitude, but flat dismissal hadn't factored in, either.

With it, her spine stiffened, that easy place where they snapped and snarled at each other a lot easier to find.

"How the hell would you know? You left."

"Yeah, I did. What did I have to stick around for?"

His voice never rose. No one in the diner would even know they were having an argument.

Yet, each word cut like he'd brandished a scalpel.

What did I have to stick around for?

Her.

Them.

The thing that never felt all the way done or dead between them.

Caroline wanted to scream all of it, but she didn't.

Nor did she even question herself any longer as to why she wanted him. Or why she could never shake her sadness that they couldn't find a way forward.

She might move seamlessly through life, morphing into whatever was needed in the moment, but she never lied to herself. And a very large part of her—the aching part she kept locked down tight—was heartbroken at all they'd missed out on through sheer, stubborn will and a fair streak of mutual idiocy.

But those regrets would have to be for a different time and place.

Right now, she needed to make him understand.

"You might have left, but I didn't. And the thug waiting for me outside my apartment the other night didn't waste time asking me questions."

Chapter 3

Raw, frigid cold gripped him with icy fingers. There was no other word for it as Caroline's comment sank in.

"You were attacked?"

Her eyes shuttered quickly, but not before Jake saw the fear as bleak and biting as the ice that still filled him.

"I got away."

He was already reaching for her, laying his hand over top of hers across the table. "What did he do?"

The mix of terror and fury was unlike anything he'd ever experienced before, and Jake fought to remain calm when all he really wanted to do was kill someone.

That anyone would dare touch her.

Caroline laid her hand over his, the warmth there doing nothing to assuage the cold fury. "I'm okay, Jake. The guy was waiting for me in my apartment parking lot. I am well trained in self-defense and I left him writhing on the floor with a nose spouting blood like a fountain."

It was a gruesome image but it went a long way toward easing the fist lodged in his gut.

Even as he hated that she'd been through it at all.

"Tell me the rest."

The instructions were terse but he added a small squeeze to her hand in reassurance.

"I've worked my contacts from the start of your father's arrest. I've handled enough high-profile cases to know how things work in town and who to pump for information."

"You do love befriending file clerks."

"I befriend everyone because I actually like everyone."

It was a trait that spoke volumes about who Caroline Esterson was as a woman. As a professional she was outstanding, but as a human she genuinely cared about others.

And no one was beneath her notice or interest.

"That extends to the feds I've worked with," she added on. That one was a bit of a dig since Jake had well and truly lived by the local versus federal mindset during his time as a detective.

A perspective that had made for a few interesting rounds of conversation with Trace and his wife, Nic, who were both ex-CIA operatives.

"We both know I don't work well with others. It's why I like dogs."

"Tell me about it."

The eye roll was expected and Jake took a small measure of satisfaction from that as he gave her hand one more light squeeze. "We digress. Go on."

"The rumors ramped back up about six weeks ago that new information was coming to light in your father's case. The trial's dragged on and there was growing concern he was going to slide or at least get out of jail while the legal process slowed to a crawl."

"Delays presumably paid for by someone?" Jake probed.

It wasn't unheard of and it would add to his ongoing speculation that the delays were purposeful. No matter how casually he'd presented his feelings to Caroline, he did care about his father's trial and had several search alerts set up to notify him of any news, no matter how small.

"That was my question. The feds have held tight to this one and add on the congressional reviews and the interstate trafficking charges and we've been shut out of most of it."

Whatever he was expecting from her, the professional distance she had from the case was a surprise. "You're not handling it?"

She shook her head. "No."

A slight grimace marred her lips before that calm visage slid right back into place.

Which might have been his biggest clue that she was in trouble. The woman could beat a world champion poker player at keeping a bland, unreadable expression.

The fact that she'd let him see even that small glimpse spoke volumes.

"Why aren't you a part of it?"

"I don't work every case that comes through the office."

She might not but she'd been a part of several high-profile ones, the DA well aware she was a rock star who knew how to win a case.

"Why not?"

"Again, Jake, I'm not on every case we prosecute."

He needed to leave it alone. No one singularly handled everything and she was no exception.

But something pushed him all the same.

"You show up here out of the blue, claiming any number of dangers, including a clear one to yourself. I deserve the whole truth."

That grimace was back, along with obvious resignation in her heavy sigh.

"There are suspicions about us." When he only stared at her she added, "You and me, us."

"We're not—" He broke off, images of that lone weekend together assailing him with searing heat. "There's no reason your personal life should spill over into your professional one."

"Maybe so, but people have grand imaginations. And we all know what happens if one protests too much. So I sat back and smiled and said I was fine with the caseload I already had."

"And worked it behind the scenes instead."

She nodded. "I got a lot more dirt that way, too. Especially when people thought I was being shut out undeservedly."

"What happened between us is no one's business. And it's not like we carried on a grand affair."

"No, we didn't."

She slipped her hands out from beneath his and Jake recognized instantly he'd misstepped, even if he wasn't entirely sure why.

There was an attraction there, of course, one they'd acted on. It had been there from the start.

The magnetic pull between them was easy. It was the rest of it that…wasn't. Being two humans who could breathe the same air outside of bed had always proved difficult for them.

Since he'd grown out of proverbially pulling anyone's pigtails a long time ago, he recognized that his behavior wasn't acceptable.

Sure, they had an attraction. And despite his inability to keep his mouth shut, he liked her quite a bit. Respected the hell out of her, too.

But the qualities that allowed people to have a high-functioning relationship?

That had never been their MO.

So he'd wrapped himself up in that certainty to avoid thinking about the way he actually felt when he was with her.

Carefree.

At ease.

And happy.

Those weren't emotions he spent a lot of time with in his life, his parents' publicly-happy-yet-awful-at-home marriage the overwhelming force of his childhood.

Once he was past that, the pressure to follow in his father's ambitious footsteps had colored his teenage years on through to college. It was a path his brother, Zack, was more than happy to follow but even he'd struggled, always coming up short of their father's wishes as the second son.

How was it possible the past he'd ignored, run from and flat out worked to forget could still manage to rear up and kick the hell out of him? With far more gusto than Orlando ever could have managed in the paddock.

Had it really only been an hour ago he was worried about training a stubborn horse?

How had it all upended so quickly?

And why did Caroline's coming to him feel so meaningful?

He'd watched his best friend fall in love with a woman from his past. One who'd been with him through something intense and dangerous and destructive. Garner and Mia had not only come out the other side of all that danger, they'd also thrived.

Garner got a brand-new life he seemed made for. One that was incredibly obvious to anyone who looked at the six-foot-three-inch ex-SEAL carrying his daughter around the ranch.

Trace and Nic had found the same. Their journey had added a teenager into the mix but they'd found their way to building a family, too.

It would be tempting to think Caroline's arrival—at this

time and place—meant something more. Especially since their brief time together felt unfinished somehow.

But he knew better.

His father hadn't just upended Jake's professional life in Las Vegas. The man had spent a lifetime modeling a feckless selfishness that Jake feared was threaded through every strand of his DNA.

One more reason he did far better with dogs than humans.

Sitting here with Caroline, her hands now tucked firmly in her lap, was one more proof point in the *Jake Stilton's an unmitigated ass* column.

"You really haven't experienced anything suspicious here?" Caroline finally asked.

"Nope. And my partners set up the security and surveillance around the ranch so that we aren't randomly surprised by anything. I've added a few tricks of my own to make that even harder."

"It won't matter."

"It all matters. We protect our own."

"You can't protect what you can't see. And you're next, Jake. You have to know that."

Caroline hadn't expected this to be easy, but she also hadn't banked on Jake dismissing the personal danger completely out of hand.

It didn't help that she couldn't give him specifics.

Her intel was strong and she believed absolutely that the shadow players who'd ensured Al Stilton found his way to the highest echelons of government were seriously pissed their investment had gone belly up.

But her instincts also screamed that there was more here.

There were still a hell of a lot of fuzzy edges, but she

had to make Jake see that there was real, tangible risk to ignoring the threat.

It was coiled and waiting right now, but it *was* real.

The thug waiting outside her apartment had been there to rough her up but she hadn't gotten a sense that he was there to do much more than give her a warning.

His mother's situation was inconvenient, but not inherently dangerous.

And his brother's house break-in had a deliberateness to it but it skirted the real edge of danger in the actual execution.

Just like her own attack, everything that had happened so far felt like a warning.

And, oddly, *that* felt more unsettling.

So how did she get through to him?

As a detective, Jake was a man who dealt in logic and facts and all she had to give him were random acts of menace. And her gut.

"I see the wheels turning, Caroline."

"Because you're ignoring the problem."

"Then lay it out for me. Why do you think I'm next? Because all I'm really hearing is that you're the one in unnecessary danger."

"I know how to take care of myself."

The flash in his gaze was the barest hint she got before he erupted.

"There shouldn't have been a damn reason you had to take care of yourself!"

The diner wasn't crowded, with only a few other people enjoying a late-morning meal, and his shout seemed especially loud.

"Jake—"

"Don't you dare ask me to calm down about this." While

she could see nothing had reduced his fury, he had lowered his voice. "You come all the way here saying this is about my family but you're the one who could have been seriously hurt. Or worse."

The *or worse* had been keeping her up at night but she brushed it off, unwilling to back down. "You don't care that your mother and brother were targeted?"

"I will talk to my family. But a curb on my mother's excessive and lavish lifestyle is hardly a problem, to my mind. And my brother's made his choices, all of which seem to be in service of his own political ambitions. He knows those risks."

"You know them, too." She pressed on, not sure of how to make him understand. "Who else can they come after? You're a natural choice to send a message to your father."

"The son who hasn't spoken to him in nearly a year? Besides, even if I bought in to the fact that I was next, to what end? My father is powerless at this point. His shady backers can be as mad as they want about that but what do they get by hurting anyone? All they risk is putting their own interests under unnecessary scrutiny."

It was logical and sane. Realistically, she knew that.

So why couldn't she accept it?

"Look, Caroline. I get we have a history and that you're not here out of some casual interest in my father's case."

It's not like we carried on a grand affair.

That direct hit still hurt. It might be true, but the simmering anger she'd tried to ignore at his earlier dismissal hadn't faded.

Nor was she willing to be seen as some simpering basket case.

"You think I'm here because we had sex? Just how big is your head, Stilton?"

"It's not about sex. It's about the fact we have a personal connection. But I want you to back out of this. Your safety isn't worth the drama my family is exceptionally good at creating."

Of all the ways she'd played this in her mind, she'd known his dismissal of the situation was one of the risks. Add on that deeply strained relationship with his family—one he now managed from a long distance—and it was obvious he'd washed his hands of them.

But to toss their non-existent personal relationship back at her as if she was sitting around pining for him? To hell with that.

"I'm not walking away."

"I'm not giving you a choice. I have no problem using what's left of my waning influence to call your boss myself to make sure you stay out of this."

The threat was real. Nothing in that implacable tone and flat, cop's gaze was joking.

Which only honed her ire into a wickedly sharp point.

"You touch my career, Stilton, and I'll feed you your balls."

He leaned forward over the table, his grin feral. "Try me."

Something large and overwhelming sparked to life, a raging fire suddenly set free.

This was *them*.

That strange push-pull of heat and tension and emotion and pure, willful force.

"I'm not walking away."

"I don't intend to give you a choice."

Caroline refused to break their locked gazes first, but she did shift slightly, pulling back from the silent battle that arced between them.

It was the work of a moment.

The simple unconscious fire of her synapses that had her already shifting position when gunshots erupted around them, the glass of the front window exploding mere feet from where they sat.

Chapter 4

In what had to be fractions of a second, Jake heard the screams that followed the sound of shattering glass as he moved into action. A career spent protecting others had his automatic response senses fairly well honed, but it couldn't do much beyond crawling out of his booth seat and moving to cover Caroline.

Her body was lean beneath his, the memories of their weekend together inconveniently leaping back into the forefront of his mind as he covered her before pushing her under the protection of the table, his own body in place over top of her.

He'd always appreciated a woman with curves, but something about Caroline's angles appealed to him.

Something that he had no business thinking about... then or now. Especially with the noise that now enveloped them as people's screams subsided in favor of a loud din as the entire diner seemed to come to life in the aftermath of the shooting.

Satisfied she was protected beneath the thick Formica table, he shifted out of the booth, his gaze scanning the shattered window and the street beyond.

Whoever had made the hit was long gone, the street empty of any traffic late morning. No matter the overwhelming urge to give chase, Jake was well aware there would be nothing to find if he abandoned her to go after whomever had shot at them in broad daylight. All he could hope was that someone local saw an unusual vehicle rushing out of Liar's Gulch toward the interstate.

Besides, he was needed here anyway to do damage control.

"Can I get up yet?"

He glanced down to find Caroline's liquid blue gaze on his, her pupils blown with the adrenaline rush. On a harsh nod, he extended his hand to pull her from where she crouched beneath the table.

He'd have done the same for anyone, but the heat that tripped off his palm and zinged up his arm was a surprise he hadn't anticipated.

Damn it.

"Do you believe me now?"

There was a distinct quaver beneath the sass and it tugged at Jake, way down deep. She shouldn't be in this mess, regardless of the reason.

But if it did have something to do with his family?

That was untenable.

His father's crimes were a public humiliation as well as a private one but they were theirs. And the one thing the Stilton family did well was keep their own baggage private.

Only now it looked as if his father's poor choices had turned dangerous.

And he wanted Caroline a million miles away from it.

His gaze hadn't left hers, but it was with some resignation that Jake admitted the truth. "It wasn't about belief, Caroline."

"Then why were you so convinced I was wrong?"

Because I already dealt with that problem and put it behind me.

Because I left all that baggage behind so I could find myself again.

Because I can't have you in my life. Ever.

Only he said none of that. Maybe he'd have admitted the first but he was prevented from saying anything by the arrival of Cage County Sheriff Dawson Kane.

Dawson nodded as he glanced around the diner, his all-knowing gaze taking in the shattered glass and the still-gossiping townsfolk. "Stilton."

"Sheriff Kane."

"Sounds like you had an eventful breakfast."

"You might say that."

Dawson's expression remained even and calm but the two of them had spent enough time together since Jake's arrival in Liar's Gulch for him to know the man was taking it all in.

And coming up with a hell of a lot of questions.

A point that was abundantly clear when Dawson extended his hand to Caroline. "Sheriff Kane, ma'am. I don't believe I've seen you around these parts."

"Caroline Esterson. I'm an old friend of Jake's from Las Vegas."

Dawson's mouth remained flat but his eyes crinkled ever so slightly as he shifted his attention toward Jake. "Seems your ranch has had a lot of old friends visit of late."

It was a direct hit and an obvious reference to Trace and Garner's reuniting over the past year with their now-wives.

And it wasn't one Jake was willing to consider.

At all.

"Caroline is an ADA in Las Vegas. She prosecuted more than a few cases I handled as detective."

Dawson nodded, his humor fading at the details. "What brings you to Cage County, Ms. Esterson?"

"An old matter I needed to discuss with Jake."

Dawson's eyebrows rose, even as his tone remained level. "Seems to me you brought a bit of big-city violence right along with you."

"Does it?"

The bark of laughter crept up his throat but Jake held it back. Dawson was more than capable of holding his own and he was enjoying—perhaps a bit too much—*not* being the one in Caroline's sights.

He suspected that would be a short-lived state, but he was determined to milk it for as long as he could.

Especially because he now had to admit that she was not only right about her suspicions and coming here, but all the family drama he diligently avoided was going to resume its role as center stage in his life as well.

His father's crimes.

His mother's outrage that he'd been careless enough to get caught.

And his brother's determination to show the world he was the faithful son.

Jake narrowly avoided shaking his head in disgust.

Apparently, Liar's Gulch, Wyoming, wasn't nearly as far away from Las Vegas as he'd believed.

Caroline considered herself a good judge of character but she wasn't entirely sure what to do with the sheriff who'd shown up and decided he needed to involve himself with their current situation.

Even if it was his job.

But damn it, she'd wanted to address the issues with Jake's family directly with him and now she'd gone and attracted the notice of the sheriff. An elected official who could hardly ignore a shootout in broad daylight.

The very fit and capable-looking sheriff, Caroline amended to herself.

Where Jake was solid yet rangy, his broad shoulders tapering down to a slimmer waist and long legs, Sheriff Kane had more of a football player's build. Solid and thick and likely able to tackle most moving objects based on the obvious muscle visible beneath his shirtsleeves. She did give him points for wearing a shirt that fit and avoiding the look she'd seen on far too many men who purposely wore one too tight.

But even without the obvious show, the man had the look of the protector written all over him.

The sheriff carried a similar stoicism to Jake's but try as she might—all while attempting to remain aloof and in control, ignoring the increasing adrenaline rush that was flooding her body—she didn't get a sense the man had a gooey center like Jake did.

Not that she had any business thinking about Jake's center, gooey or otherwise, but she'd spent enough time seeking out stories about the man to know that he had a very hard exterior that hid a deeply solid human being beneath.

She'd even witnessed the same herself a time or two.

And if she'd romanticized that a bit in her mind, well hell, shoot her. A woman who'd had the best sex of her life with someone deserved to romanticize him a bit.

All these racing thoughts were ridiculous in the extreme but as the air around them settled, that last thought hit a wee bit too hard.

Someone *had* shot at her.

Had she been the target?

Or was it Jake?

Or was this simply one more nasty warning to make it clear that Al Stilton's fall from grace hadn't fully run its course?

Even if her insides did still quake at the reality that if she hadn't moved a fraction of an inch away from Jake's magnetic stare she'd have been in the bullet's crosshairs.

The sense memories that hadn't fully left her since the attack at her apartment crawled over her skin once more. The tight hold of the masked man in her apartment complex's parking lot. The feel of his gloved hands on her body. And the fetid waves of fear that still lingered inside that whatever he meant to do to her was the stuff of her worst nightmares.

"Caroline?" Jake's tone was sharp, pulling her from the barrage of images. "Why don't we go take a seat in the far corner over there while Dawson wraps up his questions for the rest of the witnesses."

"Right." She nodded. "Sure."

His terse tone was at odds with the gentle hand that wrapped around her arm, just above her elbow, as he led her to the booth he'd indicated in the back of the diner. It was protected on two sides by the corner of the building and was the farthest spot in the room from windows. It wasn't until Jake helped her into a seat, then followed her into it, that she fully registered his intention.

"I'm fine, Jake."

"Keep telling yourself that until you believe it."

He nodded at the diner owner who'd been marching around the room with a full pot of coffee and then turned the upside down cup over into the saucer in front of her, then the one in front of him as well. It was only after the man had poured them each a cup and continued on that Jake spoke. "Sheriff Kane's a good cop. He's a good man, too."

Since that was high praise from Jake, she nodded and wrapped her hands around the steaming cup of coffee and took a sip. The hot taste scalded her tongue but along with his subtle show of protection, it was enough to push down the swelling fear that had suddenly gripped her.

"You know him well?"

"I've gotten to know him since I've been here."

It was deliberately vague and reinforced an idea she'd had as she'd driven to the ranch earlier. Jake's move to Wyoming had happened quickly. One day he was one of the LVPD's most respected cops—even with the embarrassment of the internal affairs investigation—and then the next he was putting in his two weeks' notice and leaving.

Speculation had run high he would find a law enforcement role wherever he landed, but beyond that, everyone had assumed he was one more person who'd grown disillusioned with the endless flash and luxurious emptiness of Las Vegas and left.

Caroline had wondered otherwise. Especially when she heard through an acquaintance who worked on his brother's political staff that Jake had moved in with an old friend who used to be a Navy SEAL.

Jake hadn't been merely disillusioned by Vegas. His family and his work had both shown the shakiest of foundations and in every way his leaving felt inevitable.

But his ability to dismiss his protective instincts?

Not so much.

What was he doing up here?

Because training horses felt like something he could do, but it also felt fairly empty based on how he was used to spending his days.

But if he was already friendly with the sheriff?

"Are you a cop up here, too?"

"No."

Although she and Jake were good at baiting each other, the quick, clipped response was admittedly a surprise. "So you just raise horses?"

"Didn't say that."

This wasn't the time or place to press this, but suddenly the answer felt very important. Because if he wasn't just raising horses and he wasn't a cop, what was he doing?

Caroline didn't believe her instincts were wrong about him—and the gentle way he had supported Olivia in the paddock reinforced that—but a disillusioned man with a chip on his shoulder and time on his hands could do some damage.

"What are you doing up here, then?"

"Those with a softer bent call it healing."

"What do you call it?"

His blue gaze was direct, no hint of secrets or prevarication.

"Finding justice."

Jake felt like his skin was on fire from the inside out. The unsettled feeling that more was going on back home than he ever could have imagined. The shocking reality that all of it had come crashing down on his new home. And the horror that a bullet had nearly hit Caroline.

Raging terror that refused to be sated filled him at all that could have happened to her. It only added to the still-smoldering embers of anger from the story she'd told him of her attack earlier in the week.

And all of it combined to put him on edge. A state Jake believed he'd left behind in Nevada when he'd moved here.

How humbling to realize he hadn't left anything at all. That belief that he could actually move on—one held on to with tight fists—had evaporated with all the speed of a flash rain shower in August.

Even if he was still bullishly lying to Caroline, brazening his way through the upset and giving out ridiculous answers to why he'd come here.

Finding justice.

Is that what we're calling it, Stilton?

Even as he turned that uncomfortable thought over in his mind, he had to admit—even if only to himself—that was exactly what he'd emotionally been after by coming to Wyoming.

Garner's call had come at an opportune time—the internal affairs investigation was over and he'd been fully restored to the force—but the lingering stench of his father's crimes still covered him like a blanket.

And what had he found since coming here?

A life that felt like it had purpose again. And while he might not go all the way toward saying he was whole, he was a hell of a lot more put together than when he and Hogan had driven up here a little over six months ago.

He was building something here with the Withrow brothers and their families. And if he suffered a few small shots of envy now and again that the brothers seemed to have found a way forward, ready-made families intact, well, he'd live with it.

"What sort of justice?" Caroline asked.

The fact his answer still lingered between them was one more sign he'd fallen into his head and the old musings that had stifled him into near oblivion in Las Vegas.

"Trace and Garner both grew disillusioned, too, with the way things worked in the political machines that had trained them."

"Very little is black-and-white, Jake. Which—" she gave

him a light shoulder bump "—makes it hard to separate the good guys from the bad guys."

"Does anyone fit those descriptions? Did anyone ever?"

The light press of her shoulder vanished as she turned to look at him fully. Caroline's gaze was unwavering, her voice solemn. "I'm looking at one of the best."

"I notice you didn't say *good*."

"You don't know how to be anything else, Jake Stilton."

It was a too-kind statement coming from a woman who was the epitome of good. And dedicated. And devoted.

For all their bickering, those attributes of hers were never in question.

And they were the very reason he'd kept his distance from her. Even after they'd…

Even *after*.

He rarely allowed himself to remember that heated weekend, though his dreams had managed to gin up some strong memories more often than was comfortable. He'd had an attraction to her from the start, well aware the energy he put into sparring with her was rooted in interest and fascination.

Despite the immediate interest, he also knew himself. A woman deserved a man who was clearly committed to figuring out if there was something between them, and he wasn't in that place.

He hadn't been in that place for a long time.

His father's sins had only made that point worse, but that fall from grace hadn't been the start of Jake's commitment issues. The vapid and flashy lifestyle his parents had chosen, coupled with his father's endless expectations long after Jake had made it clear he wanted the LVPD, had weighed.

Weighted, more like it. Over him like an endless demand on who he wanted to be.

There was nowhere he went in Nevada that he wasn't the senator's son. His last name was just uncommon enough that people made note of it and remarked, asking if there was a connection. Once his brother had stepped into the role of supportive son, launching his own ambitions with a star legal education followed by a run at state-level politics, the attention had only grown more intense.

His brother hadn't shied away from the press angle, either. Especially when the headlines practically wrote themselves.

Al Stilton's sons, each delivering law and order for Nevada.

It had played like gold and on the few occasions Jake had pressed his family to stop including him in the race for PR attention, he was dismissed.

Just like he'd repeatedly dismissed his mother's cooing demands he *marry well*, even if he was *determined to remain in that detestable job handling the worst criminals Las Vegas had to offer.*

No mincing words there, Jake thought without a single hint of humor in the memories.

"Clearly, you're confusing me with someone else," Jake finally said.

Caroline's attention never wavered but something did shutter behind her gaze. That same resignation he'd seen the day she'd driven him back to his car, after their weekend affair. The one that said she'd given up trying with him a long time ago.

The one that said she'd protect her heart.

Smart girl.

"Let's answer Dawson's questions and then we can get out of here."

The crowd in the diner had thinned out as Dawson dismissed each eyewitness, leaving Jake and Caroline for last. The sheriff didn't go so far as asking the owner to close the diner, but he did have a deputy at the front door keeping everyone out until the scene had been cleared.

The events of the day had brought out a horde of folks, none who seemed fazed at the risk to life and limb if they attempted a meal in the diner. Because of it, the line of people—their voices audible outside the shattered window—had grown louder since Jake had ensconced Caroline in the back booth.

Caroline peeked around his shoulder before sitting back against the thick seat cushions. A small, disgruntled frown painted her lips, but it was a serious improvement over the ashen complexion she'd worn when Jake had led her over here. "He's been so preoccupied with everyone else, I thought we might get lucky and he'd forget about us."

"Do dogs forget their bones?"

Jake kept it casual, but he wasn't going to sugarcoat Dawson Kane for Caroline. The man was one of the best and Jake had seen that in the few short months he'd been up here. He'd been more than a stand-up guy when Trace and Nic had dealt with their old nemesis at the CIA and helped rescue Olivia in the process. And then he'd actually come with Jake to San Francisco to help as Garner and Mia took down the tech CEO who'd masterminded the deaths of Garner's Navy SEAL team.

He was a good cop and a strong lawman and Jake was glad to count the man as a friend.

It also helped that Dawson recognized what Jake, Trace and Garner were trying to do up here in his county, willing to give them space to help those who needed it.

The freedom to support those in need—because they actually needed help and not because some government agency had decided they were useful—meant everything. He'd discussed it often enough with Garner and Trace and recognized the value in using his talents because he *chose* to.

He could name more than a few people from his history in law enforcement who wouldn't be willing to tolerate those choices, but Dawson had proven himself unique.

And a friend.

Which, Jake suspected as the man headed their way across the diner, was why the sheriff's gaze had remained assessing as he took in the view of Jake and the only woman from his past he cared to remember.

Caught in the crosshairs of those sharp eyes, Jake realized his biggest mistake since leaving Las Vegas.

He hadn't come to the western wilderness to atone for his sins or anyone else's.

He'd come for a new start.

But the big sin he'd committed by dragging Caroline into his life—all because he'd finally given in to what was between them—had followed him anyway.

"Ms. Esterson, would you care to tell me what you're doing in Liar's Gulch?"

The question was innocent enough. The sheriff's version was obviously skewed toward getting her to talk first and gather as much information as possible. She even employed the tactic regularly as a lawyer.

But whatever she said, Caroline had no doubt the man already knew since she'd entertained similar versions of the question from the hotel desk clerk and the nice woman at the small market attached to the gas station at the edge of town.

Which meant her visit to Wyoming was already all over Liar's Gulch.

What no one had known until the shootout on Main Street was *whom* she'd come to visit.

But now that she and Jake were ensconced in a booth together, that added tidbit was no doubt flowing up and down the line of people waiting outside to get into the diner.

Small towns.

It was a risk she'd accepted when taking off for Liar's Gulch the day before. Hell, it was a risk she ran even in a city as large as Las Vegas.

People noticed things.

When it came to things that happened between men and women, that notice ratcheted up to serious interest.

And when it involved a gun *and* a man…well, she might as well have taken out a billboard at the highway exit into Liar's Gulch.

"I came to visit an old friend."

"Jake's an old friend?"

Caroline gave the man credit, his face remained absolutely unchanged, but she heard the slightest hitch in his voice at the end of the question.

One that suggested Jake was getting a phone call later whether he wanted to answer questions or not.

"Yes, we worked together on several cases when he lived in Las Vegas."

"Cases? You're a cop?"

"I'm an ADA for the city. Jake supported me on a few leads that needed tugging as well as some evidence recovery."

Sheriff Kane nodded. "I see."

"What do you see, Sheriff?" She kept her tone light and

sweeter than the pie she'd noticed at the front counter when they walked in.

"Best I can tell, I see a woman who has a rather dangerous and unhappy individual following her."

"Why do you assume they're after me?" She allowed her gaze to pointedly skip around the diner. "There were other people eating a late breakfast, same as Jake and I."

Jake's knee, already distracting where it lay against the outside of her thigh, pressed a bit harder against hers. She ignored the warning, even if that added pressure did burn a path straight to her core.

Damn it.

She had no business getting turned on because Jake's very firm knee pressed the edge of her thigh. All that would lead to was a flushed face and an inability to keep the higher ground with the sheriff.

Jake could think the man was a good guy all he wanted, but she was the interloper, recently arrived on the man's turf.

There was no way she was getting a pass on bringing danger right to the middle of his world.

"We don't get a lot of tourists up here in Cage County. Yet, in a matter of hours, we've gotten two of them."

"I can't account for your tourism efforts, Sheriff. I came by myself."

Dawson's gaze did a drift of its own, skipping over her and Jake and straight on to the shattered front window. "Right."

Before she could say anything else, Jake doubled down on the touching and laid a hand over her thigh. Whatever modicum of control she'd managed over her body temperature vanished at the feel of that firm palm positively branding her.

"Come on, Dawson, you know I'll vouch for her. Something bad's been going down at home and it followed her here."

"I get that." Dawson's smile was grim, but there all the same. "What I don't get is why she's being cagey about it."

"She's a lawyer. You ever know one who isn't?"

"Hello," she said as she laid a hand over Jake's, squeezing tight. "I'm sitting right here."

Oblivious to the pressure of her fingers, Jake only nodded. "Yeah, you are. And since you've been a damn fool over your own safety, you've lost the right to play games with the sheriff."

The tone was harsh and unyielding, but the rush of truth was absolute.

And with it, a rush of remorse as well.

"I didn't mean to put anyone in harm's way. I had no idea I was followed here."

"How'd you get here?" Sheriff Kane asked.

"I drove. Headed out late afternoon yesterday and drove all night."

Dawson's expression did shift then. "That's a dangerous choice for a woman by herself."

"I can handle it."

Caroline pictured those long, desolate stretches of highway she covered overnight. The drive had only been about twelve hours, but parts of it had felt absolutely endless.

The thing that had kept her going was knowing Jake was at the other end.

"Just so you don't mistake my meaning," Dawson interrupted her musings, "it would have been just as dangerous for a man by himself. Someone back home followed you with a gun they have no concern about using. Bullets don't care about gender."

It galled that he was right. And it stuck a particularly hard landing that she'd brought danger here by virtue of not accepting that the attack at her home might underpin a bigger problem: an assailant more determined to do harm than she'd initially assessed.

But damn it. Her focus had been getting to Jake. On warning him of the danger, not assuming any of it was actually directed at her.

It was a serious miscalculation and one that she couldn't unmake.

But she was damn sure she wouldn't make it again.

"No, Sheriff, they don't."

"I'll put a member of my team on drive-bys past your hotel tonight and will also make sure you're escorted to your room and the hotel's fully checked out."

"She's not staying in a hotel."

Dawson only nodded at Jake's cool statement. "We'll do the same to the property, then. I'll make sure there are several passes along the perimeter."

Jake did smile at that, his casual demeanor at odds with the heated rush of ire filling Caroline like rising steam. "We've got it covered."

"Humor me, Stilton."

Caroline wondered when she'd become absolutely invisible in this conversation, the blatant brush-off of her own autonomy frustrating and slightly alarming.

Less because it was happening and more because there was a part of her that reveled in the aura of protection.

And at the idea that she didn't have to handle the situation alone.

Still, she refused to totally give in to them and held her ground, directing her comments at Jake. "I don't need permission or handling or a place to stay this evening other than the hotel room I booked."

The fact he didn't even blink galled.

But the bigger truth—that her panties began to smoke right there in the middle of the diner at that steady gaze—was the real predicament.

"Call it whatever you want, Counselor. You're bedding down with me tonight."

Chapter 5

Throughout his life, Jake had heard romantic relationships referred to in a variety of ways.

An understanding.

A coming together.

A noose.

He'd never understood any of it, mostly because he'd never really experienced any of those things, good or bad. The relationships he had attempted in the past had never felt like he was choking, but they'd never felt transcendently different, either.

One day he'd been a guy who trained his dog, went to work and managed cases. The day after committing himself to a relationship, he'd done the very same.

He'd always suspected that lack of feeling was why those relationships never worked out.

It bothered him on some level but over time he'd just come to accept that he wasn't cut out for that sort of commitment to another person. And while he could blame his parents' less-than-exemplary example, that never sat well, either.

He made his own choices and lived life on his own terms. Using his parents' example to explain away the parts of himself that he questioned wasn't the answer.

The real answer, he'd always believed, was that romantic relationships just weren't his thing.

Until Caroline.

He slowed for the turnoff for the ranch and glanced over at her. Her chin was still set in the same mulish expression she'd taken on at the diner, at his pronouncement she was coming home with him, and it hadn't faded.

Not through the end of their discussion with Dawson. Or at their walk over to her hotel to collect her things. Or in the fifteen minutes it had taken them to drive out here.

If he wasn't still reliving the feeling of covering her with his body under the risk of additional gunfire, he might have even found humor in it all.

But there was nothing funny about any of it.

Nor was there any going back.

Had there ever been?

While he'd done his level best to ignore her, there was something about her that always managed to sneak beneath his defenses. And she had from the first.

That ridiculous request to meet at an off-Strip buffet for their first introduction to each other was inspired. Their likelihood of being overheard or observed was minimal, but the selection had always suggested a woman who wasn't interested in the trappings of success.

It had tugged at him, more than he'd even realized at the time.

Especially as someone who'd grown up with access to everything and very little enjoyment of any of it.

For a woman who was almost ethereally beautiful, her feet were firmly planted on the ground. She was an excellent judge of character and a quick wit.

And she was sharp.

Almost pointed with it, but she always managed to stop just shy of being brittle or harsh.

Or maybe it was her ability to poke at herself that was what actually softened her.

He didn't know and he'd rarely allowed himself the time to dwell on those observations.

Yet, here she was all the same.

He turned onto the long drive that led to the ranch house and figured they might as well get it all out of the way.

"Everyone's going to want to know why you're here. I don't lie to them and I expect you not to, either."

"I haven't lied to anyone."

"You weren't forthcoming with the sheriff."

"Not forthcoming doesn't equate to lying. And don't BS me that you don't understand the difference."

Since he was the king of reticence—even something Olivia had remarked on a time or two—Jake avoided that trap.

But before he could say anything, Caroline turned to face him.

He was surprised to see lingering hurt in the depths of her blue gaze. "I was trying not to air your family laundry. You've made a life up here, Jake. Did you actually want me telling your sheriff all about your father and his crimes?"

"You don't need to protect me."

He shifted his focus back to the driveway but didn't miss her eye roll before he did. "Because you're doing a damn fine job of it all on your own."

Since his own temper was on a short leash—and the feel of her small body underneath his still imprinted against his skin—he refused to sugarcoat the truth. "I'm not the one who got shot at."

"Since neither of us was hit I'd say you're making an awfully quick assumption that you weren't the target."

Without thinking through the spiraling need slamming through him, he shoved the SUV into Park right there in the middle of the driveway and turned to her.

The stress of Caroline's unexpected arrival was enough to get under his skin, but all that had come since in the past few hours had done a number on his hard-won equilibrium.

Without knowing why—or maybe he knew damn well why and was just unwilling to check the impulse—he had his hands on her shoulders and his mouth on hers in less than a heartbeat.

It was rash and stupid and they'd both analyze it to death, but in that moment, he really didn't care.

All he did care about was satiating the endless fascination he had with her in the only way that made sense.

Caroline met him in the moment, one hand fisted in the material of his shirt and the other in the scruff at his neck he'd been too busy ignoring to bother with a haircut.

Her lips were just as he remembered, plump and full, as he drank her in. And as he deepened the kiss, he had a partner who met him as absolutely in the moment as he was.

The need for her Jake regularly argued himself out of rose up, hot and blazing, a blistering reaffirmation that he wanted this woman.

That he'd always wanted this woman.

One hand drifted from her shoulder down her arm before moving over to her breast. The position—him draped over the center console of his SUV—was ridiculous but he couldn't seem to care. The immense need to touch her overrode everything else.

Caroline exhaled a light moan into his mouth as he

cupped her fully, pressing herself into his palm all while deepening their already carnal kiss.

His time in Wyoming had been about emotional healing and he'd ignored this area of his life, telling himself he'd refocus after he was settled in.

And because of it, he'd gone a long time without touching a woman.

Nearly twelve whole months, actually, without feeling *this*.

Everything in him wanted that to be the excuse. Wanted to believe that he'd have this incendiary reaction to any woman he'd finally broken his dry spell with.

But it was a lie.

Because none of them were Caroline.

And as she broke the kiss, her eyes wide on his there in the cocoon of his SUV, Jake fought the damning truth.

Without even realizing it, someway, somehow, he'd been waiting for her.

"Jake."

His name wavered in the heavy breaths between them, and Caroline cursed herself a thousand ways that she'd given in to this.

And that she'd let it go so far.

Especially since his hand still pressed against her breast, exquisite shoots of pleasure radiating from where his large palm practically branded her skin.

But damn it, a woman could only be so strong.

Faced with a wall of living, breathing, gorgeous male who seemingly *wanted* her—one she already had serious fantasies about, layered on top of actual memories—how was she supposed to resist?

Obviously, she thought to herself with no small measure of frustration, you didn't.

"I—"

In all the time she'd known him, he was rarely without words but their impromptu make-out session halfway down the driveway seemed to do it because he removed his hands from her body and rearranged his large frame back into the driver's seat.

Everything in her wanted to drag him right back but she ignored the urge, savoring instead the lingering feeling of his lips on hers as she tried to resettle herself in her seat.

His low muttered curse pulled her focus off the lone button on her blouse that he'd managed to undo and she looked up to find a large truck heading straight for them.

"What's wrong?"

"Garner's headed our way."

"Um, okay?"

With his unchecked pronouncement at the diner that she was coming home with him, Caroline already expected to meet his friends. What was the big deal?

"Yeah. Right, it's okay."

"Seriously, Jake? That's all I get? Some snotty remark that suggests you want me anywhere but here?"

"What the hell?" He turned to her and if the not-so-subtle flags of her own anger weren't flying, she'd have better interpreted the vulnerability in his expression. "You're here for protection and I'm pawing at you like a hound dog."

He was sorry for what had just happened?

The sting of that had her being far too honest, her shields not quite up in the arousal still singeing her nerve endings. "Maybe I liked it."

"Maybe I—" He stopped at that and she wasn't sure if it was because she'd surprised him or because Garner was already out of his truck and rounding the hood of Jake's SUV to the driver's window.

Jake wasn't a small man by any account, but the imposing figure who came up beside his door was a mountain of a man. Broad across shoulders and chest, Jake's friend seemed to take up all the space outside the window.

But it was the wide, toothy smile that shot through the now-open window that caught Caroline up short as he made an arresting image outside the vehicle.

First the cop. Now this one, who looked like he walked out of central casting.

What was in the fresh mountain air up here?

"Ma'am." Garner nodded. "Olivia mentioned Jake had a visitor."

Before Caroline could even say hello, Jake dived in, suspicion lacing his tone. "What else did she say?"

Garner's smile only grew bigger, his delight obvious. "That you looked like Orlando kicked you in the head."

Caroline couldn't fight the shot of pure feminine excitement that layered over her already heated nerve endings.

Kicked in the head? Like it was a good thing?

All she ever saw when Jake looked at her was something akin to gum stuck to his shoe or a burning desire to get her to leave. So hearing the kid's assessment was more than a little heady.

"She's over the moon, by the way, that she got to name the horse."

"And this is how she thanks me? Gossiping about me and my friend?"

"Your friend?"

The question was bland but Garner's quick wink was anything but.

Jake turned toward her, his attitude even more surly

than when she'd arrived unannounced. "Caroline, Garner Withrow. Garner, Caroline Esterson."

"Caroline." Garner nodded. "I heard about what happened in town. You're more than welcome to stay here. Mia and Bernice are already fussing over the guest room."

The names were a mystery but she'd get caught up soon enough. "No fuss needed but thank you."

"Too late for that, but why don't you come on down to the house and fill us in."

"Word travels fast," Jake said, obviously not buying Garner's casual tone.

It never changed—nor did that smile falter—but the tease vanished from Garner's eyes. "Sure does." And then he was gone, headed back to his truck as quickly as he'd come to find them.

"Sounds like no one misses much around here."

Jake sighed as he put the SUV into Drive and followed Garner down the rest of the driveway. "No, they do not."

The large house she'd only observed earlier came into view as they crested a small ridge, and Caroline took in the place Jake had made his home.

Would she be welcome here?

You looked like Orlando kicked you in the head...

What had felt like a compliment faded as that stoic, irritated expression remained fixed across Jake's face.

She could revel in their heated kiss, but what did it really mean?

So they had chemistry.

Where had it gotten her?

Nursing unrequited feelings for Jake Stilton was where.

Only now all she'd seemingly managed to do was bring a hell of a lot of danger to his doorstep—one he shared with others, including children—and little else.

Getting all hot and bothered in the driveway suddenly felt selfish and incredibly shortsighted.

Especially when a small body pushed out the back door to the house and ran to Garner. Her arms waved in the air in her excitement and Garner bent to pick up the little girl who looked to be about two. Pigtails sprang from either side of her head and chubby hands settled on Garner's shoulders where he held her up high against his chest.

"That's Garner's daughter, Jordan."

"She's a cutie." Caroline finally spoke around the lump in her throat as she turned to face Jake. "I should go."

"Go where?"

"Away from here. You have a home and a family. There are children. The one earlier and now her." Caroline's voice trailed off as she pointed toward Jake's friend.

People lived here, just like they did in town.

A town where a gunman took aim at a diner where people were.

Followed from Las Vegas, in the dead of night.

"Oh, God!"

"What is it?"

"We have to get out of here. I have to get out of here."

He took her shoulders once more, but where there'd been heat and need and sex in the movement before, now there was just concern.

"Caroline. What is wrong?"

"I put them in danger." Her eyes darted back to Garner and Jordan and the petite redhead who stepped out the door to embrace them both. "All of them."

"We're fine."

"No one's fine. Look what happened in town? It's only a matter of time before it finds everyone here."

His hands remained on her shoulders, but Jake appeared

to weigh his words before he spoke. "We're more than capable of handling ourselves. That includes the women who live here."

Despite the comforting feel of his hands on her, Caroline stepped away, refusing the calming influence of his touch. "Handle yourselves? Against a gun? Against an invisible assailant you didn't even believe was real an hour ago?"

"I believe you now."

"Do you really? Because you keep operating under this delusion that you can't be touched. First, when I told you about what happened back home. Then, covering me in the diner to protect me from a gunman. And now, claiming nothing can touch you here. It's real, Jake."

"I get that."

"It's all real."

"Which is why you've come to the right place. These people you're so concerned about can help you. All of them."

"I can't put a child in danger."

"No one's more prepared to protect them than the people who live on this ranch."

Caroline looked around, the wide-open spaces quickly morphing from fresh and freeing to stifling and scary.

"You live on hundreds of acres of land. Do you really think a person, determined to do harm, couldn't use that to their advantage?"

Up to now, Caroline had seen myriad expressions cross a face normally kept flat and unreadable in the presence of others.

Disdain.

Arousal.

Anger.

But until that moment, she'd never seen raw, seething fury.

It radiated off him as he stalked closer, his focus never leaving her.

"No one touches my family. And for as long as it takes to root this problem out and destroy it, that includes you."

If food was love, the Withrow ranch seemingly ran on the resulting endorphins from a calorie count that could fell an elephant.

It was an odd observation but Caroline couldn't help but make it as she stared over the sea of food growing on the kitchen counter, along with the number of people who continued to fill the room.

There were the two brothers Jake had moved up here to build a horse training business with, Garner and Trace. The horses might be important, but Caroline was increasingly coming to understand all three men were here with an unstated mission.

We're more than capable of handling ourselves. That includes the women who live here.

That mission had grown and expanded since Jake's arrival based on the introductions he kept making each time another person walked into the kitchen.

She'd already met Garner, and then his wife, Mia, and the adorable Jordan out in the driveway after Jake's odd yet effective pep talk. One that continued to send delicious shivers through her at the idea he put her in the same category as his family.

Bernice, the one Jake had grouped with Mia on the guest room setup, was bustling around the kitchen keeping everyone in line as she produced dish after dish of food. The pretty, elegant Black woman she'd met earlier in the driveway had been introduced with her husband, Bennie. While it was suggested they were caregivers for Jordan, Caroline had worked far too long with cops to see anything but protector stamped on every inch of Bennie's demeanor.

The couple might want to telegraph sweet grandparent vibes, but their sharp, watchful gazes gave them away.

Then came Astrid, the woman who was formally named as Jordan's nanny. She was obviously considered a member of the group, but disappeared with the toddler after that small head had drooped down to rest on Garner's shoulder.

Bemused, Caroline had watched Garner disengage and hand off his daughter, a look of longing on his face as the nanny walked off.

Who could help but be warmed by that obvious affection?

Then Trace and his wife, Nic, had joined the fray along with the teenager from earlier.

"You're a friend of Jake's?" Olivia's assessing gaze was frank. "He doesn't have many of those."

Caroline's gaze drifted pointedly around the kitchen before returning to the teen. "There seem to be a lot of Jake's friends right here in this room. But to your question, we worked together when he lived in Las Vegas."

"Do you gamble?"

The topic change caught her off guard, especially since she was still congratulating herself on the quick riposte. "When?"

"You do live in Vegas."

"That doesn't mean I gamble. In fact—" Caroline gave the matter her genuine attention "—I don't think I've even been inside a casino in about three years."

Olivia nodded as if Caroline had passed some sort of test before continuing on. "What do you do for fun, then?"

"Come on, squirt. Cut her a break." Jake added a gentle headlock for good measure and Caroline marveled at the ease he had with the teenager. "You ask more questions than she does."

Caroline shot him a side eye. "To be fair, that is my job."

"You're a cop, too?" Olivia asked around Jake's forearm.

"I'm a lawyer who works with cops. I work in the district attorney's office and we talk to the local detectives on a lot of cases."

"And you had to come all the way here to talk to Jake?"

"Olivia." Nic walked over and laid a hand on the girl's back. "Questions are fine until they turn nosy."

Jake dropped his arm and Olivia turned to face Nic. "How else does anyone learn anything?"

"I believe you manage it by hiding out on the living room stairs." Trace's words were for Olivia but his guarded smile was for Caroline. "Welcome to our home."

"Thanks." Caroline extended a hand for Trace's. "I'm Caroline, by the way."

"Dawson filled us in on what happened down at the diner. You doing okay?"

She spent her life in and around adults and in that moment, Caroline realized just how ill-prepared she was for the far-too-interested gaze of a teenager. One who looked at her like a puzzle she was trying to put together.

And one whose expression noticeably sharpened at the mention of the sheriff.

"I'm fine. I'm just sorry I've brought it here to your doorstep."

"We're going to figure it all out," Trace said. "Dawson said you've got real concerns about Jake being in danger."

"Misplaced concerns," Jake muttered.

Since they'd circled around the same argument since

that morning, Caroline leaned in to a new audience and sought an ally in Trace. "None of this is about me. He refuses to accept that."

"I wasn't shot at," Jake argued, undeterred by her focus on Trace.

Which was enough to have her turning right back to him, that normal flare of impatience with him shooting sparks. "We were both sitting there. The guy could be a bad shot. Or maybe he got a poor reflection off the glass."

"You're quick to assume it's a man," Olivia poked in. "Women do carry guns."

It was astute and more than fair. It also had that quick flare of temper fading at the new dimension. "You're right about that and I've seen more than a few in my career. But I also think another unknown woman other than me moving through town would have caught someone's attention."

Olivia was quick to agree. "People do notice outsiders here."

"Which is what we're hoping for." Trace was quick to step in. "Dawson's banking on local attention, and that quick reflex to assess outsiders works in our favor here. Someone who saw the shooter, even if they didn't realize it at the time and can make the connection once word spreads around town."

Caroline was grateful for the help and the quick support. Even more grateful for the ready acceptance of her and the collective attitude of *we'll fix this* for the situation she'd inadvertently dropped on their doorstep.

But none of it assuaged the increasing sense of guilt that continued to creep in.

"And if it doesn't?" she asked, responsibility for it all hanging tight around her neck.

"Then I'll end it." Jake was quick to step in.

Although the question hummed through the room, every person filling the kitchen likely holding the same thought, Caroline was the one to press him on that proclamation. "End it how?"

"If I'm right and this really is all about you, we keep you safe here at the ranch and I deal with the problem."

"And if it's about you?" Caroline shot back, still not convinced she was the target in the diner.

"Then I draw out whoever wants me and deal with the problem."

"Alone?"

"Damn straight. Because if this is about my family, I'm the only one who can handle it."

Chapter 6

Jake mentally counted off the seconds in his head as he walked through the stable doors, Hogan trotting at his side. He was just on the verge of reaching *two* when the explosion erupted behind him, loud enough to stir curious whinnies out of the horses down the length of the stall doors.

"What the hell, Stilton? We're a team here. You had our backs. Now we've got yours."

He turned to find Garner already up in his face, dark eyes blazing in fury.

"This isn't the same."

"Like hell it's not!"

When the conversation had turned confrontational, Bernice had ultimately shooed them out of the kitchen, pushing them into the family room while claiming her melt-in-your-mouth rolls needed quiet to finish rising.

It was a ruse but one the woman managed well, effectively cutting the tension while also reducing exposure of adult matters—ones that actually required *adult* attention—in front of Olivia.

With the break in everyone's focus on the shooting at the diner, Mia had used the time to show Caroline the house and get her settled in the guest room.

Jake saw his opening and lit off for the stables. The

horses needed attention and Hogan had been without a solid working session for a few days. Something he normally wouldn't worry about but with the sudden focus on their collective safety, a reinforcement of the dog's well-honed skills wouldn't hurt.

If it gave him the added benefit of hiding out in the yard behind the stables and regrouping, that was just a side benefit.

"Give it a damn rest, Withrow. You've got a wife and a kid. So does Trace. Neither of you need to step foot near my family drama."

The punch landed before he ever saw it coming. Swift and furious and straight in the solar plexus so that it knocked the breath clear out of him.

Hogan went into protection mode, his low growl enough to keep Garner from making another move. The fact that he'd never even seen the punch—and needed his dog to protect him—was one more sign of how far his head had planted itself up his ass in a matter of hours.

Five hours, to be exact.

The amount of time it took Caroline Esterson to come back into his life and uproot every damn thing he'd managed to create in the past six months.

All while stirring up feelings he had no business feeling.

Protection.

Interest.

And sexual tension.

Hell, *that* was still there in spades and proof that putting a day's drive worth of distance between himself and Caroline hadn't done jack for how bad he wanted her.

With his breath still stuck somewhere below his chest, Jake waved Hogan off with the same hand signals they used in a stealth situation before rolling to his side.

Garner's extended hand met him, and his friend pulled him to his feet.

"What the hell, G?" The words still came out on a wheeze but at least he had some voice back.

"The hell is we're a team. Don't go using my family as an excuse to shut me out or claim you don't need me. Trace, too. Hell—" Garner rubbed a hand through his still-military-short hair "—Mia and Nic would come out here and finish you off for suggesting they're not up to the task of helping. And neither of them would be spooked by the dog."

"You know as well as I do this is the same family BS it's always been."

"Family BS—" Garner eyed him closely "—you keep so close to the vest it's tattooed on you."

It was hard to argue the truth.

And since it had come crashing back into his life, it was only fair his closest friend knew a bit of it. "Let's go back to the tech room and I'll fill you in."

The stables had a small office built into the back, and Trace initially set it up to manage the limited paperwork they required with the horses as well as the part-time ranch hands they carried on staff. Jake had taken one look at the space and realized he could create a second nerve center for the ranch, outside the house and accessible as an additional point of protection.

One they'd put to good use when Nic had been followed to the property. And even better use, after he'd beefed up the camera feeds, when a drone had taunted Garner and Mia after Mia and Jordan's arrival a few months back.

Although he preferred to keep his personal life to himself, Jake had loaded up all his files about his father on the shared drive in the office. It wasn't much but it was enough that if he needed Trace or Garner to access them, they could.

And it looked like the time had come.

Jake nodded toward the wall of technology. Several screens flashed through various video feeds around the ranch and, beside them, a large rack that held the server. "I stored some files in here if you ever needed access to them."

"When'd you do that?"

Jake only smiled. "The same time I upgraded the tech."

"I've never seen them."

"How often do you go looking in the drive?"

It was Garner's turn to grin. "About never."

"Besides, it's not that I don't trust you with this stuff. I do. It's why I put it there in the first place. I just—" He broke off, not sure how to make sense of it all.

His family was separate from him and had been his entire adult life. He *liked* it that way. Which was why it seriously sucked they found ways to keep pulling him back into the same old drama.

"I saw no reason to make a big deal out of it."

"Yet, here it is anyway." Garner extended a hand. "Sorry for the cheap shot."

Jake eyed the one friend he'd had longer than anyone else in his life. A truly decent human and one of the few he held dear. Instead of extending a hand to shake in return, he pulled the man in for a tight hug. "Do it again and I'll give Hogan a different hand signal."

"Yeah, yeah," Garner said, slapping him hard on the back. "I'd deserve it, too."

With that behind them Jake took a seat in the large rolling desk chair and pulled up the materials he'd collected during his father's trial. Nearly all of it was public knowledge but a few pieces were his own.

Namely the bank statements he'd stolen off his parents' computer when his father's crimes were coming to light.

He moved several items up onto the screens so he could walk Garner through the same comparisons he'd made to several public dates flagged in his father's trial.

"Deposits here, here and here," Jake pointed out with the mouse arrow before shifting focus to court transcripts he'd also annotated. "They match these specific dates flagged by the prosecution."

"He was that brazen?" Garner breathed out as he made the same connections Jake had. "Just dropping payoffs in his own personal bank account."

"Seemingly so." Jake nodded. "I still don't know how he managed to build such a reputation with this sort of rudimentary handling of money."

"How far back does it go?"

"Several years. These are the most damning but there's a pattern of it for at least a decade."

Garner stared at the screen a few seconds longer before shifting back, his arms folded across his chest. "Ten years doesn't match any specific milestone. He was already a senator at that point. You'd long moved to Nevada by then as well. What was the trigger?"

Jake had wondered the same, racking his memory to come up with what might have changed. He'd dug into staff lists and donor lists, without anything specifically popping during that time frame. Hell, he'd even looked at his mother and his brother, wondering if something had changed with them, but nothing stuck.

His brother had been out of college a few years and building his own political capital. They had several donors in common, many seeing his brother's political ambitions as a way of ensuring a dynastic approach to federal influence.

But even that had proven fruitless. Each donation had been clear and met with all campaign finance requirements.

Yet another dead end in the hunt for answers about his father.

"No idea."

"Something did it," Garner said with absolute certainty. "Even if it was just a shift in his belief that he was untouchable. You okay if Mia looks into it?"

"Another set of eyes is welcome."

Mia's former job, as an analyst for the navy, specializing in SEAL missions, made her a prime candidate to take a look for patterns.

"Might as well put the kid on it, too," Jake added.

"You want Olivia in this?" Garner's eyebrows rose.

"Since she's proven she'll dive in whether we want her to or not, we might as well give her a shot." Jake's gaze drifted back over the side-by-side data. "I can mask the stolen bank records and just give her the dates and details. How I procured them doesn't need to factor in."

"Caroline know you have those bank records?"

"No."

"You going to tell her?"

Jake didn't like the subtle itch that settled low on his neck. Nor did he care for the fact that he'd like nothing more than to keep all of this from her.

"She's in this, too. I hate she's put herself in the middle of it, but she's in it now."

"I noticed she didn't take well to your suggestion she stay safe here at the ranch."

Jake laid a hand over his midsection. "Since I'm barely back to normal breathing, I'd say that's the pot calling the kettle black."

Garner moved to the room's only other chair, his gaze

pointed on Hogan as he passed the dog to take the seat. For his part Hogan barely lifted his gaze to Garner, his disdain obvious now that the threat was passed.

It was enough to have Jake smiling his first real grin since this whole problem dumped into his lap.

"He won't bite."

"*Now* he won't," Garner said, his dark gaze in the German shepherd's direction pointed. "If that dog didn't protect my daughter with every fiber of his being we might need to have words."

Jordan loved *puppy!* as she called him and Garner was right on that front. Add on the love between dog and toddler was entirely mutual. Hogan had become Jordan's devoted protector the moment he'd first laid eyes on her, and no amount of fur pulling or ear tugging had changed it in any way.

"It was only a small growl. If he'd really meant to do you in you'd never have seen him coming."

"Sounds a bit on the nose."

Jake sensed the verbal trap but couldn't get the reference. "On the nose how?"

"Caroline. She's done you in, buddy. And you never saw her coming."

The hell of it, Jake thought as he frowned at his oldest friend, was that Garner wasn't just on the nose.

He'd hit dead center on the target.

The house should have felt like a prison. It was tastefully managed, but the technology, cameras and perimeter protection was obvious. So were the knowing gazes of every person who lived here.

Which made it funny that it was those same residents—

and their ready warmth—ensured what could have been stifling, instead, felt like a home.

And as she looked at Mia across the expanse of the guest room, all Caroline could think of was welcome.

And protection.

And a surprising amount of cunning knowledge and lethal capability hidden away out here in this small corner of Wyoming.

"You and Jake worked together?" Mia resurrected the introductions from the kitchen after peppering her with inane chatter throughout a tour of the house.

"We did."

"Garner and I worked together, too."

Caroline paused in the act of settling her small roll-aboard beside the bed and realized she had a choice to make: Play dumb or make her usual first impression.

Since she'd yet to perfect a quiet demeanor, she went with her usual bullish lack of charm. "That comment shouldn't have a hint of innuendo, yet it's dripping with it."

The petite pixie with a mane of gorgeous red hair didn't skip a beat. "It was meant to."

"Jake and I worked peripherally together so I'm not sure it's the same."

"Garner and I only worked one SEAL mission together."

"Yet, here you are, married and raising a child."

Mia nodded, her pleasure at the leaps in logic obvious. "Exactly."

"It's not the same."

"Yet, Jake's the one you came to for help."

Caroline knew what it looked like, rushing here to tell Jake about what was going on back home and then having the whole woman-in-danger shooting hours after her arrival.

But to the depths of her toes, she knew that she wasn't the target here.

Jake was in danger. Something had been brewing for a while and her exclusion from the work in the DA's office, coupled with the response to her digging around, meant something.

She *knew* it.

Even if everyone—Jake most of all—was quick to dismiss her intuition on the matter.

So maybe she was playing this wrong.

If she could get Mia's help along with support from the other women here at the ranch, maybe she had a shot at convincing him of the risks.

"I'm here because of his family. And because I believe he's the one who needs help."

"Does he know you're in love with him?"

The statement was simple—easy even—and Caroline wasn't sure if the tears pooling in her eyes were relief or sheer panic that she was so obvious.

"I… I'm not—" Since she really didn't have a leg to stand on she simply threw up her hands before dropping onto the end of the bed. "It really is written all over me, isn't it? Like an absolute fool."

Mia sat down and laid a soft hand on Caroline's back. "Love might make us foolish at times, but no, you don't look like a fool to me. And for what it's worth, I don't think Jake knows, either."

"That's a relief."

"You don't want him to know?"

"Oh, right," Caroline said, nodding and sniffling back the tightness in her throat. "What every woman wants. To say it first all while being met with stony silence and 'it's not you, it's me.' No, thank you."

"You don't know that."

"Yes, actually, I do. I'm a firm believer in the theory that men don't do what they don't want to do."

"Meaning?" Mia probed.

"Men go after women when they're interested. They don't make any effort when they're not. Jake had more than enough time to make a move on me and chose not to. Having sex didn't make a bit of difference."

With Mia's wide eyes telegraphing her delight, Caroline rushed on. "I repeat my point. The sex didn't change a damn thing."

"Or so you think."

"Or so I know."

Caroline considered saying more but stopped, refusing to dig an even more embarrassing hole than the one she was already in. Who actually wanted to admit to another woman that after a mind-blowing weekend of sex, the guy chose not to come back?

So she went on the offensive and refused to indulge a single damn minute of Mia's tempting fantasies.

"Jake and I don't have a future together and I've accepted that. In time, I'll get over my feelings. Which I've also accepted. What I can't accept is knowing he's in danger and doing nothing about it."

"We've got your back on that. Garner's outside with him right now reading him the riot act about wanting to go off on his own."

"Can Garner actually stop him?"

"I have endless faith in my husband, so it's easy for me to say yes. But reality's far more complicated."

"How?"

"Jake's one of the most honorable men I've ever met.

He's also one of the most stubborn and he's going to fight this every step of the way."

"Fight what? Facts are facts."

"They may be, but they're clouded by his embarrassment over his family's actions and his need for help." Mia smiled. "That's the stubborn part."

"And the honorable part?"

"He needs to protect you. With everything he is."

Once again, Caroline wanted to lean hard into Mia's tempting notions of Jake Stilton. Her unblemished view that said all that honor and goodness was a proxy for the emotions he didn't know how to show.

Oh, was it tempting.

And because it was, Caroline held herself back.

Jake was a protector by nature. It was who he was and how he saw the world. The man didn't know how to be anything less.

So *of course* he was going to see this through.

It was what came after that scared her. After they caught whomever was behind this. After he caught the bad guys. After he ensured she was safe.

Because she'd already experienced *after* with him once before.

And with stone-cold certainty she knew Jake would walk away again once this mess was resolved.

Jake gave Hogan the command to begin a search, adding a well-practiced gesture to the words. The dog's response was perfect, and Hogan was already heading for the shirt Jake had stowed earlier under the woodpile on the far side of the stables.

His nose remained close to the ground for the entire

thirty-yard trek, and he let out one lone bark and sat down beside the corded wood when he found the hidden item.

Jake shared words of praise as he headed in the same direction as the dog, amazed as he always was by the outcomes of hard work, patience and trust and repetitive training.

How could he be so endlessly confident in a dog and have so little of the same toward other people?

Caroline had been one of the few exceptions in his life back in Las Vegas. The crew here in Wyoming had been the other. The cobbled-together family he'd created here on the ranch wasn't perfect, but in the six months since he'd arrived he'd seen the best in others.

And it had brought out the best in him, too.

His bad relationship skills aside, that promise had been the biggest enticement to leave Vegas. Before his move, everywhere he'd looked at had seemed like his life was framed with the bad behavior of his father. Nearly a decade and a half of damn hard work for the LVPD hadn't been enough to overcome it. And even though the internal affairs investigation he'd suffered through after his father's conviction had wrapped up in his favor, it was hard to believe he'd ever be free of the taint.

Caroline had been the only sticking point in the decision to leave.

How many times had he considered reaching out to her after that weekend together? How many times had he thought of her, in spite of his resolve to forget her?

In the end, he'd left without saying goodbye. The temptation to give in to seeing her—and the potential for *more* if he did—felt like the worst sort of dick move. Especially because he knew he'd struggle to resist her.

Yet, here she was anyway.

All his running and what had it really accomplished?

He wasn't a big believer in fate or destiny or even a grand master plan, but it was hard to argue with how neatly his old life had come back to find him in his new one.

Just like your friends' old lives had come back, too.

Maybe Caroline's back for a reason.

And maybe it's the only truly good thing to come out of your father's disgrace.

The tantalizing thoughts rose up, sneaky and quick, into the back of his mind.

Even as he recognized his situation with Caroline was not the same.

Trace and Nic had been partners in the CIA, carrying on a relationship during their time together. She'd come to him for help and they'd rekindled their relationship as they battled a mutual enemy from their past.

And Garner and Mia had a child. Jordan was proof positive there had been something lasting between them, even if they hadn't found their way back to a relationship.

What did he and Caroline have?

A lone weekend, a fair amount of bickering and his endlessly surly attitude.

And heat, that same small voice whispered.

They had a hell of a lot of heat. But it wasn't the same. *They* weren't the same.

And there wasn't some happy-ever-after waiting for the two of them on the other side of whatever they were dealing with. He'd ensured that when he hadn't called her back after their weekend together.

And he clinched it well and good when he left Vegas without saying goodbye.

So he'd help her now and he'd damn well find out who was trying to hurt her. And he and Hogan would go back to the new life they were making, far away from her.

Crouching down, Jake met Hogan's solemn gaze, rewarding with praise and the special treats he reserved for their training sessions. The dog—stoic in the best of moments—preened under the attention, his entire body alert and focused.

This was right, Jake knew. *This* was the life he'd chosen and he was good at it.

Although Hogan's training had changed over time, with praise and positive reinforcement taking up the lion's share of his rewards when he accomplished tasks, Jake had shifted his approach slightly with the arrival of small humans in the house.

Olivia understood the requirements not to feed the dog but Jordan didn't grasp that *puppy!* wasn't her own personal partner in whatever she happened to get up to, whether it was playing dolls or eating mac and cheese. Add on the heavenly smells that now regularly filled the ranch kitchen from Bernice's cooking and life had certainly changed from Jake's one-bedroom bachelor pad.

A key element of Hogan's training was *not* to accept food outside of Jake's commands, for his ultimate safety and the security of his work, but Jake also recognized the dog's sacrifice. Their training sessions—and the special beef chews that were Hogan's alone—hopefully balanced the scales a bit.

With additional reinforcement via the ear scratches Hogan loved, Jake considered their next exercise.

And never heard Caroline approaching, only recognizing she was there when Hogan's attention shifted to the space behind him.

"Hey."

He regained his feet, turning to face her. The late-afternoon sun framed her from behind and he took in the long, lithe form.

She'd pulled her dark hair up into a messy knot on top of her head and the sudden itch to tug on the clip holding all those thick strands in place had him determinedly laying a hand on Hogan's head to avoid the urge.

Because it was just like everything else about his reactions to her.

Ridiculous.

He might be surly by nature but he didn't ordinarily argue with people or bait them.

Not with Caroline.

Nor did he have much trouble controlling his urges. He liked women and he liked sex when it made sense and was convenient, but something about seeing her effortlessly managed to put sex in his mind. Even now, buttoned up in a blouse and slacks that were a better fit for a legal briefing than a romp in bed, he wanted her.

"Hey."

"I, um, wanted to apologize for all this." She shrugged, her grin rueful. "You know, in that general sorry way that I'm being an inconvenience instead of the reality, which is I would still make the same decision anyway."

He almost laughed at the fact that he was able to follow her logic but ultimately let go of the dog and took a step forward instead. "I'm glad you came here. You don't need to apologize for that."

"I am sorry it's all a mess. But these are good people you're here with and I'm glad you've found them."

"I'm glad I found them, too. What about you? You haven't said much about home. How are you doing? Are you seeing anyone? McClusky was never quiet about wanting to ask you out."

What the ever-loving hell, Stilton?

In what world was he unable to control his tongue? He

was a seasoned, decorated detective, for cripes sake. He knew damn well how to strategically ask questions and keep his own counsel while doing it.

Her frown was swift and dismissive. "McClusky's a jerk. He might be a good cop but he's still a braying jackass."

"Pinter always had his eye on you, too."

"He and I eyed each other about five years ago. It went nowhere real fast."

He'd heard rumors about their short-lived affair and had always wondered what had happened. It was disheartening to imagine——

"And just so you don't mistake my meaning," she added, interrupting his dour train of thought, "nor did *eyeing each other* mean we slept together."

"Sure. Right."

"I'm not pristine, Jake. But I never made it a habit to mess around in the same pool I worked in. In my mind, I always saw my professional relationships with cops as an extension of the DA's office." She glanced down before meeting his gaze directly. "Until you."

"For what it's worth I avoided that pool, too. Until we——"

That crystal-blue gaze glittered at his hesitation. "Had sex?"

Excellent sex, his memories assailed him, the dam he'd had on them breaking fully free at the fact she was now standing here. Every exquisite detail had etched itself deeply, and he wasn't able to stop the flood.

Damn, but he itched to get his hands on her.

"Yes."

"You act like it's something we can't get past. Like it's this phantom problem still lingering between us."

"Sure. Right."

"Damn right. Something's gotten mixed in your head

and you're either dismissing me or pressing me with some sort of misguided overprotection. I'm good. I've got this. I am sorry I intruded on your life and these good people here, but I'm still not convinced you're not in danger. You need to focus on that, not the fact that I'm the messenger."

Focus on it? How the hell could he possibly focus on anything when all he could see were the risks she'd taken?

"The thug who attacked you at home is a point in the 'Caroline needs protection' column. So does whomever followed you here and shot at you."

"He shot at both of us."

That split second in the diner had lasered itself into his brain, a slow-motion replay running on an endless loop. Only each time it ran, it seemed to slow even further, his mind imagining all that could have happened.

"Damn it! He shot at you. And he'd have succeeded if you hadn't gotten mad at me and leaned back. You were the target, Caroline. You!"

That same stupidity that gripped him in the car—and continued to grip him with that mindless dating question—took hold and refused to let go.

Only this time, he had just enough self-awareness to use a bit of finesse.

Reaching out, his hand cupped her cheek, his thumb tracing her cheekbone. "It's all I can see."

Chapter 7

*B*reathe.

Caroline struggled to remember that basic function as Jake's thumb moved over her skin. The feel of his large palm, pressed against her face, instantly took her back to another moment.

In another place.

The morning after their first night together she'd sat up in his bed, thinking he was still asleep. Her intention at the time had been to quickly refresh herself and leave, not willing to wait around for it to get awkward.

"You don't have to go."

"Oh—" She turned, convinced she'd see a sort of bored certainty on his face. So it was a surprise to see a small smile and a relaxed expression she'd never observed on him before. "I'm sorry I woke you."

"You didn't. I need to get Hogan out and fed, but you don't have to leave right away." He paused, something slightly edgy pushing through his expression of utter contentment. "Unless you need to."

"No, um, I don't have to. I wasn't going to do much today." Wow, way to sell that one, Esterson. "I mean, no, I'm good."

She turned away, intending to get out of bed and past

the sudden awkward reality that she had no plans—other than the mound of work she'd intended to keep her company for the weekend—and that she'd happily stay right here for oh, about the next decade.

None of which he needed to know.

Needy much?

But it all faded when his large hand on her shoulder stilled her movements. She turned back, only to find Jake already sitting up. The sheer beauty of him—his bare torso, lightly dusted with hair, and the broad width of his shoulders—all combined to uncoil something low in her belly.

She'd touched that chest. Felt the sheer strength in those rounded shoulders as her palms moved over them before exploring on to trace the tight muscles in his back.

He was strong.

Capable.

And they'd had an incredible night together.

Whether he saw something in her gaze—the sheer indecision that she rarely felt—or was simply acting on his own, Caroline had no idea.

But his hand lifted to her face then, an infinitely sweet and soft gesture that matched the sincerity in his words. "I'd like you to stay."

"I'd like that."

How many times had that memory filled her mind's eye? How often had she mentally leaned in to those words, convinced there had been something more between them that weekend?

Only to crash right back into the reality that nothing had happened past that weekend. Nor had any of it been enough to keep him in Las Vegas.

A reminder now that while she always felt that frustrating tug of *more* with him, he didn't.

His actions had made that clear.

"I'm good." She stepped back just enough that he was forced to drop his hand. "None the worse for wear."

The sentiment might be lame, but the desperate need for self-preservation wasn't. She'd come up here, fully aware she needed to alert him to what was going on back home. That urgency to see him safe was real, but so were her feelings. And the internal pep talk on the drive here—about keeping her heart safe and her emotions out of what was happening—had seemingly flown out the window these past few hours.

It was time to double down the self-protection.

She didn't come here to resurrect something between them because there was no *them*.

There was a weekend of hot sex, nothing more.

Jake looked about to argue with her but stopped, his gaze drifting toward the expanse of land behind them. The land was impressive—she'd observed the drive up to the property twice now—but it was actually being inside the fences that she saw the sheer beauty of the place.

Rolling land and a sky beyond that framed it all in a vivid blue. She imagined it would be equally beautiful with the dark gray of storm clouds or the setting firelight of sunset.

It was nature's majesty and it was a far cry from what she'd grown up with, her entire life spent living in Las Vegas. The land was impressive there, too, the mountains rising up to the east and the west around the canyon floor that housed the city and its surroundings.

Despite that natural beauty, that was never what anyone's eyes went to when they came to Sin City.

It was always the next building. The next man-made monstrosity that drew the attention.

Whether it was mimicking the canals of Venice, the streets of New York or Paris, or the pyramids of Egypt, the goal of Las Vegas was to make an indelible stamp that proclaimed all that humans could produce.

It had dawned on her years before that her job was about prosecuting all that humans could produce as well.

Jake finally spoke, his expression once again set in those unreadable lines. "You keep saying you're okay, but we're no closer to knowing who was behind what happened."

"Have you called your brother yet?"

"No."

It wasn't exactly a shutdown but that lone word suggested Jake wasn't as ready to call his family as he'd claimed earlier.

"Then that's the place to start. You and I both know how to get information out of people. There's every chance he's seen something or experienced something recently he didn't even place with your father. It might give us a line to tug."

"You're not doing any of this, Caroline."

The argument was already working its way out of her mouth when she stopped.

You were the target, Caroline. You!

His outburst might have faded in the moment, but his frustration still lingered. Turning it all into a battle of wills neither made sense, nor would it get them where they needed to go.

Every response she had with Jake was steeped in emotion and it needed to stop. It was high time she started using the reason she was noted for.

That she could do.

No more dreams of what could have been between them.

No memories of waking up beside him, warm and naked.

She'd keep her focus.

Use her reason.

Behave with nothing other than rational behavior.

That was the mental armor she needed to get through this.

"I realize you think you've got this all under control, but you've been gone for more than six months. Things have changed in that time. So we're going to work together and figure this out. Vegas might not be your home any longer but it is mine. I'd like to know I can go back to it when this is all over."

Jake said nothing, but Caroline suspected he heard the last piece that she'd left unsaid all the same.

Without you.

Because when this was over, she *was* going back alone. Of that she was absolutely certain.

Jake kept his position, butt perched firmly on the credenza in the corner of the ranch office, as Mia set Caroline up on their tech.

The digital outpost he'd created in the stables was secondary to the exceptional war room of technology they kept in the house. Though it was initiated by Trace when he set up his home, Mia had transformed it over the past three months into a true nerve center of the ranch.

A wall of screens held video feeds on cameras placed strategically around the house, grounds and vast perimeter of the four-hundred-acre ranch. A long table held several laptops. Humming underneath it all was a server Mia and Trace managed that didn't access the cloud for data.

Since all of it had served to impress their tech maven in the making, Olivia, Jake knew it was something special. The kid regularly disappeared into the room with Trace and

Mia after dinner but before the battles Jake engaged her in when they played their favorite video games.

It had been fascinating to observe the way Trace and Nic had created a space for their child that allowed her to be fully herself. Nic was equally comfortable with the bond Olivia was creating with Mia as well, and it was one more proof point that the work Trace and Nic had done to remove Olivia from her poor home life and into theirs had been the exact right thing.

"Why are you being weird?"

Speak of the devil. Or at least a third-class demon.

Without shifting from his spot, Jake turned to Olivia. "I'm not being weird."

"Yeah, you are."

"How is sitting here waiting for Mia to call up a few web pages weird?"

Olivia stared at him, her attention unwavering. "It's the way your mouth is all screwed up. Like you're mad and amused all at the same time."

Since it was an exceptionally apt description—and one that suggested he didn't have his emotions as locked down as he wanted—he went on the offensive.

"Maybe I was thinking how I'm going to pound you on tonight's video fest."

"We're not playing tonight."

"Since when?"

Her head tilted ever so slightly toward Caroline. "Since your company arrived."

"My company has nothing to do with our plans."

"Sure it does. And it's cool. Besides, I have a date."

"A what?" Jake pushed off the counter at that news, especially when all he got in return was a smug smile and a wall of silence. "You can't go on a date."

"Yeah, actually, she can," Mia chimed in from the counter, her attention still on the screen and whatever she'd been fiddling around with since he and Caroline had come inside.

"I'm talking to Trace about this."

"Trace already knows," Nic said from the doorway. The woman basically had bat ears, a skill she'd only honed since welcoming a teenager into her life. Their discussion had obviously summoned her from wherever she'd been inside the house. "And you can be as unhappy about it as he is. In fact, maybe you can all go out and leave us alone when we help Olivia get ready later."

Jake had never questioned Nic's skills as a CIA operative. He'd already seen the woman in stressful, mission-critical situations and she had a cool head and an even cooler demeanor.

But even he questioned how the woman had managed to keep Trace Withrow from an aneurysm over the news his daughter was going out on her first date.

"In the meantime…" Nic took Olivia's hand and pulled her toward the door. "We're all going to give the two of you a bit of privacy."

Mia was already out of her chair, gesturing Jake into it. "I've got all the search queries pulled up as well as some of your historic files, Jake. I'm running a quick program through the AI agent I developed to see if there are any patterns worth recognizing."

Olivia let out a small *whoop* on her way out the door. "Woman slays the day. Again."

Mia looked momentarily stunned by the comment, her fair skin going pink under the compliment as she pointed toward the screen in front of Caroline. "The results will come onto that screen."

Caroline had been quiet up to that point, observing and taking in the constant stream of conversation they all managed to generate. "Thank you for this, Mia. For everything, really."

Her embarrassment gave way to the warmth and softness that was inherently Mia, and she leaned forward and gave Caroline a quick hug. "You'll get this figured out. You've come to the right place."

And then she was gone, following Nic and Olivia out of the office and pulling the room's French doors closed behind her.

Caroline waited until the door was closed before she turned back to face him. "They're quite a group. Impressive individually and all together."

"They're diabolical. A date? Seriously? What is Nic thinking?"

"That it's good her child has friends and people interested in spending time with her." Caroline tapped his forearm and Jake pulled his attention off the rush of images flying through his mind, including some hulking boy who might try to kiss the kid. "Olivia's fifteen. Edging on sixteen in another month based on what Nic told me earlier."

"So I'm right, then. She's too young."

The rich laughter caught him up short.

"What's so funny?"

"You. The last time I saw you was in the courts building the day they brought in the dealer who was working the worst block in the north end of town."

"Sonny Ray, who was not the proverbial ray of sunshine his name suggests."

"No, sadly he's not. But I watched you with him, as I'd seen you do in other situations, absolutely unfazed by the depraved individual you were handling."

"So?"

"If that didn't manage to ruffle you in the slightest, why are you acting like a caged animal caught in a trap over a date to the movies? Olivia's a lovely young woman. She's going out in that age-old ritual of courting."

"How do you know this?"

"Because I'm a woman and I listen. And she was excited talking about it earlier when you went and hid in the barn."

His mouth was open, an automatic response coming out about risks and Olivia's age and what boys could do when he lamely shifted gears. "It's a stable, not a barn."

"Pitched roof?"

"Yeah."

"Hay inside?"

"Of course."

"Large internal structures made of wood?"

"What's your point?"

"Call it what you want, you went and hid in it."

Caroline's smile was as smug as Olivia's and for the life of him, Jake didn't understand why he was responding to it.

Only here she was. And here he was.

And somehow, without even meaning to, he'd allowed her to do what she always managed to do.

Get under his skin.

And damn it to hell, he liked it.

Just like he always did.

"He likes her."

Nic stilled where she flipped through the clothes in Olivia's closet and turned to face her daughter.

Her *daughter*.

The thought still filled her with a mixture of terror and sheer, unadulterated awe.

She had a child, one who amazed her every single day with her intelligence, her humor and her determined march toward being a good human being.

Olivia had captured her from the first, a part of the case she was working that she couldn't separate and simply treat as part of the mission. The child's kidnapping by her uncle—a plot her mother was not just okay with but actively involved in—had ultimately brought Nic to Wyoming and to Trace for help.

It had put them on their path back to a permanent relationship and marriage. One that she'd long believed impossible to get back.

Yet, here she was all the same, picking out outfits for her newly adopted daughter while her husband seethed down the hall over the reality of their daughter going on that date.

It was heaven.

But just because she'd gotten so incredibly lucky didn't mean it was a sure thing for anyone else.

"I think you're right about that. But we need to give them their space."

"Garner liked Mia and that worked out. And Dad liked you and that worked out."

Since Nic had already headed down the same path she could hardly fault Olivia for doing the same. And realized she needed a different approach to this one.

Maybe they all did.

Because she'd already seen the clear evidence that Jake had feelings for Caroline. But she'd also spent the past six months with the man and recognized he was nursing a world of hurt that kept others at a distance. He'd slowly warmed up to her and everyone else in the house, but he still kept up an emotional distance from all of them except Olivia.

Nic sat down next to her daughter where she was giving the thumbs-up or thumbs-down to various outfits and considered how to play this. Olivia was a young woman and there was the constant temptation to minimize that because she was underage.

But she wasn't a kid, either.

She'd experienced more than most at her age, and her vast intelligence filled in the rest.

Proof as she quickly continued on with her point. "I don't want to get anywhere near their space. You and Dad and Mia and Garner are gross enough. I even caught Bennie and Bernice kissing in the hall last week and wanted to gag." Olivia frowned. "Even though it's nice to know they…you know…"

Nic pulled her close in a hug. "Yeah. I know."

Olivia hung on, her voice quiet when she finally spoke. "Which is also why Dad is so freaked out about this date, isn't it? He's being dumb because it's the movies and I don't even know if I *like*-like Nasher, and his mom's going, too. Besides, I'm not ready to…you know…"

Nic squeezed tight before pulling back. "You can call it sex. I won't scream and clutch my pearls."

"Do you own pearls?"

"As a matter of fact, I do."

Hesitance lined Olivia's face—an expression Nic rarely saw there—before she took a deep breath. "I think Jake and Caroline want to have sex with each other. And not just because there's something in the air up here."

Once again, her daughter proved that she was far more astute than any of them wanted to believe. "They probably do."

"Then she came to the right place. This ranch got you and Dad back together. And it got Mia and Garner back together."

"I know it's tempting to think there's something special here, but your dad and I got back together because we realized how much we still cared about each other. I think the same happened for Mia and Garner. In both cases we had something to build on."

"I think they do, too. Jake's just too stubborn to see it. His family sucked, just like my old one did. But he's not nearly as self-evolved as I am so he thinks he can't move on." Olivia shook her head before that calculating smile she wore far too often tilted her lips. "I should tell him that next time we're playing Fortnite."

"You tell him everything else. Why not?"

"He'll get real stubborn and squinch his face up like he does when he's mad but doesn't want to act like it in front of Bernice. I think he's secretly afraid she'll stop cooking for him."

Olivia's smile fell, that guileless expression shifting once more. "I still can't believe you're my mom now. And that Trace is my dad. And that this, here…" She looked around the room and toward the window that overlooked the stables. "That all of this is real."

"I can't believe it sometimes, either." Nic pulled her daughter close once more. "But it is."

"There *is* something special here. It brought us together. Mia and Garner and Jordan, too. It has to work for Jake. I just know it has to."

Olivia held on tight, and Nic could only hope in the intuition of her daughter's words. Especially because deep down she believed that Jake needed this place most of all.

Caroline scanned the details that kept coming up on the screen Mia had pointed out before leaving, reading through the implications the AI agent kept spitting out.

"This program is amazing."

"In case you haven't noticed, Mia's basically the human equivalent of a unicorn. She keeps up with a toddler all day, she writes computer code and has a practitioner-level understanding of game theory, she looks like a hot wood nymph and she makes a damn fine plate of brownies." Jake grinned. "But don't tell Bernice I said that or she might stop making my favorite meal every Tuesday night. Beef stroganoff."

"I won't tell Garner you think his wife's hot, either."

"Probably a good idea, even though I mean it in a highly complimentary, totally asexual way." His shoulders flinched in a shudder. "Especially because she's like a sister."

It shouldn't have lit something under her skin. What was silly, inane conversation as they sifted through Jake's files, along with other publicly available information, wasn't meant to be analyzed or dissected.

Yet, here she was, buoyed by the idea he thought of the gorgeous, accomplished woman in his home like a sister.

And one more proof point that they needed to figure this out quickly so she could get out of here and away from Jake.

It didn't matter whom he found hot *or* sister-like. None of it was her business.

"Do you have sisters?"

"So you can call them hot, too?" The words were out before she could snatch them back, only to get a rather naughty grin out of Jake.

"So they *are* hot?"

"Both of my sisters are beautiful. They also both happen to be married and have six kids between them."

"Why didn't I know this about you?"

"We haven't exactly had a lot of conversations outside of work." *Or bed.* "It never came up."

His smile fell. "I'm sorry for that."

"For what?"

"For somehow ignoring normal conversation between us. I haven't been all that great at it. Which isn't an excuse," he rushed on. "But I'm reminded of it regularly by the people I live with."

This glimpse into his life here was too tempting, and Caroline couldn't resist seeking more breadcrumbs to paint a picture of his life since he'd left Vegas. "What have they said?"

His glance drifted to Hogan where he lay curled up in the corner, relaxed after Jake gave him the instruction to sleep.

"That I'm far more comfortable with dogs than I am with even discussing the weather."

"That's a pretty direct hit. Accurate," she added. "But direct."

"So are your sisters older? Younger?"

"Both are older. I'm the black sheep, in their eyes. Thirty-three and unmarried. Eighty-hour work weeks. My oldest sister's been on me lately to freeze my eggs."

"That sounds—"

He broke off, seemingly stymied by that personal announcement, and once again she wished she had some sort of censor button. One that she could actually use to roll back time because *seriously*?

In what world was she going around telling gorgeous men she'd been mournfully instructed to freeze her eggs.

"I get they're your family, but that sounds unfair and nasty, if I'm being honest."

It had felt that way but she'd borne up under it, unwilling to create more strife in a relationship that often felt fraught with all the things she was doing wrong instead of having any appreciation for who she actually was.

"It's not the subject, to be fair. If Mandy had said it with a bit more compassion it might have felt different."

His blue eyes glittered with anger on her behalf. "But it was said to demean and belittle. I get that."

And suddenly, all that surly aloofness Jake used to keep the world at bay made a little more sense.

Toeing that slim line between humor and hurt, she asked, "Your family. The one back home? They're concerned about your eggs?"

It was enough to get a faint smile out of him. The bigger surprise was that he was willing to answer her.

"In a roundabout sort of way. My reproductive future has been less interesting up to now than poking and prodding over my political future. Had I actually capitulated there, my sperm count would no doubt have come up next. Unmarried men don't make great politicians. It's bad for the poll numbers."

"Family does put expectations on us."

"Not all families." His gaze drifted toward the doors and the rooms beyond. "I've realized lately that I was lucky enough to find a family up here. We support each other but we know how to back off, too."

"I didn't notice you backing off over Olivia's date."

"She's fift—"

"Almost sixteen and perfectly able to go on a date to the movies. It's sweet, actually."

"She's supposed to play video games and have a smart mouth. Not go places with boys in the dark."

A scroll of data caught the edge of her peripheral vision and Caroline put the arguments about Olivia's personal life aside. Jake could go commiserate with Trace all night if he wanted to, but the kid deserved some age-appropriate fun. It didn't matter that she'd only arrived this morning, Caroline would take a firm line of solidarity with the women of the house on this one.

A thought that vanished as she scanned the data on screen. "What's this?"

"What's what?"

"The dates. All of the trial dates map to big votes in Washington."

"What do you mean?"

"Look." Caroline read them again, the disparate pieces coming together as she realized what the data was saying. "Here was your father's first court appearance. The vote on the environmental dumping issue that affected Nevadans was held the same day."

Jake leaned over her shoulder and Caroline fought off the shot of warmth as his body heat seared through her thin blouse. "And here. The court date matches the really big vote on cybercrime that initiated with that casino that went under.

"And then that last vote on the drug-trafficking corridor that was uncovered in the FAA's investigation of the airstrip out at the airport."

Caroline turned to stare up at him. "Every one of these federal bills were initiated by something that happened in the state."

"All of which put extra scrutiny and attention on local jurisdictions."

"It still doesn't make sense how this matters. I mean, it's a correlation and it's hard to ignore the point. But to what end?"

"I don't know." Jake shook his head before leaning even farther forward and clicking on one of the links.

Another wave of heat assailed her, just as she was starting to get used to having him standing there, and she forced herself to focus on the matter at hand.

And *not* on Jake's impressive chest where it pressed against her shoulder. A decidedly non-erogenous zone, which had suddenly become as sensitive as parts much farther south.

Anchor yourself in the work.

Pay attention to the details that have to matter.

Do *the damn job you came here to do.*

It was that last bit that had her reorganizing her thoughts. Despite the personal moments they'd shared—and had shared all day—whatever filled the screen mattered.

The exact implications might not be clear, but Caroline hadn't spent nearly a decade prosecuting crimes not to pay attention when dates lined up. The real question was how it could happen.

State criminal cases had little to do with federal votes. And Congress was just as likely to vote on a matter one day versus another. Lining them up so precisely would be incredibly difficult.

Was it some sort of bait and switch with the media to divert attention?

Who would even make the connection? Or why?

If it hadn't been for Mia's innovative program she'd never have even questioned looking down this path.

Jake's hard intake of breath had her looking up.

"You find something else?"

"My mother's schedule."

"Her schedule's made available to the public?" Caroline quickly cycled through all she knew about Beverly Stilton and didn't think the woman had any reason to publicize her planned whereabouts.

"It's public when she's all over the news as the disgraced wife. Look here." He pointed toward the top corner of the screen. "She was in Washington, DC, on those dates as well."

Again, Caroline mentally rewound all she remembered from Al Stilton's trial. And nowhere in there did she recall that the man's wife hadn't joined him.

"She didn't go to trial with your father?"

"In my mother's eyes, going to trial meant my father was guilty."

"Yet, she's stood by him."

"Implicitly. And in her mind, standing by him is also not deigning to accept his court appearances."

"But why would she go to DC?"

"Let's put it on the list to ask her. But I'm giving you fair warning."

It seemed there was a joke hidden in there somewhere but Caroline wasn't sure what it was. "Fair warning about what?"

"You're the one who doesn't want to be shut out on the calls to my family. That you know how to get information out of people."

"So?"

"I love my mother but talking to her is the mental equivalent of a root canal. You can ask the questions."

"Getting a woman to do your dirty work, Detective?"

Jake dropped back into the seat beside her and lifted his arms, linking his fingers behind his head. "You better believe it."

Chapter 8

Olivia's date.

An impending call with his mother.

A strange series of coincidences with his father's court dates.

Jake wasn't sure where to concern himself first.

Nor was he sure that calling his mother was the best idea, no matter how tempting it was to have Caroline handle the questions.

There was a saying for times like this, he thought as he wrapped up the last few details in the stables. *Not* hiding out, but taking his turn feeding and mucking stalls as a working member of the household.

How the mighty have fallen.

What had possibly happened between 6:00 a.m. when he first did this round of chores and now with the evening closing in?

His entire world was upside down and he didn't like it.

Even if he could still feel the imprint of Caroline's shoulder against his chest where he leaned over her in the office. The scent of her still filled his head, the earthy smells of the stables unable to erase the lingering strawberry essence he associated with her.

It should have been cloying.

How the hell was a strawberry sexy?

But on Caroline everything was sexy, and that subtle scent somehow had the ability to drive him a bit wild.

What was worse was realizing that a pile of horse crap didn't have the power to erase it. Nor did the manual labor of removing said horse crap do a damn thing to ratchet down this need for her.

One day. Actually, half of one day and he had the control of a teenager.

Which only brought back images of Olivia's date and the risks Nic and Trace were inviting by allowing her to go out with some randy boy who undoubtedly had one thing on his mind.

A thing that, even with two additional decades of living, he seemingly hadn't managed to tame.

"You are a sweet boy."

The subtle crooning caught his attention and he shifted out of his morose thoughts about strawberries and horse excrement and Olivia's hulking, liberties-taking, imagined man-child only to turn and find Caroline three stalls down, talking to Orlando.

"They'll take good care of you here."

Jake took a moment to look his fill, Caroline's focus on the horse distracting her enough so that she didn't realize she had his attention.

He'd had this sort of unfettered access before, on the occasions he'd had an opportunity to observe her in court.

But it had been a while.

And now that he could look his fill, he recognized subtle things that had changed. She was thinner than he remembered. She already had a slim, athletic build, and now it looked like she wasn't eating all that much.

The smudged circles under her eyes had suggested sleep was in short supply as well.

It was a reminder of himself, if he was honest. Those last few months before he'd come here. When his job and his life had felt overwhelming.

It might be obnoxious in the extreme to think that he'd put her in this state, but her focus on his family and what she believed was criminal intention made him think this did rest with him.

What it also meant, he admitted to himself, was that he needed to take care with her. She might lay it on thick, more than able to hold her own, but there was a vulnerability underneath her bravado that was easy to overlook in the heat of the moment.

And she deserved better.

"You seem awfully sure of that," Jake said, strolling closer to where she stood with Orlando. "That we'll take good care of the demonic beast."

"Oh, I know so. That's all the lot of you seem able to do."

"He is in good hands. It's a shame whatever equine logic he possesses is convinced I'm the enemy."

Caroline looked at Orlando once more before turning to size him up. "I'm not so sure about that. I think he's enjoying testing you, but if I had to guess, I'd say you've won his trust."

That assessment shot an unexpected wave of hope through him. Orlando was the first horse he'd personally selected since joining Trace's training program and until that moment, he hadn't realized just how desperately he wanted to be right about the animal.

Not that Jake would give up on him, but more how deeply he wanted to give Orlando a better life than he'd had before coming into the rescue program.

"I hope you're right. So far he seems to prefer Olivia to anyone else."

"He senses her vulnerability and it comforts him."

"How'd you get so smart about horses?"

That subtle scent of strawberry drifted toward him once more as she lifted her head, and Jake fought the urge to inhale deeply.

"Something else you don't know about me. I was a horse girl growing up."

If the news about her having older sisters had been an overlooked detail, the idea that she'd been a horse lover was somewhat surprising.

"You mean you didn't come into the world writing legal briefs?"

"Ha ha." She kept patting Orlando's neck, continuing with those subtle croons and praising words. "Did you come into the world with a detective's notebook in one hand and dog training treats in your pocket?"

"Not quite, but I was the best dog walker in our hometown before we moved to Vegas."

"You walked dogs?"

"Had quite a business with it, too. It let me be with the animals I loved and it got me out of a house I didn't, so it was a win-win."

"Why'd you stop after the move?"

"It was way too hot in the summer to walk a dog regularly during the day. I picked up the occasional sitting job during the school year but the move put a strain on my free time anyway."

"How so?"

"My father had moved fully into senator mode by then, focused on securing his seat. We were the perfect politician's family, attending public events and smiling for photo ops."

"That sounds stifling."

"It was that. I'd also been forced away from my friends because of the move. Garner at the top of that list."

"So that's how the two of you know each other?"

"We only overlapped for a few years in the same school. He and Trace came to town to live with their grandparents after their mom exited the picture. Garner and I beat on each other at lunch his first day. We then spent two weeks after school on detention, narrowly escaping a suspension because of my father's interference. We figured out we liked each other more than we wanted to fight each other."

Caroline shook her head before turning her attention—and her question—to Orlando. "Why do men do that? Surely, horses aren't that stupid?"

"Since I saw that one nip the neck of Magnum, Trace's mount, I wouldn't be so sure."

"Marking territory, then."

Jake considered his playground fight with Garner. "Laying down boundaries is more like it."

"It's stupid."

Her dismissal had him smiling. "Probably. But millennia of evolution hasn't pounded it out of us."

Caroline dug one more sugar cube out of her pocket, giving it to Orlando, before stepping away from his stall door.

"I actually came out here to talk to you. Out of earshot of everyone inside."

"Did something happen?"

"No, but I was thinking about something. I know I don't know all of you, and I trust Trace and Nic know what they're doing as parents. But should they let Olivia off the ranch? Not knowing who's on the loose in town?"

She quickly rushed on. "I don't want to ruin tonight for her and I know I'll do that if I say anything. But I can't help but worry that it's not the best time for her to do this." Caroline let out a low sigh. "Or that I'm the one who's brought this to your door."

The unease Jake had felt about the date lessened as he considered giving Hogan a chance to sweep the movie theater. He and Caroline could sit high up in the back and remain unobtrusive as well.

And he could keep his eye firmly on the man-child.

"That's not a bad idea. We'll go with them and keep an eye."

"We can't do that to her, Jake. It's her first date. Do you want someone going out on your dates?"

How the hell long had it been since he went on an actual date himself? To a real restaurant and not just hanging out in some bar?

It was…startling, really, to realize it had been a shockingly long time. And it was a reminder of all he'd shut himself away from. Work had been the easy excuse for so many years, but it was so much more.

Sitting with someone over a meal forced intimacy. That proximity over food ensured you actually talked to someone and shared an experience with them.

Hadn't that been the secret Caroline understood on that first meeting at the buffet?

What was even more startling was to realize how easily he pictured the two of them doing that now. Dim lighting and a shared bottle of wine. Long, winding conversation over good food. Sharing a dessert.

All of it rose up so sharply in his mind that for a moment he didn't even see the stables for the vision of it all.

"Seriously, Olivia's going to hate it."

The abrupt change back to the here and now shook him out of the dream.

And the odd disappointment that they'd never had that and likely never would.

Voice harsher than he intended, Jake focused on this evening.

On Olivia's date.

With a decision on this night he could control.

"She'll hate it less than having her parents tag along. We'll bring Hogan, too. My work with him entitles me to bring him into any number of scenarios for training. That will be our excuse."

"She's so excited and I'm ruining this for her."

He recognized the concern but refused to be deterred on this one.

"It's the price you pay for being a part of this family. She'll understand."

"No way! This is beyond unfair! I can't take him! And a dog!"

Tears streamed down Olivia's face—how was it they refused to stop?—as she screamed the same words over and over. The only thing that changed was the octave.

And it kept getting higher.

Jake stared at her across the family room, somewhat taken aback by the sheer vitriol that continued to spew his direction. He'd originally sat on one of the large sofas but after the first outburst he'd moved toward the bookshelves that lined the far wall. If he was honest, he was scared by the transformation.

Where had Olivia gone?

"Come on, sweetie, it's a good idea." Nic continued to press Jake's same points on safety and security, her steady hand on Trace's forearm a deliberate move to try to handle this.

"No, it's not." Olivia shook her head.

The hard sobs of earlier had turned into hiccups, and Jake still couldn't believe the absolute transformation in his video-game opponent and partner in all things ranch snark.

"Come on, squirt. Hogan and I need to—"

"There! Right there! Nasher will see you and the dog and you'll call me squirt and I'll look like a child!"

"You *are* a—"

Caroline had remained silent up until now but moved forward, her hand firm on his lower back, cutting off his words. The feel of her hand was enough to distract him but the added grip on his forearm, her fingernails deliberately digging into flesh, shut him up.

"Olivia, before you get mad at them, it's only fair you know that I'm the one who brought this on."

Olivia turned to Caroline, her red eyes scrunched up in confusion. "You?"

"I'm so sorry but it's bothered me since you and your mom mentioned your date this evening. I can't stop thinking that the man who shot at me is still on the loose. And I can't put you or Nasher in danger like that. We need to tell his mom, too."

"And what if she says no?" Olivia wailed. The tears still fell but now they were just a steady stream spilling over her cheeks. "Because you know she'll say no."

"We can have a movie night in the stables."

Jake wasn't sure where that idea came from and he nearly asked Caroline where she'd come up with such a ridiculous notion when Nic perked up from the couch.

"That's a great idea. Mia brought the computer projector with her when she moved in. We can get you set up in the back of the stable on the big wall beside the office."

Olivia's skepticism didn't waver but the tears did slow slightly. "You all will want to watch."

"No, we won't," Nic and Caroline said at the same time, cutting off anything Jake or Trace might add.

That mulish expression Jake had never seen directed *at* him before still rode Olivia's face but the tears had stopped, even though her face was still red and splotchy. "I guess I can text him and ask."

"Why don't we go into the kitchen and I'll call his mom. She does need to know about this." Nic ran a hand over Olivia's hair. "I'm sorry it sucks and I'm even more sorry I didn't think about it earlier. But Caroline is right. If the situation was reversed I'd want his mom calling me."

Olivia didn't look entirely convinced, but she did nod at Nic's suggestion. Without a backward glance she followed Nic out of the family room and Jake felt the cut.

Deeply.

"Why the hell am I the bad guy over this?" Jake still watched the doorway to the kitchen, surprised to realize watching all those tears actually stung.

"It's a change since I've been the bad guy since this whole date nonsense started last Wednesday." Trace's smile was fierce and a bit edgy. "But damn it, we should have figured on this when you both got back from the diner."

Caroline's hand had already fallen away from his back when Nic and Olivia walked out, and Jake felt the loss of her touch.

Funny how easy it had been to feel like a united front to Olivia.

"You've been distracted, Trace." Caroline took a seat on

the couch. "It's a big deal, navigating this stuff. But her date isn't nonsense. And how she feels isn't, either."

Trace let out a few choice expletives under his breath before dropping his head. "I know it's not. It's important to her and I want her to experience these things. But it's so damned confusing. Is he a good kid? Will he treat her right? Is she vulnerable to him if he makes advances, which I have no doubt he will." That fierce smile was back. "I've actually been a teenage boy. A point Nic keeps ignoring."

"She shouldn't ignore it. I was a teenage boy, too. I know what we're capable of if given the chance." Jake realized how quickly he was able to recall those feelings. The confusion of it all, along with that steady interest in the opposite sex. And the mix of fear and awe when you finally did get to kiss a girl. Even more if you were lucky enough to touch her.

Had anything actually changed?

Caroline's arrival had put all of those feelings into sharp focus. A fact that chafed at his pride. It also made him realize how little attention he'd paid to that part of his life since coming here.

He'd chalked it up to maturity and a focus on getting his life back together, but now, looking at her, he wasn't quite so sure.

Because for reasons that made little sense, he mentally divided his sexual experiences before and after Caroline. He'd tried to pick up a few women after his weekend with her and both times hadn't managed to seal the deal. It had all felt…empty.

And while the flirting in the bar had felt good, even right in the moment, when the decision to leave so they could continue spending the evening together, he'd found a way to disengage.

And went home alone.

Why hadn't he realized it? Clearly, his subconscious had, but until this moment he hadn't related his abstinence to Caroline.

Only now that he'd made the connection, he couldn't unmake it. Just like the vision in the stables of taking her on a date, the only person he could see sharing any of it with was Caroline.

And what in the ever loving hell was he supposed to do about that?

Never have sex again? Never actually go on another date?

Because moving back down that path with Caroline wasn't fair or right. She deserved far more than he could ever give.

Hadn't he already proven that?

Nic walked back into the family room. The harried sense of concern she'd left with had vanished, a fresh calm in its place.

"Nasher and his mom are both coming over here this evening. The kids will watch their movie in the stables and I even got the agreement Hogan could play watchdog."

The plan felt like a good one, but it didn't explain Nic's expectant smile as she stood there, hands on hips.

"Why are you looking at us?" Jake finally asked, already aware he wasn't going to like the answers.

"You and Trace need to grab Garner and get out to the stables. We've got movie night to set up."

A hum filled the house as everyone moved around, waiting for the evening's guests to arrive. Despite not knowing anyone very well, Caroline had been put to work and she was grateful for the distraction.

She still felt horribly guilty for the part she'd played in nearly ruining Olivia's date, but with the new plans in place, the tears had vanished and Caroline had even been invited up to Olivia's room as she primped for the evening.

"I remember that feeling," Mia sighed as she scrubbed at a ketchup handprint her daughter had left on the hem of her T-shirt at the kitchen sink.

"Getting ready for a date?" Caroline asked.

"The date, yes. But the possibility of it all. It felt so big at that age. So monumental. Not that it doesn't now," Mia quickly rushed on. "It's just different when you're experiencing it for the first time."

Mia stared down at the stain she'd only managed to turn into an orange blob on her shirt. With a soft sigh and a big smile she tossed the dish sponge she'd been using into the sink. "And then life gets so much better."

Clearly excited by the topic, Mia's smile widened. "Where was your first date?"

"A bowling alley a few blocks off the Strip."

"As in the Las Vegas Strip, with casinos and tourists?"

"Afraid so. We lived in a more suburban area of the city but my date was clear on the opposite end of town so we picked a place in the middle."

"That's so wild. But of course it's your home so I'm sure it didn't feel that way." Mia turned and leaned back against the counter, the conversation easy. "Did your mom have to take you?"

"My older sisters drove me and even though they promised me they'd leave and come back two hours later after going to the mall, it was all a lie."

Jordan picked that moment to come racing into the kitchen, a slightly manic quality to her laughter as she ran straight for Mia's legs.

"Mama!"

Mia scooped up the handful of wiggling child, one who had a matched ketchup stain on her pale purple T-shirt, and hugged her tight before seamlessly shifting back to the conversation.

"Your sisters? That's brutal. But even more reason you understand Olivia's mortification that she's got a slew of people watching."

"Liv!" Jordan waved her arms.

Mia kissed the side of her daughter's head. "Yes, your Liv. Let's go get you cleaned up so you're at least presentable when company arrives."

Caroline reached over and ran an abstract hand down Jordan's back. "You are a cutie. How come I can't pull off ketchup stains like that?"

Jordan preened under the attention and Caroline took full advantage of the few moments of simplicity with nothing more to do than enjoy the company of a small child.

And, sweetly enough, reveled in the idea that it did get better.

Her own experiences with her family had been limited, both of her sisters quite regimented in their parenting style. It wasn't wrong and she didn't want to judge their choices, but neither had been quick to let her alone with the kids or allow her to take them out for something as simple as ice cream or cupcakes.

It was only now, staring at a bedraggled toddler who looked happy, healthy, well fed and deeply loved, that Caroline realized how much she'd missed by not having that.

And how much her family had missed, too, by restricting it all.

Jordan waved at her over Mia's shoulder as they headed off to get cleaned up, Mia's questions and comments still ringing in her ears. Caroline spent a lot of time in her head—a state she'd accepted long ago when she'd made the decision to become a lawyer—and used the quiet time cleaning up the last of the cupcakes she'd contributed for the evening's festivities to puzzle through it.

And what struck hardest was how little she'd considered her sisters' behavior through any other lens. She'd always taken it as some sort of reality as the youngest child that she'd be tormented and babied in equal measure, but long before her career had become their handy excuse, they'd found reasons to make her their punching bag.

How did family manage to do those things? The people who should love you more than anyone could manage to hurt the most.

How different it was to look around the Withrow ranch and understand that everyone was there because they wanted to be. And everyone contributed to everything, from the running of the house and the ranch, to helping out with cooking and upkeep, to the work Trace, Jake, Garner and Bennie had done out in the barn to get it set up for Olivia.

They weren't a family by blood, but they'd created something by choice.

Choice…

Unbidden, an image of the data scrolling through Mia's AI agent filled her thoughts.

Jake's mother had chosen to stay away from Nevada.

In my mother's eyes, going to trial meant my father was guilty.

Was it possible staying away meant something else?

"You okay?"

Caroline glanced down to realize the pan she was toweling off was bone-dry. And looked back up to find Jake standing there.

Oh yeah, she admitted if only to herself. *Things got so much better.*

"Your mother's trips to DC." Caroline actually got the words out without adding the breathless sigh that always threatened when Jake walked into a room. "Did she make them often?"

Oblivious to her struggle, Jake considered her question. "Often enough. She always accompanied my father when Congress was in session. She loved all the events as well as entertaining. I never got the sense that the move to Nevada was out of a love for hundred and ten degree temperatures for months on end."

The desert wasn't for everyone but she couldn't deny the slight sense of affront at the way her home was so often maligned. The region did have beauty if you looked for it.

"I hit a nerve with that one."

"Never mind. People just don't complain about any of it when they flock there in January, is all. Anyway." Caroline waved it off. "How did she feel when it all dried up? After your father's behavior came to light? Assuming it did."

"Oh, it did, even though I can't say I asked much about her life. I'd been out of my parents' day-to-day for a long time at that point, but I know it was hard."

"Right, of course it was."

Caroline wasn't sure why it nagged at her so badly, but something about the implication of his mother being in DC felt significant.

Here was someone who wasn't a power player on her own. Especially since her social star was linked to the senator's.

"Want to go look at the results again? We left the program running."

Caroline glanced toward the family room and the steady conversation coming from there. "Everyone's getting ready for guests."

"Right. So they won't be worried about us. We'll even swing through the dining room and avoid the crowd."

Without waiting for a yes, Jake took off and Caroline followed, only realizing as they walked into the office that she still held the dish towel. Setting it on the desk, she took the seat she'd had earlier, her gaze focused on the program they'd left running.

The AI agent had pulled additional details, including news stories featuring his mother. Photos from galas or even quiet dinners around DC could be found on each link Jake clicked.

It was only as he pulled up the third link, featuring a dinner in Georgetown with his mother and three of her friends, that a small shriek of awareness crawled up Caroline's throat.

"There!"

Jake leaned forward, his body again covering her with that distracting warmth.

But even with that shot of sexual awareness, it didn't distract from what she saw on screen.

"Right there. That man." She pointed to a guy in the background of the photo, sitting at a table just nearby.

Watching behind Jake's mother and her friends.

Like a bodyguard.

"That guy's the one who attacked me the other night."

Chapter 9

All the anger and raw, seething fury Jake had carried since Caroline described the attack at her apartment complex finally had a place to land.

On a man who spent time with his mother?

What the *hell* was going on?

"I'm calling her now."

"Jake, wait."

He was already reaching for his cell phone when Caroline's urgent plea stopped him.

"Really, wait. We need to think this through. Even try to find out who he is before you attempt to get answers from your mom. Especially because we've finally got something to go on."

Caroline was right. In every way, it was a bad idea to fly off the handle and confront his mother without doing his due diligence to figure out what was going on.

To understand what she could possibly be up to.

But had he really underestimated the desire to maintain her lifestyle so much that he'd ignored very real warning signs? That his *mother* was sending men out to make hits on innocent women?

Or was it worse? Had his father's public disgrace—something he'd laid firmly at his father's feet—been the catalyst for his mother to act the same?

"Did I overlook her all along?"

Caroline's voice was quiet when she spoke. "She's your mother, Jake. It's less about overlooking something and more about not wanting to paint her with the same brush as your father."

"Maybe." He shrugged. "But why not look? I never had a clue what he was up to and that's on me. As a kid, fine, there'd be no reason to understand it. But I'm a trained detective. Yet, I saw nothing."

"After his behavior came to light, I'm sure you wondered." She laid a hand on his arm, that gentle comfort a soft reminder of all the reasons he'd gone it alone.

His family had been a burden and an embarrassment to him, just as he'd been to them.

How did you bring someone into that?

Up until Caroline, he'd never considered his family name with respect to relationships. But as soon as he realized there was something special about her—and that his response to her wasn't like any woman before—he'd put up an emotional block.

She had a vocation and was damn good at it.

Bringing a career prosecutor into the orbit of a family desperate to create a political dynasty seemed foolish in the most basic sense.

"I looked into my mother and brother, quietly and on my own. Every line I tugged came up with them clean." He'd been exceptionally discreet, not even using any of his contacts, as he dug into the rest of his family. "Whatever pockets my father was in, he'd protected Zack and my mom in the process."

The heavy ring of the doorbell echoed through the house, announcing the moment everyone had been waiting for.

Olivia's date was here.

That inward clanging that he needed to call his mother and straighten things out didn't abate. Nor did the need to keep digging on Mia's computer program, seeing what details they could get on the man in the background of that photo.

There was no reason he and Caroline even needed to take part in whatever was going on outside the office. The kids were going out to the now-decorated barn for the movie, and Trace and Nic were entertaining the kid's mother for the evening. Garner and Mia had already made plans to take Jordan to an evening dinner and playdate with another toddler's family they knew in town.

He and Caroline could do what they wanted.

And what he wanted was to call his mother and raise holy hell her bodyguard was trying to hurt an innocent woman he cared about.

That last bit reared up and clamored for his attention but Caroline was already nodding toward the closed office doors.

"You might want to introduce yourself to Olivia's friend and his mom. Especially if Hogan's playing guard dog all night out in the stables."

Olivia's tears from earlier and his role in the evening's festivities slammed back into him.

Once again, it was proof of how his family managed to get under his skin and disrupt his life. Putting miles between them hadn't changed anything. Ignoring them hadn't, either.

He glanced at Hogan, who'd come to sentinel attention at the sound of the doorbell. The dog had stuck close all day. Ever since Jake and Caroline had returned from town with the news of the shooting, those elite senses had remained on high alert.

It was a departure from the way their lives had changed since coming to Wyoming but was a clear reinforcement of the dog's continued training and conditioning.

Hogan's adjustment to having more people around had gone well, but in the beginning he'd remained close to Jake, rarely venturing out of his sight. It was only after Olivia and Jordan became a fixture in Hogan's life that the K-9 started to remain wherever they were to keep watch over them.

And as Jake looked over to where his partner now sat straight up in the corner of the office, relaxed but fully aware, he nodded at Caroline's underlying point. "He makes an impression."

"That, he does. It might be worth an introduction to Nasher and his mom. Give them a chance to get used to Hogan while you explain his training and how he keeps watch."

"You sure you don't moonlight as a press-relations expert?"

"Now, what fun would that be when I can be a mouthy lawyer all day every day instead?"

Without giving him a chance to argue or suggest a different approach, Caroline headed out of the office and toward the kitchen.

Just like out in the stables, Jake gave himself another one of those moments to look his fill—especially since the sway of her hips made such an enticing picture—before he turned to his dog.

Hogan's raised eyebrows and steady gaze suggested what Jake already feared.

Caroline had already gotten under his skin.

And the only person he was fooling about it was himself.

Nasher was a nice kid.

That lone thought kept rolling through Jake's mind as he smiled through introductions with their new arrivals.

His imagined man-child from earlier was actually a respectable teenager, gangly and skinny and nearly as tall as Jake was, with tousled hair that flopped over his forehead in a fuzzy bush, and jeans that looked like they needed to be held up with duct tape.

He met every adult's eye when he spoke to them.

He was kind to his mother.

And he was totally infatuated with Olivia.

In a way that was actually sweet and nice, Jake admitted to himself.

Not that he was ready to suddenly trust fifteen-year-old hormones, but he could admit that whatever he'd imagined had been flat-out wrong.

The kid got serious points for how he greeted Hogan, too. He asked smart questions like how best to speak to Hogan and the right behaviors around him so as not to interfere with the K-9's training.

It was all…civilized and a far cry from the teenage frat party he'd envisioned.

So with the promise of pizza when they came back in, he and Caroline headed out back to set Hogan up while Nic and Nasher's mother, Ella, got the kids settled with their movie and snacks.

"He's a nice kid. And I'm really glad they're here tonight. I feel a lot better about it all." The relief was palpable in Caroline's voice as she kept up a steady pace beside him.

She remained close as he walked Hogan through several exercises outside the stables. They made a perimeter sweep as well as a check farther out into the yard before they doubled back and did a route in and around the paddock.

It was only when he started the same process a second time, more to give Hogan some exercise before he settled in to watch over Olivia and Nasher, that Jake shifted to the question that had been nagging at him.

"You're sure the guy who attacked you was the same as in the photo with my mother?"

"I wish I could give you a different answer, but yes, I'm sure."

"I've never seen him before but if he's an honest-to-God bodyguard then what's he doing going around hurting women?"

"And if he's a hired gun?"

The question was reasonable.

Rational.

And devoid of any sense of fear or anxiety.

The nonchalance with which she spoke about her attacker continued to haunt him. Caroline had been at risk, yet to hear her talk about it all you'd think was she simply tripped at a garden party, twisted an ankle and was now on the road to recovery.

The bastard in the photo had *attacked* her.

"Then why's he so damn stupid that he got himself photographed?"

"Why would he have ever worried about a connection? We'd never have found it if it weren't for Mia's computer work. There's no reason he or anyone else would think we'd make him in the way we did."

Caroline paused, obviously considering it further as Hogan stilled, waiting for them at the edge of the stable doors. The light of the overheads painted her in stark relief, and while the harsh fluorescents should have made her look nearly ghostly, he was reminded of a different time.

A different place.

The parking lot outside her favorite dive bar. The one she'd taken him to the night they made love.

The overhead lights had been garish then, too, glaring high above them. But then, just like now, all he saw was her.

All he wanted was her.

It wasn't the right time or place. And just like that night so long ago, taking a step toward her was a bad idea.

Only just like then, Jake moved in anyway.

He dropped Hogan's leash, unconcerned the dog would go anywhere, and placed his hands on her hips as he moved into her.

The need for her was a harsh pounding inside, but the sheer longing he had for her somehow smoothed it out, and he pulled her close with far more ease than he felt.

And then his mouth was on her and she was opening beneath him and everything faded away except the two of them.

Her tongue met his in one long, carnal stroke and Jake would have sworn he saw stars if his eyes were open. She was bold and determined and took exactly what she wanted.

It was sexy as hell.

And suddenly, he was frantic for her.

That empty desolation he lived with—the one he deftly ignored most of the time—filled and then faded when he was with her. Having her in his arms was the sweetest victory and spurred him on to take the kiss another level deeper.

Through it all, heartbeat by heartbeat, Caroline met him fully.

Her palms splayed against his chest and stomach as he kept her pressed against his body. With one hand he explored the length of her spine while the other settled at the base of her neck, an anchor to hold them both in place.

This wasn't the time and it sure as hell wasn't the place, but he couldn't stop touching her.

Wanting her.

But it was Hogan's loud bark that pulled them both apart.

That bark wasn't for show—Hogan was working—and it was the reminder that he needed to work, too.

They'd set up this situation, putting a damper on Olivia's plans for the night, for a reason.

He stared down at the dog, both of them now on high alert, before looking back at Caroline.

Sexual need still painted her features, from the pink that heightened her cheeks and neck to the heavier breaths that filled her chest, lifting her breasts with each inhale.

Even with the marked signs of her own need, she'd shifted to focused and alert, just like him and Hogan.

"Does he see something?" Her hands had settled lightly on his waist at Hogan's bark, but she dropped them to step away and look in the direction of the house where the dog's attention was focused.

He felt the absence of her touch as keenly as he felt the tension from his K-9, and Jake struggled against the weight of disappointment.

This wasn't the time for screwing around or a grand make-out session where anyone could find them. He needed to stay focused and sharp and protect his family.

But with the sudden realization something was out there, he needed to protect Caroline, too.

"Get behind me and then slip into the stables."

"Jake—"

"Now. I want Hogan to investigate and I can't worry that you're exposed out here."

He heard the intake of breath and expected an argument, but only got a small "fine" before the stable doors slid open behind them.

As soon as he heard them slide back home he gave Hogan the quiet order to move.

It was time to hunt their quarry.

Man and dog.

Two sentinels standing guard in the night.

What a joke.

Like either of them had any idea what—or who—waited just beyond the house lights.

It had been easy enough to set up his little surveillance equipment. A few payoffs in town with a freelancer looking for work and he was in business.

The camera—hidden high on the lamppost at the edge of the driveway—had given him a clear view of the comings and goings in the Podunk town his brother had vanished to.

And given him unfettered access to watch the Revered One's movements.

The eldest Stilton son.

Their father's great disappointment.

Just as it always did, his brother's audacity to simply walk away from the family, coupled with his father's inability to see what lay in front of him in Zack's attention and devotion to the family legacy, combined to infuriate him.

Even now, he remembered the fights that echoed from the family room as his father and brother went round after round about Jake's future.

Jake wanted a criminal justice degree; his father wanted him to pursue law.

His brother was insistent on spending his weekends working at the local animal shelter while his father seethed when the family wasn't all in attendance for an event that promised a series of photo ops.

And in the end, Jake had refused to be cowed and entered

the LVPD, working whatever hours he needed to—including beat cop work on the Strip in the August heat—to have the life he wanted as a detective.

Through it all, their father never saw what was standing right in front of him.

Zack *wanted* the political arena. He loved it beyond reason and thrived there. Shaking hands and holding babies and giving of himself to his constituents was his *life*.

And it was never enough.

Because he wasn't Jake.

Zack pushed back hard on the edge of his desk, his well-polished rolling chair falling to the floor behind him as he stood.

So far he'd resisted going to visit or making too big a deal about his brother's new address. It was easy to beg off with a busy schedule and a steady drip feed of soulful stories about standing by the old man and not wanting to go too far out of town or be too far away.

Jake hadn't questioned it, the limited, perfunctory texts they managed to exchange once or twice a week showing just how little interest he had in whatever was going on back in Las Vegas.

Just how little he cared about what he'd left behind.

That utter dismissal had been perfect and it was the distance from his sainted brother Zack had craved all his life.

He moved around the desk and headed for his sideboard, pouring the one drink he allowed himself each day. The spiced rum over ice wasn't the classic Scotch his father favored, but it was Zack's.

It was a new path.

A more modern path.

And in a small way, it was his own.

Zack took that first small sip and considered the past six

months. The overwhelming relief he'd first felt when Jake left had been palpable.

He'd finally be out of the shadow of his big brother.

And then a few months ago the old man had gone and changed his tune again. Saying how he needed Jake back home and that *he* could fix everything.

Zack had kept his finger in the dam for a few months, increasing his visits to his father in prison and amping up his own messaging in every public appearance he could find.

It had worked, too.

Zack's solemn, soulful rhetoric was catching on. That his father's disgrace actually shed light on a real problem: the seediest areas of politics, driven by outside interests and corporate greed. He'd stayed on message, unrelenting in the approach of just how difficult it was to lead in a time that demanded so much of politicians.

The message was gaining traction and the local kingmakers were eyeing him once again for his ascendance. The restoration of the family name and a focused effort to put him in his father's empty senate seat in another two years.

And then his father damn near blew it all up with a local interview that caught national attention.

All his regrets and the shame he brought his family, including his eldest son, who even moved away because of the embarrassment. One of Las Vegas's finest cops, leaving his home and his job because of the disgrace.

It was never Zack.

His father never saw what was right in front of him.

Only what he'd imagined for Jake.

Drink in hand, Zack crossed back to his desk and considered the video feed coming in crisp and clear on his laptop.

Jake and that ferocious dog of his stood on alert in front of the barn, looking around, trying to assess the invisible threat. The woman was gone, likely ordered away by Jake so he could play hero with his puppy.

But it was the woman Zack kept coming back to.

He'd always kept close tabs on Jake's life, well aware a love interest would provide another opportunity to put pressure as needed. His mother had sure as hell paraded enough *suitable candidates* at Jake over the years, but nothing had managed to stick.

No one who would provide the glue his parents needed to pull Jake back into their vision of a political dynasty.

It was only in the past few months, as Zack had searched for a new plan, that he'd caught wind of the woman.

Caroline Esterson.

And the small nugget of gossip his wife had snared one night at a charity event for the local hospital system. Charmaine's chatty seatmate had told her all about the legendary sparks that went off between Jake and the assistant district attorney whenever they got within a few feet of each other.

He'd been tempted to write it off. Jake was gone for Wyoming by that point and since he didn't have any obvious relationship with the woman—certainly not one that would keep Jake in Vegas—it hadn't seemed important.

But when Esterson's name had come up again a few days later, in conjunction with the prosecution of a local murder Zack was using in his stump speeches, he couldn't ignore the coincidence.

And learned that she was one of the brightest minds in the DA's office.

So he'd quietly asked around, his focus on local events providing that special blend of access and gossip that ran rife in every community. And in the asking, had learned that she was keeping tabs of her own.

Her steady requests for information on Senator Stilton's

case; her keen interest in the ongoing—and ever-expanding—state and federal charges brought against him.

And the very interesting news that the DA had opted to leave her out of the case they'd built on one of his father's racketeering charges.

There was no way she'd been left out by accident, and that was the linchpin for Zack.

Someone had recognized the woman's personal interest and it had given Zack a way in.

If Esterson was that interested, she'd either had something real with his brother or she'd manufactured it in her mind.

Either way worked for him.

Because either way, all he needed to do was get her to Wyoming and she could take the fall for Jake's *accident*.

The tragedy practically wrote itself.

Her nosing around in the senator's case had put her in the crosshairs of some very nasty people. People determined to tie up loose ends. And in their getting rid of Jake, she'd be collateral damage.

So sad, too bad.

The fact both of them were out of Las Vegas was the real bonus.

The cops up in Jake's neck of the woods would have no reason to connect his brother to the murders. The likelihood they'd even have the skills to consider it was low.

The only question was how.

He'd figured that Caroline was just a hanger on, his aloof brother's departure from town without the woman a sign she hadn't been nearly as important as she'd hoped to be. But the lusty make-out session in front of the barn, along with the way he looked at her, visible even in the black-

and-white surveillance video, suggested Zack might have been too presumptive on that count.

So he'd give them a test and see what shook out.

The shooting this morning at the diner had been a hasty order—one he'd given too quickly to try to get things over with. That was a mistake, and his gun-for-hire had already beat feet to Jackson Hole to let things settle down for a few days.

Since it had all been random and there hadn't been any reason to associate it with Zack, he wasn't worried. Antoine was rock-solid, and the promise of a key role in Zack's future dynasty ensured his loyalty.

Besides, he didn't need him right now. The camera he'd had planted on the ranch wasn't the only surprise he'd built in for his purposes.

Pulling up a new program on his computer, Zack considered the next test.

And with a last fortifying sip of his rum, he initiated the program sequence to self-destruct.

Caroline walked around the stables and tried to focus on what the guys had created in the barn for Olivia's date. The place positively glowed, the work they'd done in a few hours transforming a well-kept stable into something out of a movie.

White twinkle lights draped over bunting on the ends of stall doors. A dark sheet rigged over the back wall functioned as a movie screen. And lawn chairs had been strategically placed for optimal viewing.

A picnic table flush with the opposite wall held several bottles of soda and bags of chips waiting to be opened. Even her cupcakes had made it out here, courtesy of Bernice's setup while Caroline and Jake had been in the office.

All in all, the adults had created a suitable movie theater on very short notice.

It was special and sweet and beautiful, and Caroline was enamored with all of it before reality reared up once more in her mind.

They had to do all of this because of what she'd brought into their midst.

For all her concerns that Jake was at risk—and she stood by that—she'd also forced herself into this situation. The ongoing interest and her refusal to leave well enough alone put her squarely here.

Along with whomever had followed her.

Images of what Jake and Hogan now faced outside filled her mind and she ruthlessly pushed it aside. If there was something going on, she'd hear it. And if he needed help, he had several very large, capable men inside the house to address the problem.

Even knowing all that, it stung that she'd been sent to hide inside the barn.

A few times already she'd considered going outside to check on them but held back at the last minute.

Because that damn loop of truth kept whirling through her mind.

She was the one who'd brought this to Jake's doorstep.

And by extension, the wonderful people he shared his home with. The least she could do was allow him to manage a possible risk to their home without worrying about her getting in the way.

She felt rather useless and that wasn't a state she was used to.

But what had Hogan seen or sensed?

That deep, ferocious bark had pulled her and Jake apart, effectively dousing the flames he'd lit with that kiss.

And wow, was it some kiss.

Just like earlier in the front seat of his SUV, she'd been shocked into blazing sexual need the moment the man's lips touched hers.

Why was it so easy to fall back to that place?

The one she'd told herself over and over was well and truly *done*.

Was she that desperate for him she couldn't keep her hormones in check? Because damn it, she'd been down this path before. She'd taken what Jake had offered and believed she could *handle* it.

Yeah, right.

Instead of handling it, she'd become a needy version of herself she didn't like very much.

Not that she'd let him see that.

After their weekend together—and the lack of follow-up that suggested he wanted to see her again—she'd diligently avoided reaching out to him. She had no interest in coming off too available or needy.

Even if the memories of that weekend haunted her.

It was the reason—the *only* reason she told herself repeatedly—why she couldn't let any of it go.

A woman intuitively knew when a man was relationship material and when he wasn't. And as much as she believed he'd be damn good at one, Jake Stilton had *no commitment* written all over him in bright, blinking neon.

The smart, rational part of her got it.

Which made it exceptionally frustrating that her heart couldn't manage to get the message.

The stable doors rumbled from the opposite end of the building, and Caroline stepped away from Bernice's beautiful table scape to find out what Jake had discovered. Only to find Nic and Nasher's mom, Ella, along with the kids, heading straight for her.

Nic was pointing out a few details on the horses and the rescue and training operation to Ella when she caught sight of Caroline.

"Oh, Caroline. I didn't know you were in here."

Caroline weighed how much to say as she didn't want to alarm Ella. But in the end, there really wasn't any other way to say it. "Jake asked me to wait in here. Hogan's attention got caught on something and they went off to look into it."

Nic's concern flashed briefly before she deftly shifted the conversation. "I hope it's not a skunk. I know Jake loves that dog but there's no way we can deal with a smell like that inside the house."

"Hogan knows better than that," Olivia piped up before obviously realizing the mention of a skunk was a ploy. She gave a small shrug and pointed toward the back and the table full of food. "But he's also a dog so who knows."

"Who knows." Nic smiled at the kids. "Go on back and help yourselves. I'll put the movie on after you get some snacks."

The mention of food got the kids moving, and Caroline was left with Nic and Ella. Ella's gaze followed her son until he disappeared past the last stall door with Olivia before turning back to Nic. "It's amazing what you set up in here."

"My husband's been a little apprehensive about the idea of a date. So thank you for the quick change in plans."

"I'm glad they didn't have to cancel."

"I'm glad, too." Nic shifted a bit to include Caroline in the conversation. "And I appreciate you understanding our concerns and coming over here with Nasher."

"I'm sorry you're going through all this. Why would

someone follow you from Las Vegas?" Ella asked, her sympathy for Caroline's situation clear.

"I work for the district attorney's office. Unfortunately, people do get disgruntled with the justice system."

It was the truth and, sadly, Caroline realized, it actually fit the situation. Jake's father *had* committed crimes. All that had resulted since his arrest was an outcome of those poor choices.

Ones his son was now paying for.

"The shooting this morning has been all the talk in town. I'm just glad you're okay."

"We all are." Nic rubbed a warm hand over Caroline's back in support. "Since I also made sure we kept our fair share of the food back in the kitchen, how about we have some pizza and a glass of wine and let them get to their double feature?"

"I'd like that."

Nic walked off to help set up the superhero movies the kids had decided on and Caroline was left with Ella. "We moved here about a year ago. It's been nice to see Nasher settle in and find some new friends."

"Where are you from?"

"Born and raised in Seattle. After my divorce I was looking for fewer people and a lot less rain and we found ourselves here."

Caroline smiled and nodded as she deliberately kept her tone conversational. "It's beautiful here. And I can see where leaving the rain would be a most welcome change."

Along with whatever you ran from back home, Caroline silently added in her mind.

She'd worked with scared people for far too long not to recognize the signs.

The nervous eyes.

The slightly restless hands.

And the oh-so-practiced explanation for their move that said very little.

The temptation to say something was strong, but Caroline left the woman to her privacy.

Despite whatever lingering fear Ella carried, she was here and had still given her son a chance to enjoy his evening.

That spoke volumes about the life she was trying diligently to have.

Nic returned with a smile. "I'm not sure we put enough cupcakes on the table but I'll come out and check in a little while. In the meantime, our pizza awaits."

The three of them headed toward the exit, the swelling orchestra music coming up on the movie filling the barn with that dual sense of excitement and anticipation.

Which was exactly what a first date should be, Caroline thought as they started across the expanse of driveway to the house.

It was a happy thought. One that was matched by the easy lope of Jake and Hogan as they walked down the driveway from the opposite direction.

They were okay.

Maybe the skunk excuse wasn't too far from the truth. She didn't doubt the K-9 was well trained, but there had to be scents and smells here he wasn't used to. And dealing with animals skulking around *could* mimic an intruder.

It was an easy thought.

And obviously the wrong one as a huge explosion filled the air behind Jake and Hogan, fire erupting into the sky.

Chapter 10

Jake felt the wall of heat at his back as the air filled with fire and smoke and the deliberate menace of a bomb. The force of it all was enough to push him forward and he barely maintained his footing from the power of it all.

Damn it, Hogan had been right.

That thought filled Jake's mind through the chaos and the searing heat before stark fear filled him to his core.

Where was Caroline?

He'd seen her along with Nic and Nasher's mom coming out of the stables, and now he couldn't see anything for the thick clouds of black smoke and the suddenly dark night. Hogan's solid body pressed to his side and he reached down to touch his treasured partner, satisfied when he got a low bark in return.

"You okay, buddy?"

If the dog was shaken he was far better at focusing through it than Jake was. Whatever had caused the explosion had taken out the high spotlights they'd installed around the driveway. It was a situation Hogan would navigate far quicker than he would and with that foremost in his mind, he gave the order to find the others.

The dog took off at the order and Jake forced himself to stand still for a moment and take stock of the situation.

His ears rang from the explosion and his pulse hammered hard in his chest, all while that endless heat continued to roll through the air.

That moment of stillness paid dividends, and beyond the heavy ringing he could hear shouts.

And then Trace was suddenly visible, rushing toward him through the clearing smoke. The lights hadn't come back on but the fall evening still had a bit of sky left to it, detectable once again as the smoke billowed upward.

"Jake!" Trace came up beside him. "What the hell happened?"

"Where's Caroline? Where's Olivia? And Nic? The others?" The image of each person in turn struck him with edgy panic. "Where are they?"

Bennie materialized out of the lingering smoke. "Safe, man. They're safe." The older man laid a hand on his shoulder, the fatherly gesture going a long way toward lessening that roiling panic. "Saw them with my own eyes. They're okay."

He needed to see them for himself but the confirmation they were all okay helped to dim that endless throbbing in his ears.

God, he needed to get it together for a moment. The fierce adrenaline spike from the explosion had nothing on the wild emotions that couldn't find a place to land as he imagined each person he loved hurt or worse in this blast.

Bennie's hands never left him as the older man expertly kept contact, ensuring he remained grounded in the moment. "Bernice called it in. Sheriff's on his way and I trust she's got the rest going with the county's volunteer fire support."

"I need to see—"

He broke off as Olivia steeled through the smoke, slamming into both him and Bennie as her small arms came around his waist.

"Hogan found me. He was barking and carrying on and he—" She buried her face in his chest and clung tight as a burr around his waist. "You're okay."

Bennie stepped back, patting Jake's shoulder before giving them space.

"Yeah, squirt. I'm okay." He held on to her slim shoulders, taking comfort in the small, solid feel of her body and the evidence she was unharmed. "You're okay, too."

"I'm totally fine. It's not exploding or burning back there. The horses are upset, though."

All the words were a garbled rush against his chest and all he could manage to do was hang on, relieved Olivia was unharmed.

"It's okay." He couldn't seem to stop murmuring those words. "We're all okay."

Olivia stepped back and Trace was right there, at her side, pulling her close. "Dad. Mom and I are okay."

Trace barely let her get the words out before he was crushing her against his chest.

And then Caroline was there, like an apparition reforming out of the still-lingering smoke. "Jake."

His gaze raced over her face and body to reassure himself that she was, in fact, whole and unharmed. But when he looked into her eyes he saw the abject terror that had settled itself deep inside that crystal blue.

Her pupils were blown wide, her pulse throbbing hard at her throat. She hadn't started shaking yet but Jake knew it was only a matter of time.

Like their stolen moments in front of the barn—had it only been less than fifteen minutes since he and Hogan had left her in the barn to investigate?—Jake moved back into her, pressing his body to hers.

Caroline didn't say a word as she clung to him, and a big part of him was okay with that.

What could they say? That if things had gone even minutely different they wouldn't be here?

Just like only that morning when a gunman's bullet could have changed everything, too.

Two close misses.

And a matter of inches that could have had markedly different outcomes.

There were no words to make it better and very little beyond the need for human touch that could alleviate that stark, undeniable truth.

So he held her close and willed his strength into Caroline as he took the same right back from her.

And as Jake held tight, refusing to consider the alternative outcomes of their near misses, he remembered the desperate thoughts that had filled him as he and Hogan rushed from the blast.

The litany of names rushing through his mind as he fervently hoped each and every one of them was okay.

Because the people he loved most in the world lived on this ranch, all save one.

And now that Caroline was here, it was getting more and more impossible to think about letting her go.

Police and fire and EMS services all found their way to the ranch, like a parade in and out of the driveway. Caroline had spoken to a member of each team at least once, as had everyone else in the vicinity of the blast.

But it was Jake who bore the brunt of the questions.

From protocols for a possible concussion to a physical exam, he was the center of attention.

A state he hated if his repeated attempts to pace the kitchen—all met with the instructions to sit back down—were any indication.

Trace, Nic and Bennie remained outside with the sheriff and the fire chief, walking the property and assessing the damage. After setting out more food for everyone, Bernice headed for the stables with Ella and the kids to make room for the commotion in the kitchen.

Caroline had remained with Jake, keeping watch over him and Hogan.

So far she hadn't done much other than add her voice to the steady orders to sit down.

"I need to be out there," Jake said yet again, his mulish expression making it clear he was near a revolt. "I can tell Dawson where Hogan and I searched."

Caroline caught the eye of the EMT who was busy placing a bandage over a gash down the back of Jake's forearm. To the woman's credit, her facial expression never changed, but Caroline saw the solidarity—and genuine pity for Caroline's role as kitchen babysitter—all the same.

"You can tell him once he comes back in."

"But he needs the information now," Jake insisted.

"Jake, you need to get that cut looked at and cleaned up. Trace has it well in hand."

"Trace wasn't there. And I'm fine."

Since talking to Jake was the equivalent of banging her head against a rock, Caroline shifted focus to the EMT. "Any morphine in that bag of tricks there?"

Again, that visage never changed but the humor ticked low under her reply. "No, ma'am."

"I'm not picky, you know. You can use it on him or me, just please put one of us out of our misery."

The woman stood, dragging off her rubber exam gloves and pointing toward Hogan. The dog had settled in the corner of the kitchen and despite his best efforts to remain alert, his eyes drooped.

"I'm not a vet and I'd suggest getting him formally looked at, but I did spend all of my high school summers with one of Cage County's best vets. I can take a look at him if you'd like."

The shift in attention to Hogan was well played, and Jake's frustration for his own situation vanished. "He's stoic and won't give you much information to go on."

"I don't need much. If you think he'll let me I can do a light once-over on his body and see if he's got any sensitive spots or if I can feel any lumps or bruises forming."

Jake called the dog over, his commands low and gentle. Even with the exhaustion, Hogan's training was impeccable and he came forward immediately.

Caroline knew the bond between Jake and his K-9 was strong, but she fell a little harder for him as she watched how gently he touched his partner, using soothing words and more of the gentle commands to allow the EMT's ministrations.

After receiving Jake's all-clear, the EMT settled down beside Hogan on the floor.

"You're a good, brave boy, aren't you? Keeping your family safe."

Caroline didn't speak dog and she hadn't been lucky enough to have a pet growing up, but she was warmed by the woman's steady, soothing demeanor and care.

And couldn't resist a solid poke at Jake once the woman finished her exam. "He's a better patient than you."

"Jordan would be a better patient than me. I don't set a particularly high bar."

The EMT closed up her things, pulling out a few additional rolls of gauze and tape and setting them on the table. "You're set until tomorrow but you do need to change the bandage after you shower."

"Thanks." Jake was already on his feet when she stepped up beside him, all hints of mild-mannered goodwill gone. "Do you run your K-9 into the ground?"

If the situation weren't so dire, Caroline might have laughed at the look of pure offense painting Jake's face.

"Of course not."

"Why not?"

"Aside from the fact that it would be wrong to treat him that way, his skills aren't as sharp if he's too tired to work."

"Sound bit of advice, don't you think?"

She turned on her heel and left before Jake could sputter out an answer.

It shouldn't have been funny, but after the intensity of the past hour, her laughter bubbled up all the same.

"Mad she didn't leave you any morphine?" Jake's attitude was surlier than usual and he eyed her as she got up to walk to the counter.

The drawer she'd seen him rummage in earlier held some dog treats and she pulled out the bag, ignoring the question. "Mind if I give Hogan a few?"

"Dog deserves the whole bag."

Hogan's tail did a hard thump from where he lay near his dish, his gaze hopeful on the package. "That, he does. But maybe we can give him a few and then let him rest."

"I can do it."

Caroline pulled a few of the beef chews from the bag before turning to face Hogan. Even when she'd spent the weekend with Jake, she'd kept a solid distance from the dog. Partly in deference to his training and not wanting to overstep in any way, but more because the K-9 cut an impressive figure. He was beautiful, but powerful and she had a healthy attachment to all her limbs.

"Hold it in your palm."

Caroline did as Jake instructed, then waited for more, but Jake only nodded his encouragement.

And then she was on her own.

She had no actual fear Hogan would hurt her, but she wasn't sure he wanted anything to do with her beyond taking the treat.

So it was a serious surprise when, after gently nipping the treat off her hand, he settled his head against the underside of her hand.

When the dog made no move to leave, she turned her hand over and stroked his fur, giving him the same praise as the EMT. "So, so brave."

Caroline shifted her gaze from the soulful brown eyes staring up at her to the piercing blue ones that watched from across the room.

And in his steady, fathomless gaze, all the stress and strain of the explosion finally found a place to land.

Not the rush of adrenaline and emotion from outside when she'd run to him in the driveway, desperate to know he was okay.

But a different need.

One that asked a different kind of question.

Earlier, she'd worried about being too needy. About falling back into old patterns wanting someone who was emotionally off-limits.

It was only now, with the reality of what could have happened, that she recognized the folly.

She wanted him.

And there wasn't a reason on earth—not even the reality that she'd leave him when this was all over and go back to Las Vegas—that she wanted to stay away.

She could be sad and bereft later without him.

For now, she'd prefer to be whole and happy and alive with him.

Duty.

Responsibility.

Action.

They were the qualities Jake lived by. The principles he'd always believed in and, over the past few years since his father's crimes had come to light, they were the values he believed set his life apart.

Over and over, both professionally and personally, those principles were the base for all of his choices.

Yet somehow, someway, Caroline's presence in his life upended all of it.

He'd never believed that his responsibilities as a person ended because he wanted sex. He treated women with respect and honor and, most of all, he'd always chosen partners who wanted the same things he did.

Even the few relationships he had tried hadn't been grand declarations of love but more experiments in trying one another on and seeing how each other fit.

And no one ever had until Caroline.

She was one of the smartest and sharpest people he'd ever met, male or female, and she had a sense of honor of her own that he respected beyond measure.

He respected *her* beyond measure.

Which made it unreasonable to think that he could carry on an affair with her and keep it casual.

She wasn't a woman you *tried on*. She was a woman you committed to and married.

And he wasn't cut out for any of it.

Nor was he some lonely bachelor bemoaning his lack of luck in love.

He simply wasn't built for the sort of emotional nakedness required to let another person in.

Caroline hadn't moved from Hogan's side since giving him the treat, but Jake sensed a change in the air all the same. It had been the same way that night at the bar before they went back to his place.

The sexual tension humming between them was electric, but it was so much more.

She had *expectations* of him.

His father had expectations of him, too. Ones Jake had never lived up to or wanted. And because of it, he'd failed.

Because love was all about expectation.

And he'd never found his way to meet any of it.

Not for his father and the man's wishes that his son emulate his choices. Certainly not for his mother, who only carried an endless frustration with him. Hell, he didn't even have the basic ability to maintain a healthy relationship with his brother, their fraternal bond summed up in terse text messages and biweekly phone calls that were perfunctory at best.

It was easy to look at it now and blame all of it on his father's public disgrace, but his familial relationship had died long before his father was outed as a paid-for criminal.

Which always brought him right back to Caroline. She deserved so much more than he could give.

Hadn't he proved that very point by walking away?

And now she was only here because she needed his help.

He didn't get to pick and choose the easy parts.

Because falling back into bed with her would be oh so easy. Effortless, really.

It was what happened outside of bed that was the real challenge.

"Jake!"

The kitchen was suddenly filled with noise and motion, Garner and Mia rushing in with Jordan. Garner's daughter was groggy on his shoulder from the car ride home but rapidly coming awake at the tension gripping the house and grounds.

The fire had already been put out but the emergency crews had set up large spotlights in the driveway to aid the work. Add on the tension everyone carried at the mysterious explosion, and sleep was going to be elusive for all of them.

Mia came to him first, her hug more of a tight, fervent hold. She was a small woman but in her warm, motherly way managed to make the gesture so much more.

And vastly bigger than she was.

After one final squeeze Mia turned and repeated the same with Caroline before then bending to pet Hogan, who was so tired he did little more than lift his eyes. He did thump his tail in greeting.

"What happened?" Garner asked after all the necessary hugs and confirmation that everyone was unharmed had passed.

Jake filled them both in, detailing Hogan's initial awareness of something beyond the stables and their subsequent pass around the house and surrounding yard to check it out.

Garner's frown deepened as he resettled Jordan on his shoulder. Now that they'd shifted to conversation she'd settled back down, her head nestled against her father. "Hogan's trained in bomb detection. He didn't smell it?"

"Nothing registered. But he was restless. Kept pacing

the same area up and down the fence line, but each time I looked I couldn't find anything."

Jake glanced over at the dog, fully asleep, and knew his well-trained and highly sensitive sense of smell had found something.

"I figured we'd look again in the morning and turned him around to come back to the stables so he could play guard dog for the big date."

Garner did smile at that, his and Mia's decision to leave for the evening steeped in Mia's insistence they not overwhelm Nasher and his mom with too many people.

And instead, they'd gone and had a major incident smack in the middle of the ranch, with a bomb blast. The kids would have been far safer at the mall, thirty minutes away.

Garner's smile faded fully, his face somber once more. "Dawson did say it started in your house."

"Damn it."

That was the final confirmation he needed. Especially because Hogan's focus had been around that section of the property.

Without checking the impulse, Jake let out a low, harsher string of expletives.

His house?

Mia took Jordan from Garner's shoulder. "Thank God you and Hogan turned around. If you'd waited any longer I hate to think—"

She shook her head. "You did move and now we'll deal with whatever this is."

"We've got this, Jake," Garner vowed. "All of us."

Caroline had remained silent since they'd come in, her gaze repeatedly landing on Jordan. He couldn't claim clairvoyance, but he already knew she worried about bringing this problem from Las Vegas to their home here.

Only a bomb changed things.

A bomb that *wasn't* planted today, upon her arrival.

Which meant she was absolutely right in her assessment that he was the real target.

Whatever was lurking out there had been aimed straight at him all along.

Caroline had seen Jordan's room briefly when Mia gave her a tour of the house, but the small room felt different now that she understood what had happened outside.

What risks lay just beyond the pink, purple and blue frills and big stuffed animals and the old wooden rocking chair.

The little girl was mostly asleep, her eyes droopy as Mia gently laid her on top of the dresser that doubled as a changing table. Jordan might have sensed the excitement earlier, but here, in her own room within her mother's care, gently removing her clothes and preparing her for bed, she had no idea of what had happened outside the house.

No understanding of just how close the danger had come.

Danger Caroline had brought to their door.

"How are you doing?" Mia was a deft hand with the diaper and in moments she was snapping a line of closures on a sleeper outfit that ran from Jordan's foot up to her neck. It was impressive and on top of Mia's computer skills and gentility, Caroline was reminded of Jake's compliment earlier.

The woman really was a unicorn.

Maybe it was all that perfection that had the dam bursting, but the tears and the words spilled out in a rush. "Very, very sorry I came here."

If either was a surprise, the human unicorn didn't miss a beat.

Nor did she try to *there-there* away the tears.

Instead, she finished taking care of Jordan, pressing a deep kiss to the child's forehead before she settled the toddler into her crib. It was only then that she crossed back, took Caroline's hand and led her down the hall to the room she shared with Garner.

Also part of the tour earlier, Caroline had somehow missed the sitting room on the far side of the overly large king-size bed and realized the cozy couch was their destination now.

Mia turned on a lamp and snagged a few tissues from the box on the end table as she gently settled Caroline into place. Taking the seat beside her, she remained watchful but unfazed as the tears continued to fall.

The sheer kindness and understanding of it all was enough to make the sobs heavier and harder before they finally subsided. When the rush of adrenaline and emotion and absolute fear had finally worked itself out of her body.

Not that the fear didn't find a place to linger, but those hard stabs of awareness—and the constant concern something would happen to someone on the ranch—had dulled a bit.

Even as Caroline had no doubt they'd be back.

"Everyone is okay," Mia finally said, her tone gentle. "You can take comfort in that."

"And if they hadn't been? I brought that here. Me." The agony of it all spewed from her chest as hard as the tears. "This morning, someone could have been seriously hurt or killed in the diner. Jake is of course my biggest concern but anyone else there could have been harmed."

"But they weren't."

"And now? Tonight? You said it yourself, Mia. If Jake and Hogan had been a bit closer. If Jake hadn't decided to move along and instead given Hogan one more chance to read the perimeter."

"But he didn't."

"But he could have."

Those steady arguments were the curse of her intellect, both the one that had trained in the law and the core of who she was.

Caroline saw possibilities. She always had. And while it might be a trait others made clichés out of and TV shows scripted for that bulldog-like tenacity, it was the way she saw the world.

What if?

Where, when, what, why and how.

The tenets she lived by.

Mia's gaze was gentle, but something hard and certain glittered in her green eyes. "I'm an analyst. It was my job for a very long time to consider every scenario. To imagine every variable. And almost three years ago, I failed in that and by extension, failed Garner's SEAL team on a mission. The three other SEALs on that mission died. Garner was the only survivor."

"I didn't know."

"How could you?" Mia's smile was soft but that glittering determination remained. "Aside from the fact it's classified, it's not a story I or Garner share broadly. I'm telling you because I know you'll understand."

"Thank you for trusting me with it."

"I believed for a long time I was solely responsible. That all my work was flawed and I could have prevented what happened."

Caroline pictured the clever AI program from earlier and the cool calm that seemed to define Mia. There was no world where this woman dismissed threats and put people in danger.

"Of course you couldn't have. Things do happen out of anyone's control. And presumably something was faulty by design in the intel you were given."

"A truth you settled on a heck of a lot faster than I did. It took me a long time to believe it. And because of that, I kept my child from her father. I also believed I had to work alone, fixing the problem."

"How do you fix something that's so far beyond you?"

All that glittering hardness softened at the question, doing nothing to hide the triumph in her smile. "That's my question back to you. You can't take ownership for something nefarious happening on the part of others."

Caroline wanted to believe she might have seen the neat trap if she wasn't so far gone with worry, but that likely dismissed those very real unicorn skills of the woman sitting opposite her.

Skills that were wrapped up, at their core, in the deepest level of care and compassion.

"You came here to warn Jake. I shudder to think what would be happening right now if you hadn't."

"There wouldn't be bullets in the town diner."

"But there still would have been a bomb in his house. The one he's building on this very property."

Mia reached for her hands once more, her grip tight. "*Think*, Caroline. You didn't bring this here. It's been here all along, brewing in silence. You're the one who sent up the warning and it's one I'm deeply grateful for."

"It's one I'm grateful for, too." Jake stood in the bedroom doorway. "*I'm* the one who's put my family in danger. And now that I know it, I can do something about it."

Chapter 11

Jake had listened in on the end of Caroline's discussion with Mia. He'd eavesdropped without remorse, taking a page squarely out of Olivia's book.

And as he'd stood there in the hallway, shamelessly hoping Mia could smooth over what he'd handled so poorly up to now, he heard the deep anguish and fear that lay beneath every word Caroline spoke.

She believed herself responsible for the events of today when all she'd done was take the problem in hand and come to warn him.

Come to make sure he stayed safe.

And all he'd done was brazen his way through it, claiming he was fine and that whatever she was worried about had no impact on him.

And yet somehow, someway, someone had planted a bomb in his home.

One that could have killed anyone on this ranch.

So it all had a hell of a lot of impact.

Caroline had been crying and he was sorry for the tears he'd caused there, too. But as she stared at him across the expanse of Garner and Mia's bedroom, Jake took solace that there was a renewed conviction in her gaze.

Whatever had happened today hadn't snuffed out the essence of who she was.

Caroline Esterson was a woman who would always fight another day.

"Dawson would like to ask us a few more questions before he leaves."

She only nodded and got up from the couch. But before she could walk away, Mia laid a hand on her forearm to stop her.

"Please remember what I said. Even in the big, overwhelming moments, it doesn't make any of it less true. You've shined a light, Caroline. One that's protecting us all."

"Thank you."

She remained silent in the walk downstairs to the kitchen and Jake struggled to find the words to make it better. Instead, all he felt was an emotional sort of clumsiness that butted up against his usual desire to remain aloof and quiet.

He needed to *say* something to her.

But what?

That reminder of the raw panic he'd felt when he stood in the driveway, in the midst of the smoke and fire from the blast and didn't know where she was or if she was hurt, broke through the indecision.

Stopping in the middle of the family room, he turned to face her. "Dawson will help us. You can trust him in whatever you need to say."

"I won't lie to him."

"I know, but you can really trust him. We've proven ourselves to him and he's done the same in return. He's a good guy."

"I'll keep that in mind."

It wasn't a dismissal, exactly, but her flat words and empty expression were proof that whatever was going on had finally taken its toll.

That clumsy feeling didn't fade so Jake simply stepped aside, giving her the room to continue on to the kitchen.

He needed to follow but Hogan caught his eye where he was curled up on the oversize pillow that served as his bed in the corner of the family room. Jake walked to the corner, ostensibly to check on his furry mate, when he took in the tableau the sleeping dog made, juxtaposed next to a small cloth bin of Jordan's toys.

A doll in a pink dress lay next to an army man in fatigues. Stacking boxes—covered with numbers and letters and colors—nestled together and Jake knew when they were ordered smallest to largest they represented various sizes and a guide to counting. And finally, one of Hogan's favorite chew bones stuck up out of a colored stack of rings.

His *life* had mingled with this family.

They cared about him and had made a place for him, even though he wasn't blood.

And tonight it had become clear that *he* had been the one to put them in danger.

A check mark in the column of how his hubris and resistance to seeing his father's choices for what they were was far more insidious than he ever could have imagined.

And it brought to mind what Nic and Trace and then Mia and Garner had come up against over the past months. In each case, they'd encountered a nameless, faceless threat outside of themselves. A puppet master in the wings, manipulating events for their own gain.

He wanted to say this was the same. He sure as hell didn't know *who* was doing it.

But he damn well knew why.

And all of it centered on his family and his father's awful choices in his insatiable need for political power.

Which only served as a reminder of all he'd struggled with earlier.

It was fair and right for your loved ones to have expectations of you. Decency and fairness and a regard for living with morals and a code of honor were all good things.

But expectation that came with a price—that love or understanding or empathy would be taken away if a set of criteria wasn't met—just wasn't the right model.

And those feelings he'd pushed against all his life weren't about whether or not he wanted to enter into politics to make his dad proud. They were about having his parents' love and acceptance for who he was and who he chose to be in life.

And that was where *they* had failed.

Over and over.

Understanding that didn't suddenly change all that had come before with Caroline. But it did change how he wanted to move forward.

He had a choice.

Just like he'd had a choice to come here to Liar's Gulch and build something with his friends. A decision that had led to the relationships he now treasured so damn much it hurt.

And had created dog bones in toy boxes and video game battles with mouthy teenagers and a trusted inner circle.

He couldn't make up for what had come before, but continuing to equate time with Caroline to his family situation was unfair to them both.

Most of all to her.

He didn't deserve her forgiveness simply because he'd decided he wanted to change. But he could change his attitude and tell her how he felt.

And if he was lucky, get a chance to try again.

It was a start.

And if he crashed and burned? Then he'd find a way forward there, too.

Caroline had a right to high expectations. The highest of the high.

Maybe it was time to find out if he was the man for the job.

"Can you walk me through the dog's reaction outside the stables?"

Caroline knew Dawson was only doing his job, but she'd grown increasingly uncomfortable with his questions knowing her answers would inevitably circle around to making out with Jake in front of the barn.

Stables, she mentally corrected herself.

That large wooden structure that housed animals and which likely still bore the imprint of her heated skin on its sliding front door.

"Jake was leading Hogan through a series of exercises, checking the perimeter of the stables before he was going to set the dog up with the kids while they watched their movie."

"Did something specific set him off?"

"I don't know."

"Did you see anything?"

Heat crept up her neck since the answer to that question was a big fat no.

Because her eyes were closed.

All because Jake Stilton was attempting to reach her tonsils with his tongue.

A point that felt especially salacious since the owner of said tongue chose that moment to waltz into the kitchen.

"She didn't see anything, Sheriff Kane. She was otherwise occupied with me."

"I see." Dawson clicked the end of his pen and closed his notebook.

"What exactly do you see, Sheriff?"

She might be as red as a Christmas present, but she was still a lawyer.

A damn good one.

And ending his questions with some sort of final click of his pen like it was *game over* wasn't going to work for her.

"What other questions do you have for me?" Caroline pressed.

"I don't have any other questions. Whatever else I need to ask can wait until tomorrow after you all have had a chance to rest and recoup. It's been a bad day."

Hadn't Jake said Dawson was a good guy?

"I can keep going," Caroline pressed, his acknowledgment she was exhausted—especially after the long drive she'd made the day before—suddenly drawing a yawn.

"Not to worry. I'll be back tomorrow and we can talk again. In the meantime, let this simmer in the back of your mind. Things back home ultimately set you off and sent you up here. I'd like to know more about those things because they've no doubt got an impact on what's happening now." Dawson stood. "We'll start fresh in the morning."

Jake saw the man out and it was only as he once again stood beside the table that Caroline realized she'd fallen asleep, her head propped on her palm.

"Time for bed."

"Yeah, it probably is." Caroline glanced around the kitchen. "Did I really only get here this morning?"

"Yeah, you did."

"Bet you wished I'd stayed home." She felt his strong but gentle grip on her forearm as he pulled her up from the chair.

"Bet you'd be wrong."

Before she even realized what he planned, he had her up in his arms, carrying her toward the stairs. She came awake fully on the realization that she was lifted in the air and being carried to bed. Like… Like a soap opera heroine.

Or like someone treasured.

"I'm too heavy for this."

"I'll be the judge of that." His voice was husky against the side of her neck, the heat of his breath sending shivers racing down her spine.

Was she still asleep at the table and this was just a powerful and glorious dream?

Because it felt like one.

And as Jake carried her into the guest room Mia had shown to her earlier, Caroline decided to be brave, like she was in dreams, and ask for what she wanted.

"Stay."

Jake stared down at her, the light from the hallway reflecting behind him. "I shouldn't."

"Maybe not. But I'd like you to all the same."

When he only nodded and turned away she figured her dream had taken a turn. Not quite a nightmare, but an embarrassment she'd be happy wasn't actually real tomorrow.

Until he closed the door, effectively shutting off the light, along with her fanciful notions.

Because this wasn't a dream.

And Jake wasn't going anywhere.

Stay.

Caroline's request seemed to linger in the room.

As he crossed back to shut the door. As he toed off his work boots. And as he slipped onto the bed, pulling her against his chest.

She needed rest. They both did. But that quiet request, a powerful lure in the dark, was impossible to resist.

His body had already reacted to her nearness, the raging need for her hard and insistent against his fly. And yet… even with that determined reminder his body wanted so much more, it was easy to set it all aside.

Because he needed to hold her even more.

To reassure himself that she was whole and safe and *alive*.

Caroline turned into his chest, one hand pressed against his heart and the other at his hip. He wrapped his arms tight around her, marveling at how easily she fit, nestled there.

And wondering how he'd walked away all those many months ago.

"Sheriff Kane is a good guy." Caroline's comment broke the silence.

"I'm glad you think so."

"So are Trace and Garner."

Her words were sleepy but Jake sensed there was some point underneath. So he continued tracing lazy circles over her spine as he answered her. "Right again."

"You're one of them, you know."

"It's good of you to think so."

"I know so." She looked up at him, her gaze solemn in the limited light from the small crack in the curtains. It wasn't much, but his eyes had adjusted well enough that he could see her face and the conviction that painted her wan features.

"What makes you so sure?"

"You don't know how to be anything but good, Jake Stilton."

It was an earnestness he didn't deserve and sure as hell hadn't earned.

But to his earlier thoughts as he'd checked on Hogan in the family room, he could start making up for it.

"I haven't been very good to you."

"What do you mean? You've helped me since I got here. You've taken care of me and everyone else."

"I mean before, Caroline. After we got together. I owed you a hell of a lot more than a 'thanks for dropping me off at my car' and then walking away."

The exhaustion still rode her features, but he sensed an alertness that had broken through the need for sleep.

And along with it, a level of indecision before she finally spoke.

"Yes, you did."

"I'm sorry for it. For running away. And for being too big a jerk to tell you how I really felt."

"Which was how?"

It was the moment of truth. The one he'd avoided in every way, from pretending it didn't exist to telling himself speaking it into words wouldn't make any difference.

Only it did matter.

And she deserved to hear it.

"Scared."

They lay there for a long time, his confession hovering between them. The very big, very vulnerable, part of him wanted to snatch back the words.

But the other part of him—the part way down deep that had wondered about her, even after telling himself he'd moved on—waited with bated breath for her answer.

Because he'd never forgotten their weekend together. Or how good it was between them and how *right* he felt when he was with her.

Or how wonderful it had felt to be whole.

All those feelings lived in the part of himself that refused to forget her.

And the part that really scared him was if she felt anywhere near the same way he did, he was in real trouble.

Rest of his life trouble.

Share all those dark, vulnerable, naked parts of himself trouble.

"I'm scared, too." The hand that rested on his hip lifted to press against his cheek. "The way I feel about you scares me because it makes me forget a part of myself. And I can't forget how to be strong. Or how to stand on my own."

"Even with all these miles between us, you found me anyway. You pushed and pushed until I saw the truth. Until I realized the danger. How can you say you're not strong? It's all I see when I look at you."

"And all I see is a woman running after a man who doesn't want her."

In all the months since they'd spent the weekend together, nothing could have prepared him for those words.

"How could you think that? Or believe I don't want you? How—"

And that was when he stopped himself and really looked at all of it.

Because he *had* walked away. Thanked her for the ride and gotten out of her car and never called again.

What the hell else was she supposed to think?

"I thought all of it because you walked away."

Her low tone quavered at the edges, but the strength was unmistakable. A perfect example of who she was to her very core. Even when something was difficult, she did it anyway, no matter the cost.

"From the weekend. From me. From your home. One day you were just gone. So I told myself I needed to keep doing what I was already doing. Forget you and whatever could be between us. I had to forget the fire and the sparks and the laughter and the orgasms." She dropped her head then against his chest. "So many orgasms, you bastard."

It should have been funny, especially since he recognized her attempts at humor were meant as a shield.

Only he couldn't find it inside to laugh. Or even puff up at the suggestion he'd left her well satisfied.

Instead, that juxtaposition of Hogan's bone in the midst of Jordan's toys filled his thoughts once more.

He could have a different life. A better life. If he made the choice.

"I can't take it back, Caroline. Any of it. Including the orgasms. And you can call me a bastard any time you want because I deserve it. I will likely always deserve it."

He pressed a knuckle under her chin, bringing her gaze back to his.

"But please, whatever you do think, don't ever question yourself. You bring out the very best parts of me. The ones I didn't even realize were there. They also happen to be the parts of myself I'm not very good at. But my running from them has never been about you."

Jake pulled her close, pressing his lips to hers. Caroline leaned into the kiss, falling into the dream of being with him again.

He hadn't fully erased all the anxiety she'd carried the past year, but there was something about a man saying you brought out the best part of him that went a long way toward assuaging negative feelings.

What it couldn't manage to erase was the worry from the day.

"I must be doing this wrong." Jake murmured the words against her lips.

"You're doing this exactly right. I'm just—"

Caroline considered Dawson's parting words and admitted the sheriff had distracted her.

Things back home ultimately set you off and sent you up here. I'd like to know more about those things because they've no doubt got an impact on what's happening now.

Jake was from back home, too.

And all of this did center on him, the bomb on the property on the same day she arrived proof that the situation had been building for some time.

What didn't make any sense was how anyone could possibly connect them.

No matter how much angst she'd personally carried over their sex weekend, to the outside world they didn't have any relationship to speak of.

So who put them together or even recognized a connection beyond the same professional relationships she shared with the rest of the LVPD?

Jake shifted slightly and turned on a bedside lamp. "What are you working through? Especially since it's putting a real damper on kissing me back."

The joke was just that—a statement meant to tease her, nothing more—and in it Caroline recognized yet another facet of Jake's personality that pulled her in.

He had a healthy ego, but it wasn't predicated on how someone else behaved.

Instead, he could see the bigger picture and not pout or mope over being ignored.

While she'd been in a bit of a dating desert the past several years, she'd been rather successful through college and law school. And in that time had found several men who—despite also seeking their own degrees—had little time or tolerance for her devotion to seeking hers.

Anything that pulled attention off their goals or their needs had been met with frustration and dismissal.

A trait she'd never seen in Jake.

Since this wasn't about his kissing—which was amazing—Caroline leaned in and laid a hot one on him, pleased when his hands tightened on her shoulders and he pulled her hard against his chest.

When they finally surfaced, she couldn't resist a tease of her own.

"My distraction has nothing to do with the kissing."

"Then what does it have to do with?" The husky timbre of his voice nearly sent her right back into his arms, clamoring ideas aside.

"Dawson asked me to think about what happened back at home."

The stiffening of his shoulders was immediate. "You were attacked."

"I mean before that. Way before it. You and me before it."

"What about us?"

"Exactly. There wasn't an *us*. There was you. There was me."

"There was a hell of a lot of *us* in my bed for an unforgettable weekend."

That growly voice shot straight to her core once more and Caroline diligently fought back the undeniable urge to just jump the man.

Focus on the problem, not on the way his chest feels under your palms.

"Yes, there was a lot of *us*. I didn't mention those orgasms for funsies or to stroke your impressive ego. But other people don't know about that weekend, Jake. We weren't dating or public in any way."

"It's no one's business."

"No, it isn't. Yet, somehow you and I've been connected by someone back home. That message in my parking lot a few nights ago was about you. Whoever followed me to Wyoming is here because of you. And whoever's behind all this went and proved it by planting a bomb here in the midst of your life."

"Which is why first thing tomorrow we're digging into that guy in the photo with my mom. He's the key to this."

"Or maybe he's just a tool. All of what's happened feels awfully personal to come from the hands of a man you don't even recognize."

The ideas flew through her mind so fast Caroline knew she was missing an important piece.

But it all *felt* important.

"Someone went to a lot of trouble to set up a bomb on this property, especially with the volume of surveillance and the collective skills of everyone in this house. That's not something to take lightly."

"Lightly? It's a freaking breach."

Jake's anger flared sky-high once more and Caroline quickly rushed on, doing her best to smooth out the frustration.

They needed to focus on the point underneath. The one that spoke volumes about whomever was plotting against Jake. It was the idea she kept furiously digging at, even as it felt like all she was doing was moving around a hell of a lot of dirt.

"That bomb was a plant, likely done weeks or months ago, set up in advance for just the right moment."

"So what made today the right moment?"

"Me. I was the catalyst. My coming here put it into motion."

"But you didn't decide to come here until that guy attacked you."

"Because I got too close. I asked the wrong question or I tipped off the wrong person but I set it into motion with my questions. Dawson's right. The answer is back home."

"But the problem is here."

"No, Jake. The problem is wherever you are. And until we figure out why you're in danger."

"No." He shook his head. "As long as I'm the target, I'm a danger to anyone close to me."

"I don't think a single person in this house will see it that way. And not one of them will let you face this alone."

"There was a time when I could have agreed with that. I might not have liked it, but I would have understood. Trace and Nic. Garner and Mia. Even Bennie. They know how to handle themselves and have worked in dangerous situations."

"Then trust them to know how to help."

"I do trust them. But now there are children in this house. Bernice, and Jordan's nanny, Astrid, too. I can't put them in danger."

"You have people here who will help you."

"Right. They will help me. It's why I want you to stay here while I go deal with this."

She'd accepted it earlier, when Jake had told her to stay inside the stables while he and Hogan went to suss out possible danger and she'd hated it.

There was no way in hell she was going to face days wondering if he was okay or risking his life from a faceless threat.

"I'm not staying here."

"You have to. I can't worry that you're hurt."

"Right back at you, Jake."

With his jaw set in implacable lines, Jake pressed on. "I left you behind because I couldn't deal with how I feel about you. Facing a situation that you might not survive? I can't live with that."

"Are you so blind you can't understand I couldn't live with it, either? The whole reason I'm up here is because I can't stand the idea of you being in danger. Of a world without you in it."

"This isn't your battle to fight."

"No, Jake. It's our battle."

"I want you safe. That's the only thing that matters."

He believed what he was saying. Caroline saw that clearly.

But she couldn't see her way to agreeing.

Nor was she going to change her mind.

"Either we're an us or we're not. I'm not looking for halfway."

"This isn't about halfway. It's about me fighting a battle that's only mine to fight."

"No, it's about you continuing to shut me out. For a different set of reasons you've decided I need to follow."

Without checking the impulse or giving herself a chance to back down, Caroline stood and headed for the door.

"I've lived my life without you, Jake. I'm actually pretty damn good at it. It might not be my preference, but I can do it. What I can't do is accept only the parts of yourself you're willing to dole out to me."

"This isn't the same, damn it!" He came off the bed, standing before her, anger flashing in his gaze. "Knowingly putting you in danger isn't the same as being afraid to start a relationship with you."

"Leaving me here while you go out to fight the problem isn't a relationship, either."

Chapter 12

Caroline stared at the clock on the stove, the digital numbers flashing as another minute passed. For someone who was past exhausted, she had no idea how she was sitting upright, let alone watching the clock, but here she was.

"You look like you could use something stronger than water."

She turned to find Bernice padding into the kitchen, her feet clad in thick, fuzzy slippers that matched an equally plush, fuzzy bathrobe.

"I'm sorry if I woke you."

Bernice waved a hand as she grabbed the kettle on the back burner of the stove and headed for the sink. "There are ten people and a dog in this house. At any given moment of any given day, someone's awake."

Caroline couldn't help but smile as the older woman took the now-filled kettle and set it back on the stove, flipping the burner on in one practiced move.

"I should be asleep."

"That's nearly always the case at three in the morning." Bernice winked. "Unless a body's getting up to more interesting pursuits than sleeping."

"Yes, well, there are no, um, pursuits…happening."

Bernice sniffed at that. "Shame."

Her legal training kicked in and since she had no actual

response for Bernice's sniff and what passed as a pointed criticism, Caroline opted to remain silent.

What she hadn't banked on was that Bernice not only possessed the same set of skills but the woman seemed to take great delight in taking the chair opposite Caroline and waiting her out.

"Do you like living here?" Caroline finally gave in and asked.

"It's been the right choice for my Bennie and me. We love Jordan and Mia and followed them here from DC."

"Wyoming is a long way from DC."

"In some ways." Bernice nodded. "But distance isn't everything. We—"

She broke off, her deep brown eyes troubled. "We're estranged from our son. Lived five miles from him back home and we might as well have been a thousand miles away."

"I'm sorry for that."

"I am, too. More than I can say. But when Mia and Jordan came into our lives…" At the mention of the baby Bernice lit up once more. "Well, some prayers do get answered."

The kettle whistled and Bernice got up to get it. In a matter of minutes she was carrying two mugs of tea back to the table, the comforting scent of raspberry floating from the mugs. Bernice busied herself with pulling a few sugar cubes out of the bowl and Caroline realized she wanted to know the answer to the question the older woman likely wasn't even aware she'd left hanging.

"What were you praying for?"

"A chance to be useful again. Time with young people who need us. A family." Bernice looked around the kitchen, her small smile not quite erasing the sadness from when she'd spoken of her son. "The Lord was generous and I am grateful."

"And what about your relationship with your son?"

"I'm greedy enough to keep asking for that, too."

"Loving people isn't easy."

"That's where Jake gets tripped up." Bernice dunked her tea bag a few times before placing it on a small saucer already on the middle of the table. "He thinks he's not any good at it."

"He's told you that?"

"He hasn't needed to. And whatever he came from never taught him that way more than half of love is about showing up."

Jake was a man who showed up. From that very first day, when he'd agreed to meet with her at the buffet, he'd proven that. On the case that followed and the others she'd asked his help with as well.

And then today.

He hadn't hesitated to make sure she was okay.

The only place he had hesitated was after their weekend together and even that choice he'd fully taken on himself.

"He watches over everyone," Bernice continued on. "That precious baby adores him. Olivia thinks he walks on water. The dog is devoted to him."

"Jake doesn't know how to be anything else," Caroline said.

"And he still doesn't give himself much credit." Bernice let out another little sniff. "Seems to me it'll take a rather impatient woman to make him see the light and recognize what he's worth."

"I thought patience was a virtue?"

Bernice's smile was knowing when she picked up her mug and gave Caroline a considering look over the top of it. "When it comes to dealing with stubborn men, virtue's highly overrated."

Thoughts of virtue and patience and stubborn men accompanied Caroline a half hour later as she headed back for the guest room. She wasn't any closer to answers but the raspberry tea and conversation went a long way toward getting her ready for bed.

One that still had a man in it, she realized as she walked into the guest room.

Jake's long form was stretched out on the bed, his head turned in to the pillow and his feet nearly hanging off the bottom. His features had smoothed out in sleep and she gave herself the briefest moment to just look at him.

She'd always thought he was an attractive man, a point just as evident in sleep as when he was wide-awake. But as she observed him, Bernice's reminder rang loud and true over all the rest.

More than half of love *was* about showing up.

He might need to work on the rest of it, but the man had the right foundation.

After crossing around to the other side of the bed, she got in and pulled the covers over herself. They were still miles apart on how to fix the problem that lurked in the shadows, but tea and conversation and those hearty sniffs of disdain from Bernice had galvanized her in a new direction.

Because she was a person who showed up, too. And she damn well wasn't going anywhere.

It was the second to last thought in her mind as she drifted into sleep.

The very last was how nice it felt when Jake's arms came around her, pulling her tight against his chest.

Jake woke up with a breast in his hand and a warm woman pressed against every inch of his body and figured he'd either won the lottery or died. It was only as he considered it, coming awake now that he realized where he was, that he didn't need either.

Because with the right woman, money was overrated and he sure as hell wasn't ready to die.

And Caroline was most definitely the right woman.

Deciding to put his good fortune to the test, he bent his head and pressed a line of kisses on the curve of her neck.

Since his reward was a warm wiggle where her butt pressed more firmly against his most determinedly awake body part, Jake doubled down.

And got a small shriek as the object of his morning attention leaped out of his arms and the bed in one smooth move, like a cat doused in water.

"What are you doing?"

Jake adopted the same innocent face he'd seen on perps the world over. "Saying good morning."

"With your hands. And your lips. And—" She glanced down where his joggers hid absolutely nothing.

"*And* is right." He leaned forward, quick as a whip, and snagged her hand, pulling her off balance toward the bed. "*And* is very, very good."

She was lithe enough to keep her feet, even as she left her hand in his.

"*And* is off the table until I brush my teeth and shower and—" she glanced down at herself, suddenly frowning "—and look far better than I do right now."

"You're perfect."

"Your *and* is talking."

He tried one last valiant attempt, but recognized the futility when she snatched her hand back and crossed her arms to prevent another tug forward. "But it has so much to say."

Caroline had already snuck around the bed and headed

for her suitcase. He decided that watching her without her knowing was highly overrated and instead settled back against the headboard, his arms behind his head, to watch her deliberately.

She rummaged around her suitcase, her incredibly attractive backside—the one still indelibly imprinted on his *and*—sticking straight up in the air.

"Why are you staring at my ass?"

"Why are you bent over showing me your ass?"

She swung around from her hunt for items, an armful of clothes, a small tube of toothpaste and a toothbrush in her hands. "I'm not a baboon showing you my rump."

"You most certainly are not. But I think the sexual principles remain unchanged, Counselor." He made a show of scratching his chin. "Come to think of it, I don't think we managed any monkey sex on our weekend together. Perhaps we need to get reacquainted and put that one to the test."

She shook her head but he didn't miss the edges of a sexy smile that lurked at the corners of her mouth. "Now's not the time for this."

"Sweetheart, now is always the time."

When she only rolled her eyes and headed for the guest bathroom down the hall, Jake figured his powers of persuasion weren't nearly as well honed as he believed. Which left him two choices.

He could mope here or he could mope in the stables.

And since he wanted to get a look at what remained of the small cottage he was renovating, he'd quickly run through chores and then get Hogan sniffing through the bombed-out remains.

On one last sigh—all while imagining a delicious round of *and* with Caroline—he got up and headed for his own room to clean up and change.

And couldn't deny the promise that lingered heavily in the air because Caroline had said only *not now.*

Which meant *later* was most definitely on the table.

Jake might have looked forward to later, but *right now* stunk to high heaven. He wrinkled his nose at the heavy, ashy scent that filled the air as he and Hogan gingerly moved through the mud that now surrounded the remains of what was going to be his home.

The fire chief had promised to return today with an inspector from the county, and Jake wanted Hogan's take on the situation before they arrived. The sheer volume of mess and debris that covered the ground felt insurmountable, but Hogan already quivered beside him in readiness.

"Jake!"

He turned to find Garner striding toward them from the house. He wore a thick blue sweatshirt with a navy insignia in the corner, jeans and heavy work boots. If Jake had to guess, his oldest friend was coming to give him a hand through the debris.

The fact he had no one else with him meant he was offering a side of persuasion with it.

Obviously, Jake wasn't the only one angling for something this morning.

"You're up early."

"Jordan's bright idea." Garner grinned at that, the besotted joy that seemed to be his perpetual state since Mia had arrived with their daughter showing no signs of dimming.

"Where is she now?"

"I believe tossing bites of her pancake on the kitchen floor and screaming 'Puppy Ho, come here!' at the top of her lungs."

He glanced at Hogan, still primed and waiting for Jake's

signal. "I'd say we're sorry to miss it but the big guy's been working overtime. Having to turn down Bernice's pancakes is an exercise in torture."

"I'm sorry about that." Garner shot Hogan a pitying look.

"Since Jordan makes up for it when she uses him as her pillow to watch her shows, I wouldn't feel too bad. He secretly loves it."

"Speaking of secrets. When the hell are you going to try and sneak out of here?"

That broad grin and smart-aleck humor that were Garner's trademarks were in full effect.

"What makes you so sure about that?"

"Because I know you. I know how you think. And I suspect you've already figured out just how you're going to sneak away."

Jake's attention flashed back to the house. Although he didn't see any faces peeking out of windows, he knew each and every character who lived inside. "The crew send you out here to rag on me?"

"I was already coming to do it myself. But Mia did give me her opinions on my way out the door."

"And?"

"And I quote, 'If you let that jackass sneak off this property alone you're on diaper duty all by yourself for a month.'"

Jake fought the shiver. "I've seen those diapers."

"So you know what I'm up against. My wife will make good on the threat, of that I have no doubt. And my healthy-as-a-horse daughter will deliver. Every day, Jake." Garner let out a shudder of his own. "Every damn day."

"Sounds like a you problem."

"Maybe." Garner shrugged. "But what you're dealing with? It's an us problem, man. It has been from the start."

Garner meant well. And in every way that mattered, his brotherly bond with the man was stronger than the familial one he should have had with Zack.

But it was because of that bond Jake had to walk away. Had to do this by himself.

"You can't ask me to do this."

Garner's brows slashed over dark eyes. "Do what? Let me in? Let Trace and Nic and Mia and all the rest help?"

"I can't put them in the crosshairs."

"Then you disgrace every member of this family."

"That's bullshit!"

The words ripped out of his chest with so much force Jake hadn't even realized how hard they'd clamored for release.

"Look at this! A bomb has been sitting in this building for who the hell knows how long!" He flung a hand at the gray wasteland that spread out beyond them.

"*Yards* from the house. With you, Trace, Bennie all tromping around in here over and over again. With Mia carrying Jordan in here. With Nic and Olivia and Bernice and Astrid, all visiting to nose around and make sure I'm taking their inputs on everything from lights to Wi-Fi to kitchen appliances to big enough windows."

Under it all was that tortured image that refused to leave his mind.

Of Caroline, leaning across the table in the diner, their faces so close together as they clashed over her safety back home. And the explosion of glass and bullets just as she pulled away.

It was all much too close. And it was only by sheer dumb luck none of them had been hurt yet.

Or worse.

"You disgrace me if you think I can stand by and put everyone at risk."

"Then you've not been paying attention to anything we're doing up here. You've talked a good game, helping Trace and me when we needed it, but it's all been an act."

The same urge to just haul off and hit Garner—the one that had ridden him hard that very first day they met all those years ago at recess—reared up but Jake held it back.

He wasn't a kid any longer.

And he didn't hit people when he knew, way down deep, they were right.

But hell and back, the fear twisted his guts into knots.

"That's a cheap shot."

"Is it?" Garner asked, the carefree smile nowhere to be found. "We're all here for the same reasons. Every one of us was done with the shady characters and the bad actors and the entities that are so damned structured and restrictive they don't function if there isn't a bad guy."

It *was* the reason he'd come.

The lure of leaving Las Vegas and finding himself once again in the western wilderness with people he trusted. Doing work that mattered. That had value and purpose.

The fact he'd gotten a family out of it was the part he never expected.

But none of it meant Garner wasn't absolutely right.

"We all made a vow to help the people who needed it. Here." Jake glanced at the house once again.

"On our own terms," Garner added.

"Don't you see, G? That's the part I need you to understand. I need to handle my family my way. If I can do that, I can come back to the one I actually care about."

"Don't *you* see?" With his own question ringing back at

him, Jake wasn't prepared for Garner's direct hit. "If you don't let us help you, you might not come back."

Zack signed his name to the prison sign-in sheet and headed for the metal detector screening. He dutifully emptied his pockets of his keys and cell phone, undid his belt and placed it all on the conveyor. He exchanged jokes with the two guards on duty—the same ones he saw each week when he visited his father—and picked up his items on the other side.

The early-October day was hot as blazes as Zack headed for the visitors grounds. His father preferred meeting inside but the man needed some sun and vitamin D. Since it was becoming increasingly obvious that Zack did know better when it came to Al's best interests, he'd already put in the request to meet outside in the yard.

His father might not like it, but he'd come outside for the visit. Not like he had anything else to do.

Zack kept his focus on the empty table in the middle of the yard, but he did recognize some of the other prisoners as he walked past the various groups gathered together. He wasn't the only family member to visit regularly and he gave a few halfhearted waves as he walked.

It galled to realize that even in this place he needed to glad-hand people, but they were still voters.

And anyone who realized that Zack Stilton was a good, devoted son would no doubt give him higher consideration next time they saw his name on a ballot.

The sun was high and several prisoners had been given outside privileges, even without visiting guests. Zack took a seat and considered them now as he waited for his father.

This prison had a mix of criminals, all with varying levels of sentences for a variety of crimes. Although his father's lawyers had argued for something with minimum security, the state had ultimately won out on a harsher penalty.

Especially when the sex trafficking details had come to light.

People got skittish when minors were involved, after all.

Sunlight flashed off the high towers that surrounded the yard, men in each visible at their posts, long-range rifles in plain view.

Zack took comfort from the watchmen, grateful they did an insufferable job for terrible pay.

His father shuffled toward him and Zack kept his gaze level and steady, refusing to break eye contact as Al moved ever closer. The orange jumpsuit was a supreme insult for a man used to wearing custom-made suits, the corresponding ankle chains an added indignity.

"Zack."

"Dad." He nodded as his father took a seat. "You're looking well."

"Cut the crap."

Zack only smiled, his father's direct approach far more preferred to the ridiculous charade they played in public.

Or for his mother.

"The DA's been busy. His hive's humming with activity as they work on their case against you."

"They don't have enough."

They actually had more than enough—especially with the anonymous files Zack himself had ensured found their way to those eager prosecutors' desks—but there was no need to share that.

"They seem pretty confident." Zack inclined his head, the deferential bent one he'd practiced his entire life. "But Radner's been hard at work building your defense."

"He damn well better be. I pay him enough." Al looked around, his attention briefly distracted by the groups of people huddled around. "He hasn't been here in a while. Find out why."

Zack knew why.

He'd laid just enough breadcrumbs there to make one of Nevada's highest paid attorneys think good old Aloysius Stilton wasn't good for the money.

And since the funding source—the shady crime boss who'd fronted Zack's parents' lifestyle—had quit paying the bills, it was a perfectly natural assumption on the part of William Radner, Esquire.

"Your mother hasn't been here in a while, either."

"She's been indisposed of late. Claims she doesn't want to be seen in public."

It hadn't stopped her from making two trips with him to fundraisers in DC, but again, information dear old Dad didn't actually need.

Not that it was going to matter.

"She and I discussed this when everything started. This—" Al waved a dismissive hand over his jumpsuit "—is all temporary. I've been mischaracterized and set up as a scapegoat. The party hasn't liked my votes on a few items and now I'm paying the price."

Was that the story he was telling himself?

Zack briefly wondered if it was a trait specific to his father or something the human mind could manufacture with far too much time left to consider one's own sins.

Likely the latter, Zack figured. Judas himself probably came up with a perfectly reasonable excuse as he'd taken all those pieces of silver.

Since his father was waiting for an answer, Zack gave

him the exact one he sought. "The mercurial nature of politics, no doubt."

"Damn right." Al tapped on the top of the table. "Have you talked to Jake?"

"We've both been busy. Texts only this week."

"When's he coming back for a visit?"

"I have no idea."

"Did you tell him I want to see him?"

No. "I've told him each time you've asked me to."

"And?"

"And he's busy. Claims he can't get away, though who knows why. He's just living on a ranch in Wyoming, playing with some horses."

Since this was most certainly not the answer his father was looking for, Zack took the fleeting pleasure in watching Al's face turn a bright shade of red.

"He needs to get his ass back here."

"I'll pass on the message."

"Rumor has it he could have a shot at my seat in a few years."

Whatever congeniality he'd armed himself with fled at his father's words.

Just like always, it was Jake.

Never *him.*

Never the one who'd stayed.

"I've got a shot at it, Dad. Me!"

"You don't have the experience." The dismissal was swift and immediate. A brush-off that didn't even acknowledge Zack's rising ire.

"And a dog-walking cop does? One who's never had a moment of interest in a political career?" Zack couldn't hold back the bitter laugh. "Have you lost your mind?"

"He's the heir, Zack. Voters want a dynasty."

"Voters want stability. Security. And someone they believe will get them there. That's me."

Zack stood up then, self-righteous venom swirling in his veins.

He'd made his choice, even before walking in here. He'd known what he'd needed to do from the start of his father's fall from grace and hadn't deviated once from his plans.

He knew what needed to be done.

But all along he'd wondered if he would feel remorse.

Only now, looking at that haggard face, the eyes still blind to what was in front of him, Zack felt nothing at all.

Even the usual cold, icy fury seemed beyond him.

"I've got to go."

Moving around the table, Zack pulled his father into a tight hug. His gaze scanned the distance, the ever-so-slight nod from the guard on the north tower the signal he was waiting for.

His gaze moved lower, to the group of men moving their way, their exercise time in the yard obviously at an end. The largest one, on the far end, nodded as well.

With a press of his lips to his father's cheek, Zack patted him on the back and turned away.

He walked the length of the yard.

Crossed back into the prison building.

Moved through the exit.

Just as he cleared the door, the heavy sound of sirens went off, accompanied by shouts from all the guards on duty.

He kept on walking, one thought foremost in his mind.

Unlike Judas's kiss millennia ago, Zack didn't feel a moment of remorse.

Chapter 13

"You're doing great!"

Olivia's encouragement winged across the paddock as Caroline led Orlando around on his halter. The kid had looked skeptical when Caroline had offered to tack him up, but had grown more and more impressed as Caroline had patiently walked the horse through the steps.

She'd initially not wanted to dampen Olivia's excitement at how Orlando was coming along by boasting of her own experience, but Olivia caught on fast.

And her overriding hunger to learn more about the horse made her a quick study.

"You really were a horse girl when you were my age?" Olivia walked toward them.

"I really was. Any excuse to be near a horse and I took it."

"Did you have one?"

"I was never lucky enough to have my own. But I had a favorite at the stables I took lessons at. His name was Arthur."

"Seems like a formal name for a horse."

"I liked it."

"So why'd you become a lawyer?"

"I liked that, too." Caroline leaned forward. "I like asking questions, too. Which brings me to my biggest question."

"Oh?" Olivia looked leery but Caroline also didn't miss that small part of the kid that loved to spar.

And recognized the kindred spirit.

"How was your date with Nasher?"

"You mean besides the whole *a bomb exploded at Jake's house* part?"

"Yeah. I really mean the you and Nasher part."

"He's nice."

Although Caroline agreed, she took the Bernice route and held her tongue.

And was rewarded with Olivia's rush to add more details.

"He's really cute and we're science partners in school. He's new, too. I mean, he's been here a little longer than me but not much. And he's really smart and he doesn't seem to mind that I'm smart."

"Why would he mind that you're smart?"

Olivia stilled at that, the carefree smile vanishing. "You know not everyone likes a smart woman. Or girl."

"Yeah, I do know that. And no, not everyone does. It's their loss."

"Maybe so, but it's real."

It *was* real. Caroline had experienced it herself with those guys in college she'd long since put out of her mind. But she also experienced it with her sisters who were considerably harder to forget or dismiss.

"My sisters tell me sometimes I need to shut my mouth more and quit being a know-it-all."

"That's harsh."

"Yeah, it is."

"Jake likes your smarts."

Caroline reached out and ran a hand down Olivia's braid. "He likes your smarts, too. So do your mom and dad and aunt and uncle and everyone else inside that house."

"I think that might be all that matters." Before Caroline could ask for more details on Olivia's lofty pronouncements, she kept on.

"That we find people who appreciate us. I didn't have that before I came here and I thought I had to be something different. Better or quieter or dumber or whatever was going on in the moment." Olivia stopped. "Do you know about that stuff?"

"Jake said you had a tough time with your old family, and Nic and Trace helped to get you away from it. The rest is your story to tell. If you want to."

"My birth mom was really shady and so was my uncle. My dad was out of the picture a long time ago. And they figured they could trade on my computer skills to do bad things."

Olivia looked down at the ground, toeing the dirt with the tip of her riding boot. "I'm not proud of it but I did some of what they asked me to."

"It's okay you're not proud of it. But it's also okay if you give yourself a bit of room to accept that they weren't giving you a lot of choice."

"Even if I thought it was fun? I'm smart and I liked figuring that stuff out. Especially because it meant I was smarter than my dumb family." The tears filling Olivia's eyes spilled over as she looked back up. "Doesn't that make me guilty?"

Caroline knew virtually nothing about raising children beyond what she'd seen in social media posts over the years, but it didn't take a psychology degree—or having an actual child—to know what to do with this one.

She reached out and pulled Olivia close in a hug. "It doesn't make you guilty, sweetie. It makes you human. You were in a bad situation with people who were supposed to care about you."

"You did what you could, squirt."

Caroline looked over her shoulder to realize Jake had joined them in the paddock, Garner following just behind.

Olivia's eyes were wide as she stepped back from the hug. "You weren't supposed to know about that stuff. Or hear any of that."

"Why not?"

"It's not a good part of me."

Jake opened his arms and pulled her close. "Good and bad, Olivia. I'm here for all of it. And for the record, being good at hacking doesn't make you a bad person. Enjoying it doesn't make you a bad person, either. You helped Dawson and me find Garner and Mia in San Francisco. And you used it to get to Nic, too, so we could find you."

Caroline watched as Jake enumerated all the ways Olivia had helped and was reminded yet again of Bernice's wise counsel the night before.

Way more than half of love is about showing up.

Everyone here showed up.

Jake was worried about putting them in harm's way.

What he hadn't realized yet was how much stronger they were as a unit. Because working together, they were greater than any individual member of the team.

Now it was time to convince him.

"Who is he?"

Jake stared at the raft of information Mia had displayed across the various screens in the office. Several held photos of the guy who'd attacked Caroline, from the photo with Jake's mother to others Mia had found of him on social media.

"Low-level muscle in a Las Vegas crime family. Derek Jensen is his name." Mia read a few more details off her legal pad full of scribbles. "He's twenty-three but he's already amassed quite a list of probables. That includes arson of a small off-Strip casino and suspicion of murder in a gang death last year."

"And he's protecting my mother?"

Jake tried to match Mia's description of a deeply unsavory young man with his mother's predilection for perfection and overall snobbery and it just didn't play.

Unlike Jensen's other crime of attacking Caroline in her apartment parking lot, which fit a hell of a lot better.

While Mia walked through the details she'd discovered, Caroline had set up with her laptop and logged in to her work database to see what else she could find. It was technically legal but he couldn't quite shake off his discomfort that she was helping him with city resources.

And then he reminded himself that the same hulking menace had actually attacked her, and his conscience shut the hell up.

Caroline tapped the top of her laptop screen. "He's also got a prior on an attempted murder out near the small private airstrip that services the local bigwigs."

Garner spoke up from where he was sitting in a chair beside Mia. "So how the hell did he suddenly become a bodyguard in DC?"

Jake had always known the local crime bosses in Vegas had long tentacles. Their interests were vast and extended well beyond the desert oasis that was Sin City.

But they were also smart about who they hooked up with

and that included not jumping into situations that drew attention.

Politicians, as a general rule, didn't practice staying out of the limelight.

"If he's low-level it actually makes sense," Caroline said. "No one would have predicted Mia's AI program would make a match here off a photograph. It's just additional bad luck I made the guy standing in the background of a photo. Your mother might have stature in DC but if there's been an effort underway to get her out of town it would be an easy job for the kid to handle."

"He's not a power player," Mia added. "Which makes him invisible in DC."

"So we don't go after Derek Jensen?"

Nothing about that felt right but Jake also recognized Mia and Caroline had an approach in mind.

"Oh, we go after him," Mia said, her smile broad. "And we use his age against him."

"How?" Garner asked.

"Our resident hacker," Jake said at the same time Caroline said, "Olivia."

"Kid can do it, too," Garner piped up. "She can sell a hustle."

Mia turned to face her husband. "Yes, well, maybe we don't position it to her quite in that way. She is fifteen. And we need to loop Nic and Trace in, too."

"We're not hustling *her*," Jake stressed. "We need to set up a bit of fake dealing to get Jensen distracted and off his game. She can make it look legit."

"We're not doing anything until we talk to Trace and Nic," Mia said before turning to her husband. "And don't forget Olivia is the primary role model for our child. What if it's like witchcraft and whatever skills we take advantage of come back on us threefold?"

Garner's grin was unrepentant. "Then we'll count ourselves lucky and lock down the Wi-Fi every night."

Caroline waited until they were both gone, the office doors closing behind them, before she spoke.

"I know I should feel some bit of remorse for mapping out a plot to take down that little weasel but I haven't found it yet."

"I've never felt any remorse when someone gets what's coming to them." Jake swiveled in the office chair so that he could reach out and grab Caroline's hand.

Unlike earlier in the bedroom, he'd truly caught her off guard and she wasn't able to keep her footing.

Which gave him a chance to neatly catch her in his lap and get what he hoped they both had coming.

That delectable spot beneath her ear beckoned him and he pressed his lips there, delighted when he got a breathless moan for his efforts.

"Jake."

Her tone held the slightest bit of protest but it was quickly squashed when she lifted her arms and wrapped them around his neck. "We shouldn't be doing this."

"Why not?" He used his tongue to trace a small line from the side of her neck to her earlobe.

"Someone might walk in."

"Then let's go upstairs."

"We… Ohhh."

The temptation to go straight up to his bedroom warred with the simple pleasure of sitting right where they were and making out. The office wasn't exactly private, but the curtains on the French doors kept them out of view of anyone sitting in the family room.

And really, why risk someone in the house adding further distraction when he could just stay here and revel in more of those breathy moans that kept spilling from Caroline's lips as he continued to vary the angle of his lips on her skin?

His hands gripped her hips and he used his thumb to tease the sensitive skin of her stomach, just under the thin T-shirt she wore. She rewarded him with another breathy moan, deeper than what had come before. Intrigued, Jake increased the pressure, his hand drifting higher to tease the underside of her breast.

Obviously pleased with the idea, Caroline leaned into him, pressing herself into his touch.

She was sheer perfection and Jake was fast forgetting people hovered right outside the office door, with an ability to—

The office door slammed open so hard the handle hit the wall as Trace marched in.

"Stilton! There's no way in hell my daughter's running an Omaha Hustle or an Alabama Slide or any sort of damn honeypot so get it out of your ever-lovin' mind!"

Caroline wanted to find an elegant way to slip off Jake's lap but hadn't yet worked out the how. There was no delicate way to hide what the two of them had been up to and no delicate maneuvering was going to change that.

The *why* she needed to get up, though, was obvious as Trace stormed into the office, Nic, Garner and Mia on his heels.

For his part Jake looked unperturbed, by either the shouting from his friend or the fact they'd been caught. He just tightened his hold on her and stared up at his friends. "None of us are suggesting Olivia does any of those things.

And no one runs Alabama Slides any longer. Too difficult with modern technology."

"What is an Alabama Slide?" Caroline asked, still trying to find a way out of Jake's lap.

"It's a con you run on a con. Not something my daughter will take part in." Trace folded his arms, his gaze never leaving Jake. "And I'm really pissed you'd even ask."

Jake eased his hold, allowing Caroline to smoothly get off his lap, before he stood and met Trace head-on. "For the record, you leaped to specific cons. All I want her to do is gin up a few fake text messages that someone closer to her age will think are legit. I can handle the rest."

"Guy's a menace and I don't like the idea of her anywhere near this."

"You think I do?"

"No." Trace stood there a few beats longer, his chest puffed up before he dropped the facade. "Damn it, no, I really don't think so. It's just—"

Trace put his arm around Nic. "We just got her and now she's on dates and helping with cons and it's changing. It's all changing."

"Yeah. It is."

"And then you go and think you're going to run out of here without pulling us in? Not happening, Stilton."

"You just got done reading me the riot act at the idea of putting your kid in danger. My staying here actually puts her in danger."

Caroline recognized there was a high degree of macho maneuvering going on, but what she hadn't figured on was how wrong it felt for Jake to turn his back on these people and ignore their help. She'd barely passed the twenty-four-hour mark with all of them and it had taken her a fraction of that to understand what they all shared was special.

Their bond might be unbreakable, and if that was all they shared Caroline might see her way to Jake's point. Why put everyone in danger if you didn't have to?

But for a group of highly trained ops professionals who understood how to mitigate the very risks Jake faced?

There was no reason to walk away.

Yet, Jake wanted to all the same.

He walked away from you and didn't look back.

That small voice she'd believed quieted by Jake's confession the day before reared up once more, in many ways louder than before.

Was she really going to believe a few pretty words so he could maneuver her into bed?

Because really, what had changed since yesterday? A confession that she didn't believe was a lie but wasn't a commitment toward a future, either.

Yes, he'd told her he was scared. And he'd stressed that it wasn't her, it was him.

You bring out the very best parts of me. The ones I didn't even realize were there. They also happen to be the parts of myself I'm not very good at. But my running from them has never been about you.

But he hadn't actually made a commitment. Just a sincere acknowledgment that he thought well of her.

Her boss thought well of her. So did her landlord and her damned dentist.

Being thought well of didn't mean forever.

Which meant whatever was going on here with these people—whatever decision they ultimately made as a team—didn't concern her.

So she'd leave them to it.

And as soon as possible, she'd pack up her things and go away until this was done.

Jake was the one in danger, not her.

She had a few weeks of vacation coming so she'd book a ticket and go somewhere to lie low.

When this was all over—when she could come back to her home and live in peace, without any external threats—she'd start the important job of healing herself.

And getting over Jake Stilton for good.

Jake had late-morning duty in the stables so he headed out for that, leaving Mia and Garner to work on a few more details for the text message scam they wanted to run on Jensen. Caroline had excused herself earlier and he figured they could regroup when he got back inside for lunch.

Only by the time he'd returned from his chores he'd gotten the news that Caroline had driven into town with Nic and Olivia.

It went like that all day; each time he thought to find her she was somewhere else, and it wasn't until he hit the kitchen after a late-afternoon meeting with the fire inspector that Jake started to get concerned.

Where was Caroline?

And how had he gone from an armful of willing woman in his lap to radio silence in the span of a day?

Bernice had made a nice dinner but when he realized Caroline wasn't there to eat it he begged off and headed upstairs, claiming he'd fix himself something from the fridge later if he got hungry.

Only Caroline wasn't upstairs in the guest room, either.

Puzzled, he walked into the room, oddly relieved to find her suitcase still on the floor and the outfit she'd worn earlier hanging over the small chair that filled the corner by the window.

Something caught his attention through the window and

he finally got a clue to her whereabouts. If he'd been two minutes too late he'd have missed her, but right now, he watched her struggle to get the stable door open before slipping inside and pulling it closed behind her.

After ducking out of the room, Jake headed down the front stairs and on out to the barn, bypassing the kitchen entirely and the pairs of curious eyes that would no doubt want to know where he was going.

Why was she hiding out? From him, yes, but from all of them? She was more than welcome to join the group for dinner yet she'd chosen to slip out by herself.

The air had taken on the decided bite of fall and Jake huddled into his coat as he crossed the driveway and pulled the large sliding door open to the stable. The horses greeted him as he worked his way past each stall door, but it was only as he got to the end of the row of doors that he finally understood her destination.

The area they'd set up the night before for Olivia and Nasher was lit up, the small white lights giving off an ethereal glow as Caroline stood beneath them.

She hadn't realized he was there yet—or he assumed she didn't—as she gently meandered around the space.

"Why are you hiding in here?"

With her airy stroll interrupted, Caroline turned back to look at him. The T-shirt and jeans she'd worn earlier had been traded out for an oversize sweatshirt and yoga pants and she still wore the vest that she'd added over the thick material of her top.

Nothing about the look should have been sexy or enticing, but as he looked at her set off against the small white lights, he knew he'd never seen anything more beautiful.

"I'm not hiding."

"You sure about that?"

"I'm very sure. I'm not part of that family inside. I don't want to intrude any further on their lives or their meals or their home."

"What's got you so upset?"

"Nothing important."

He heard the warning signs but had no interest in stopping. "Of course it's important if you're hiding out in here. What's wrong?"

"Me, Jake. I'm wrong! It's all me."

"How can you say that?"

"Because you didn't want me here. Then you gave me some sob story about how all that went sideways between us back in Vegas was you, not me and here I am, right back to falling for you."

Although her retelling of their discussion the night before didn't paint him in a particularly good light, it also wasn't wrong.

Or not exactly.

He did leave because of his own mixed-up feelings. And she did deserve to know. But he hadn't shared any of it as a way to sleep with her.

He'd wanted her from the first and he knew he'd want her until the day he died.

Wanting her had nothing to do with the fact that his apology has been a long time coming.

And deeply necessary.

"It *was* me. It was all me, which is why I told you that."

"Yeah, and then you tried to maneuver me into bed. And here I am, going right back to it all without thinking about myself. Without protecting myself."

Her anger was a living thing, and it broke his heart to realize how much of it was inwardly directed. "I got hurt yet I climbed right back on your lap without a second thought.

A ridiculous idiot who went straight back for more, all because of a few pretty words."

He was willing to own his part in all that had come before, but he'd be damned if he was going to stand there and be called a liar.

Especially about something as important as what was between them.

He'd never ever lied to a woman to get her into bed and he wasn't about to start now, no matter how badly he wanted a second chance with her.

"It wasn't some lure, Caroline. I told you the truth. Something you deserved to hear a hell of a long time ago."

He took a few steps closer, surprised to see the feral look in her eyes grow sharper.

Despite the clear signs to back off, he pushed forward. "What do you have to protect? And why?"

"My heart, you idiot! The one you walked away from. The one you're going to walk away from again, just like you want to walk away from all of those good people sitting inside eating tacos."

"I need to protect them!"

"No, you need to protect yourself. It's always about protecting yourself and it doesn't matter who the hell gets hurt in the process. Believe me, I know."

"Don't compare what's between us with the danger of what's going on. They're not the same."

Only he was beginning to think that yes, they actually were the same.

And that all she accused him of was correct.

Because he'd behaved selfishly. He'd believed he was acting with some sort of noble righteousness, but in the end, it was a lie.

He was more afraid of all he'd lose than putting in the work and believing he stood a chance to actually win.

"I'm leaving in the morning. I can go somewhere quiet and off anyone's radar while you go off and deal however you see fit. But I need to leave."

She pushed past him and headed for the stable exit, only to be intercepted by Garner, who laid a hand on her shoulder to stop her.

"I need to talk to you for a minute. Both of you."

Caroline looked ready to balk but something in Garner's tone seemed to change her mind.

Or maybe it was the "please" Garner added onto the end of his request.

"G?" Jake looked at his friend, unable to imagine what was coming next.

All he did know was that it wasn't good.

"I'm sorry, Jake. It's your father. He was murdered today."

Chapter 14

All the air seemed to rush out of the stables as Caroline struggled to process Garner's announcement.

An endless parade of questions cycled through her mind, but all of it vanished when she looked over to see Jake's face.

Ashen and devoid of anything other than shock.

A shock that was deepening as his pupils grew wider inside the blue of his eyes.

"Jake." Their argument—one that had seemed so necessary in the moment—faded away as she moved to his side and took his arm. "Jake?"

Garner moved in and took Jake's other arm and they led him to the chairs set up the night before for Olivia and Nasher.

Jake was quiet, taking the seat that was offered but saying nothing, so Caroline pressed Garner for details. "What happened?"

"The specifics are fuzzy but it made the news. Mia confirmed the rest on her phone. Apparently, there was some sort of fight in the prison athletic yard. He was jumped by another prisoner."

"And no one stopped it? He's still a former senator and public fig—"

The words faded out as Jake reached for her hand. "He's

not a senator any longer. He's a loose end and they wanted him taken care of. Whoever the hell *they* even are."

Caroline considered how little they actually knew. Besides the kid, Derek Jensen, they still had no idea who'd followed her from Nevada and shot at them in the diner. Even less idea where the bomb planted in Jake's fixer-upper came from.

And now this?

What had started it all?

Because tempting as it was to say all of it began with the attack in her apartment parking lot, the dangerous things that were happening weren't impulses.

They were a product of time and attention and planning.

And the attack at her apartment had simply been the beginning.

She'd been digging around in the senator's case for months and, as an ADA, had every right to. Yet suddenly, she was attacked last week, seemingly out of nowhere.

The bomb in Jake's house wasn't set recently. Someone had found a way onto the property, either as a plant or during a time when there was enough activity they could go unnoticed.

And now a murder inside a federal facility? She'd worked cases for far too long not to understand bad things happened in prison, but for the senator to have been killed so easily, someone was paid off.

All the steps were too methodical.

And it no longer felt just like a crime family who was pissed off their pocket politician got caught.

"I need to call my brother and my mother." Jake was already up and out of the chair. "I need to know they're okay."

"Take it easy, Jake." Garner was already by his side but Jake was shaking him off.

"I need to talk to them."

"Jake. Wait."

He stopped at her words and Garner moved past them, allowing them their privacy.

A host of emotions painted Jake's face but it was the stark grief and shock that knitted his brow in a sort of dazed confusion.

"I know it isn't much," she started in. "Especially in light of all I just said. But I am here for you."

"It's actually quite a lot, so thank you." He tilted his head in the direction of the house. "I need to get inside."

"You go on. I'll be right there."

A part of her ached to watch him walk away but even if everything had been rock-solid between them, this was a chasm he had to cross himself.

Ten minutes ago he believed he had a father, and in the work of an instant that was taken from him. The relationship might be strained, but it existed. Al Stilton was his father.

And no matter how much that bond had created the hurt places inside him, his father was gone.

Before and after.

One of the defining moments of Jake's life.

Caroline needed to get inside, but there was something about the settling noises of the horses and the pretty white lights that soothed her. She'd come in here in a flurry of emotions and the earthy smells and calm lights went a long way toward giving her the space to think.

Before and after…

She'd lived with the same. Her own father's death in a car accident her junior year of high school had been devastating for them all. Life had been one way one day and then upended the next.

The life—all she knew—was taken in a deadly instant.

Jake had worried about bringing danger to this ranch and all the people in it, but danger actually lurked everywhere.

Life, in all its glory, often paced a matched race with death.

The horses stirred enough to clue her in someone was coming, and she turned to find Mia clearing the center walkway. "I wanted to check on you."

It was one more example of the woman's kindness, and Caroline was touched that Mia had come to find her. "I'm fine. Just thinking about Jake and the starkness of it all. An hour ago, in his view of the world, he had a father. Now he doesn't."

Mia gestured toward the chairs before heading over to take one. "Death never gets easier. And when it's threaded through with violence the added senselessness of it all is difficult to process."

Mia shared what little was publicly available as Caroline settled in the seat opposite her. "There's something personal about all of this."

"You see it, too?" Mia asked, her attention clearly caught.

"I didn't at first, but with each act it gets harder and harder to unsee. I've worked in Las Vegas my entire career. For all the perceived glitz and glamour of the city, people live there, work there, die there. They also commit crimes there and they're not a heck of a lot different than crimes anywhere else."

"Meaning?" Mia probed, easily following Caroline's thoughts that felt like they had a destination just out of reach.

"Meaning there's not a lot of glitz and glamour behind the crimes. Just the standard motives of greed and opportunity."

"The classics."

"Exactly."

Recognizing she had a real sounding board, Caroline

kept going. "All along it felt like the crime family that funded the senator's lifestyle was behind this. And maybe they are. But I also questioned the cabal of powerful people who were rumored as backing him."

"All would fit and who says it has to be either-or. Both parties certainly have greed." Mia seemed to consider it before adding, "And powerful people working with a local crime boss would give specific connections in the city to create those opportunities."

"What if that's too easy?" Caroline asked.

"Sometimes it's easy because it makes the most sense. And Derek Jensen does work for a crime boss."

"True."

Mia's analyst training meant she could catalog the data quickly and see patterns. But it was Caroline's ongoing professional study of human nature that had her thoughts seesawing.

Yes, the loss of the senator's influence would matter very much to the people who wanted him—and paid for him—to be in place.

But wouldn't they be colder about executing their plans?

Which brought her right back around to the attack in her apartment parking lot.

"When I was attacked last week. That was the incident that got me here, but there was something missing."

"Missing how?"

Right *there*. That was the level head and clear eyes Mia brought to this. Each time she'd spoken of the attack, Jake had immediately seen red. She appreciated him for it, but it hadn't moved the conversation along.

But Mia got it.

"It was as awful and as terrible as you could imagine, but it was only after that I realized how quick it was. And how much it felt like a warning instead of an attempt to do me harm."

"That's a pretty narrow distinction."

"And a hard one to explain. The man held me and put his hands on me and I certainly didn't think about anything but getting away. But after he was gone, I couldn't stop feeling like it was more of a performance."

"Did he say anything?"

"Just that I was a nosy bitch who needed to keep out."

"Original." Mia rolled her eyes before seeming to think better of it. "But if he said that and he was hired with the instruction to rough you up, it makes sense. And if he was hired then maybe he has a sense of why. We could tweak those text messages Garner and I created to figure out who gave the orders."

"He's not going to fall for that."

"Actually," Mia said, smiling in triumph, "he might. Olivia came through again, after Nic and Trace talked to her. She's already found his three hidden social media accounts as well as his ridiculously easy email password."

Caroline knew she shouldn't feel quite so excited about the teenager's sleuthing, but with the memories of the guy's arms tight around her and his breath on her neck, she couldn't find it inside to feel guilty, either.

And for the first time in her life, she wasn't trying to preserve a trail of evidence.

"Should we be afraid of those skills?"

"We should be very afraid." Mia smiled broadly. "And I might be if I weren't so damn proud of her."

"Let's go see what she's got."

What Olivia had, Caroline realized an hour later, was a thorough set of details and a methodical approach to data collection.

They'd all moved into the dining room, plates of chocolate chip cookies set out on each end of the long table, and two large monitors with a mirrored connection to Olivia's laptop.

Jake was still upstairs talking to his family and had told Trace to start without him.

Caroline hadn't seen him since she and Mia had come back inside, but she didn't take his lack of interest in what they were doing as a bad sign.

Give him time.

They had been Bernice's gentle words as she brought in the cookies while they were getting set up, and Caroline took comfort in them now as they all settled themselves around the table.

And while Jake might need time, Caroline recognized that the rest of them needed action. She could only hope when Jake was ready for the same, they'd have something for him.

Olivia toggled through the social media accounts, explaining how she found them and why. "Dude loves the gym and guns and women. That's all he posts about."

"Why keep the accounts secret? Or separate?" Trace asked.

"Different friend groups most likely. The gun one he probably got when he was still underage and hiding it from his parents. The gym one's for showing off so it's probably not that big a secret. And the girl one is because he's a douche."

"Olivia—"

Nic started in when Bernice held up a hand. "Don't censor the child for the truth. Young man's clearly got a disgusting view of women if this is what he's spending his time engaging with. I don't need a sugarcoated version of it."

"And the email?" Caroline asked, before mentally adding, *You know, the part that violates every oath I made as a lawyer.*

"I got the idea off his gun account. He posted a picture of an email he got, complimenting him on a good day at the range. His email was up on screen so you could see the address. In the bottom corner was what looked like a scribbled piece of paper with the last few letters of his password."

"Is that photo public?" Caroline asked as Olivia toggled to it on screen.

"Yeah. You can pull it up right now and take a screenshot. I didn't do anything special on this. Honest." The kid's gaze was solemn. "Everything here is publicly available." She shook her head. "Doesn't even have two-factor on the email. I got right in."

"There's dumb and then there's primordial soup dumb." Garner pointed toward the screen. "Who does this?"

"Someone more focused on bragging than on common sense," Caroline said as she stepped closer to the TV screen to look at the piece of paper. The only two letters visible read *AT*. "What did you get out of that?"

"Gym rat was the first thing I tried." Olivia shrugged. "It worked."

"What's in his email?" Nic was sitting next to Olivia and had been quiet up to now watching her daughter put it together, step by step.

"I didn't click on anything. All I saw were a lot of gross subject lines and I didn't want to look at any of them."

"We can handle that part," Trace spoke up. "And I'm not sure much of that will be relevant anyway. We're looking for an email with instructions."

Olivia's eyes widened as she looked at her father. "Oh, those subject lines had instructions."

"I'll just bet they did," Bernice said under her breath.

It was the joke they all needed and was enough to break the tension over what Olivia might have seen if she'd gone further. And it was the way Jake found them a few minutes later when he stepped into the dining room.

"Hey." The laughter quieted as he moved into the room. "You all look hard at work."

"Olivia found a treasure trove of information," Nic said.

"That's great."

Jake stood with his back against the wall, there with them but separate, and Caroline recognized she had a choice.

Before and after.

She could go to him or she could maintain that distance she'd claimed to want when she told him she was leaving. Allow all that had come before to color every choice. Every action.

Or she could try to start building something new. And prepare for what might come *after* all of this.

Without questioning herself or the choice, she stood and went to him, wrapping her arms around him. "How's your mom? And your brother?"

He was stiff and unmoving, his voice robotic. "Shaken up. Shocked."

"Of course."

And then he moved into her, pulling her close and clinging to the comfort she offered. "It was bad. They did him really bad."

That last part was just for her, a quiet retelling of what he'd learned.

"I'm so sorry," Caroline whispered against his ear.

He kept talking, the words spilling from his lips, vague expressions of grief and shock.

Caroline let him get it all out as she quietly watched over his shoulder as everyone moved out of the room to give them privacy. One more obvious sign of the family they'd all made together.

A unit who understood what each member needed and gave it in kind.

And a tight-knit team who would be waiting for him when he was ready.

Before and after.

He might not understand it, but Caroline had no doubt he felt it. Jake had found the people who would see him through the after. The ones who would be there long after she'd gone home.

That certainty she'd come to in the barn with him hadn't changed. She would leave after all of this was over.

Which was why she would take all she could of the *now*.

Jake had lost all sense of time.

Between his discussion—argument? Fight?—with Caroline in the stables and then Garner's arrival with the news of his father, Jake struggled to keep it all straight.

And now?

With Caroline's arms around him and her murmured words of comfort, he wanted to believe they'd taken a giant step past whatever had happened to make her want to leave.

But wanting to believe it and knowing it for truth wasn't the same.

Hadn't that been the trouble between them from the start?

That translation between what was in his head and how he acted.

And she'd paid the price.

Caroline passed over one of the bottled waters on the end of the table. "Why don't you drink this."

"Thanks." He took the bottle, taking a long sip before gesturing toward the table. "Sit with me for a minute. Please."

She did as he asked, that fierce determination he'd felt in her when she had clung to him nowhere in evidence as she played with the edge of a napkin.

"I heard what you said. Before. In the stables," he started in, not sure if this was the right approach but figuring action was his best bet. "I have protected myself. Every choice I made when it comes to you was about me. About staying in a comfortable bubble of my own making and not wanting it to burst."

He reached for her, suddenly desperate to make her understand.

"Caroline, please, I need you to know this. I want you. In every possible way, I do. But I'm not telling you any of this to romance you back into bed."

The deep, crystal blue of her eyes met his. That gaze was so compelling—so honest—and he couldn't look away. "Then why are you telling me?"

"Because I don't want you to leave. Not today and not after. I want to see what can be between us. I know that seems hard to figure out now but I'm committed to finding the way forward."

"I am, too."

He leaned forward and kissed her, the sharp sense of relief he expected at sharing his feelings never quite materializing.

But she was here and she agreed with him.

It should be okay.

It would *have* to be okay.

"Why don't we bring them all back in here. Olivia can

walk you through what she found. We were just about to look at Jensen's email."

Facts.

She shared a string of them and after calling the rest of the crew back in, Olivia filled in the gaps.

And through it all, Caroline kept her hand in his, never breaking the contact between them.

It should have been enough.

He'd explained himself and apologized. And he would make up for the clumsy way he'd treated her. They had a path forward.

Together.

And for now? Well, it was weird because they were processing a lot but they'd get through it.

Bernice's sweet authority cut through the discussion going on around them about the social media accounts and the hack into Jensen's email. "I trust you know about the ways of the world, sweetie, but why don't you and I give them some time to get through those emails."

Olivia nodded and leaped up from the table. "I think that's a good idea. I might even watch Jordan's shark video with her and let that song earworm its way in to distract my brain from those gross subject lines."

Jake didn't miss the way Trace and Nic reached for each other, or the subtle relief that flooded his friend's face at the reality that his daughter wasn't quite as grown-up yet as he feared.

And then Mia took over the controls and flashed up the email account that would give any father nightmares.

Various subject lines leaped out, one promising pleasure of the oral variety, another using a slang term Jake had even been hard pressed to hear all that frequently when he worked a beat.

It reinforced why they'd wanted Olivia out of the room and why none of them were all that eager to probe into the sick mind of Derek Jensen.

"Keep scrolling," Caroline said, her focus on the screen. "Those dates are still too recent. He attacked me five days ago and he'd have been contracted before that. If it was in email."

Mia kept going through the list, picking up speed as she understood what to pass by.

Intermingled in the subject line come-ons were ads for strip shows and several porn sites.

"Guy's a real peach," Garner muttered as he rubbed a hand over Mia's back.

"Sorry, Mia, but slow down," Caroline said. "You're getting to late September and a few of those emails don't look entirely pornographic."

"His training schedule at the gym," Mia read off before scrolling a bit farther down. "A haircut, which may prove useful if we need to call someone and confirm his whereabouts. Wait." She stopped and took her hand off the mouse. "Here. Subject line reads JOB DETAILS."

Jake had scanned up and down the page as Mia scrolled, but he was already a few steps ahead of her.

Because he'd already seen the email address on that JOB DETAILS email.

And he already knew who'd sent it.

"Open it."

Every pair of eyes landed on him, but it was Caroline who spoke first. "Why that one?"

"Because the sender? ZS95? That's my brother."

Chapter 15

Zack?

His baby brother was behind all this?

Jake hadn't been able to do much beyond stare at the email, stark and far too *real* up on the screen, and compare it to the man he knew.

Or thought he knew.

One he'd spoken to less than an hour ago, his voice full of grief and rage and utter sadness.

Was it all for show?

Because in what world was Zack hiring men to attack Caroline? How the hell did he even *know* about Caroline?

And why did he have connections with a man like Derek Jensen?

His brother had never made any secret of his political ambitions, but Jake couldn't understand how he could have been blind to Zack's ruthless streak.

Because anyone who could plan out an attack on an innocent woman was…a problem.

"Jake?" It was Bennie who finally spoke. "This is a terrible tragedy. On your family and on everything you believe. However you need to handle it, we're here for you. And whatever you need, we'll do what's in our power to help you. You are not facing this alone."

Just like last night, when Bennie had been the steadying hand after the bomb blast, he saw the traits he'd wanted to find so desperately in his own father.

Honesty.

Compassion.

And unwavering belief.

However he'd cataloged the danger since Caroline had arrived in Liar's Gulch—from thinking her fears were nothing more than a nuisance to a danger directed solely at her to a problem he needed to battle alone—it all meant nothing now.

All that mattered was what he did moving forward.

Those dark eyes were as unwavering as his beliefs as Bennie looked at him from across the table.

And Jake could only nod around the lump in his throat and the reality that somehow he'd been given a father figure when he needed one most. "Thank you. Because I know I'm not facing it alone."

Jake looked down to find his hand wrapped in Caroline's.

She hadn't wavered, either. She'd pushed and poked, believed and berated, but she hadn't given up on her fight to get him to understand.

"Thank you, too." He lifted her hand to his and pressed a kiss to her knuckles before looking at each and every person who sat around the table. "Thank you all."

There'd been pain that his adult relationship with his brother was so empty.

Only now he had to wonder.

Was it empty because he hadn't tried? Or had Zack pulled away long ago, initiating this journey that Jake could neither understand, nor sanction.

A beep echoed from Mia's laptop and she flipped to

whatever program had dinged. The screen with the emails went dark as her hand went to her mouth, a hard breath dragging through her lungs.

"Oh, my God."

Mia looked up from her laptop before quickly tapping a few keys. Whatever she was looking at now projected for all of them to see up on the wall.

And with unmistakable clarity, Jake saw a picture of his brother, dressed head to toe in a cowboy hat, jeans and work boots, right beside a guy in a work shirt. They'd been captured on one of the house cameras that caught footage in the driveway, both standing next to a truck with an electrician's logo on the side.

"He was here," Caroline said.

"Three weeks ago." Jake nodded. "When we had the guesthouse rewired with electricity."

Caroline didn't know what to do.

Jake, Mia, Garner and Bennie had set up time to talk to the sheriff.

Trace and Nic had gone off to do a sweep of the property after reviewing camera footage for the few days around Zack's stealth visit to the ranch. They'd thankfully found nothing else, but it hadn't stopped them from riding the property.

Bernice had buried herself in the kitchen, claiming she wanted time to focus on dinner.

So here she was.

Sitting in the family room, idly thumbing through a book she had no interest in and wondering how to be a productive human if she didn't have a laptop at her fingers and a legal brief on her mind.

It was *ridiculous* but it also seemed a fitting topper to a heartbreaking few days.

And brought a lone truth painfully to light: Caroline didn't know what to do with herself if she wasn't working.

A fact that sat rather uncomfortably, if she was honest.

And she was always honest.

Always looking for…

"Caro!"

Caroline just managed to set her book aside as Jordan ran to her and leaped at the couch. Since she had half a second to react, convinced the little girl was going to fall, she scooped her up instead.

"Caro!" Jordan giggled before planting both hands on Caroline's shoulders.

"Jordan."

"Puppy Ho!"

Since she'd already figured out what that meant, Caroline shook her head. "Hogan's outside with Jake and Daddy."

"Puppy Ho! Woof!"

The belly laughs at making a dog bark started just as Astrid came into the room, a basket full of laundry in her arms. "I'm sorry. She raced off just as I was disposing of a rather unpleasant naptime deposit."

"She's no trouble. I can play with her for a bit." Before Astrid could argue, Caroline added, "I'd love the company."

"And I'd love a cup of tea. Can I get you one?"

"No need. Please, take a bit of time for yourself."

Astrid looked about to argue when Bernice hollered to her from the kitchen. "Get in here and have your tea!"

"I'd go if I were you. I don't think she's going to take no for an answer. Besides—" Caroline tickled Jordan's belly, getting an immediate laugh "—I need a bit of toddler time and you need some tea time. It works nicely."

The nanny didn't wait to be asked again and headed off to the kitchen.

And for the next hour, Caroline found herself immersed in a series of fascinating games including block stacking, a tea time of her own with an army man and a Godzilla action figure, and a dance session to a kids sing-along show that was as good a workout as her Zumba classes.

She hadn't had this much fun in forever and had her little toddler taskmaster to thank for it.

"Caro! Blue." Jordan pointed to the T-shirt she'd stripped down to when her sweatshirt had grown much too warm.

"And Jordan's wearing green," Caroline said, pointing in turn, tapping Jordan's belly and the green shirt she wore.

They'd done a similar exercise earlier with the blocks and she was fascinated to see how much the little girl already knew, from counting to various colors. They'd just moved on to puzzles when Jake walked into the room, Hogan in his midst.

"Puppy Ho!"

Whatever points Caroline might have won contorting herself for the cartoon sing-along were forgotten as Jordan raced to her true love. Flinging her arms around the dog she hugged him, the words, *ho*, *love*, *puppy* and *shark* repeated several times as Jordan plopped onto the floor.

Seemingly understanding the drill, Hogan did the same, rolling to the side so he could lie beside her.

"They're a match."

"From the very first moment," Jake agreed.

Caroline took the slightest solace in his smile as he gazed at Jordan and Hogan. It wasn't much but it beat the bleak emptiness that had filled his face before heading out for his meeting with Dawson.

"How did Dawson take the news?"

"He's looking into everything, that electrician at the top of the list. We did vet the guy, for what it's worth. He came highly recommended so I'm not sure if Zack conned him as a way to get inside or if the dude was in on it."

"He'll get some answers."

Jake nodded, his gaze jumping around the room as if looking for some place to land.

"Why don't we sit down. I've been sitting on the floor too long and my butt's sore."

Jake followed her to the couch and Caroline was tempted to ask him more questions but stopped herself. He'd no doubt been handling details all afternoon and probably didn't want to talk more about his brother's actions.

"Jordan's impressive. I think Mia and Garner may have an Olivia-in-training on their hands. She named every color I pointed to, counted to seven and beat me in block stacking twice."

The talk of playtime made for the right diversion, and Jake smiled at the matched pair now laid out on the floor side by side as Jordan watched more of her singing cartoon.

"She's pretty amazing."

As if she sensed she was being discussed, Jordan sat up, her interest in the two of them piqued in some way. She walked over to where they were, climbing up between them.

Just as she had before with Caroline, she moved to Jake's lap. Only instead of putting her hands on his shoulders, she laid them on each side of his face.

"Scratchy."

He got her to laugh by tilting his head and rubbing his day's growth of beard against her palm.

As the giggles died down, she moved closer, looking into Jake's eyes. "Jake."

"Jordan," he said with a small smile.

"Jake sad."

Caroline could do nothing but watch as that large body crumpled forward, his arms wrapped around the little girl as he pulled her close.

"Yeah, sweetie. Jake sad."

"Jordan kiss." She twisted up into his arms so she could give him a kiss on the cheek, then scooched back down to sit in his lap.

Settling her head against his chest, Jordan simply sat and kept him company as the tears rolled silently down his face.

Taking the child's cue, Caroline pressed a kiss to his cheek, salty tears mixing with the light scratch of his whiskers.

And then rested her head against his shoulder and gave him the gift of silent support, too.

Jake had never gone in much for the whole men couldn't cry BS that came from his father's generation. He wasn't overly sentimental by nature but he wasn't a robot and he didn't go out of his way to hide his feelings, either. He'd had several cases that had shaken him and if the urge to cry struck, he took it.

But damn it, he hadn't expected to blubber like an idiot with a two-year-old on his lap and the woman of his dreams at his side.

Everyone else gave them the privacy of the family room couch and it was only when he realized every other member of the house had sequestered themselves around the kitchen table that he finally got up.

Jordan had dozed off and he settled her on the corner of the couch, tucking her in with her blanket. Caroline hadn't slept, but he'd brushed a kiss on her forehead and told her to stay and have dinner.

And then he'd fled to his room.

They were all walking on eggshells and he hated that.

In a matter of hours he'd gone from member of the team to fragile human betrayed by his family.

It sucked.

And worse, he could hardly get pissed about it because if he was in any of their shoes he'd be doing the same.

The light knock on his door was quickly matched with the distinct scent of bacon and he hollered "come in" before anyone could ask.

"I can't get the door."

Which was how he found Caroline on the other side, an oversize tray in her hands.

"Bernice made BLTs. And I'm not good at waiting. And, well—" she glanced down at the tray before shrugging "—bacon."

He took the tray from her and set it on the nightstand. "You don't have to wait downstairs."

"Good, because I'd like to eat with you." Caroline reached over and snatched a slice of bacon from a heaping dish of extra Bernice had prepared for him. "And I'm so hungry I might have bent down and eaten a piece with my teeth."

"Why didn't you come up sooner?"

"I wanted to give you privacy."

"I'm not very good company, but you don't need to stay away."

It was true but he could see how it might not have come off that way, especially in light of his historic behavior with her.

So he picked up a piece of bacon and handed it to her. "I'm glad you're here. And I'd rather have dinner with you, you know, assuming you're willing to have dinner with a blubbering idiot."

"Oh, Jake—"

He waved a hand. "No need. I get that I'm falling into inappropriate assumptions about gender norms and that crying over my family, or actually crying at all, isn't a sign that my masculinity is—"

She picked up a piece of bacon and shoved it into his mouth.

"Shut up, Stilton. I wasn't going to say any of that and I sure as hell wasn't thinking it." She shook her head. "No one outside of bad daytime TV psychologists think it, either."

"You don't know that," he said around a mouthful of bacon.

"I'm pretty sure I do."

He swallowed his mouthful of salty perfection. "What were you going to say? After the *oh, Jake* part?"

"That I'm here for you. And that I lost my father suddenly when I was sixteen and it's awful and terrible and nothing prepares you for it."

"Oh."

"And what I was also going to say is that I'm here if you want to talk about it but I'm not going to be one of those people who pressures you to talk about it. I can respect your privacy and your need to handle this in your own way. I'm good with whatever—"

Going on instinct—and banking on the same sort of response he got the last two times he did this—Jake leaned in and took. The taste of bacon lingered on both their lips and he smiled as he came up for air. "Tasty."

"I really should go brush my teeth."

"Walk out of here and I may be forced to tackle you and shove a piece of bacon in your mouth."

"We wouldn't want that, now, would we?"

"Now you're catching on."

Caroline lifted a hand and rested it at his nape. The position was intimate in its simplicity, her touch so powerful he felt it down to his knees.

He'd missed this.

And he'd missed her.

As he stared into her eyes, he finally understood why he'd failed so miserably those nights at the bar when he'd tried to bring someone home.

He'd told himself it was only because they *weren't* Caroline.

But that was only half the truth. The other half—the much bigger half—was because he was in love with her.

"I'm sorry I walked away."

"When you left the dining room?"

Her confusion was as sweet as it was genuine, but he shook his head. "When I left to come here."

"I've missed you."

"I've missed you, too, Caroline. And I'm glad you came here. Glad you came to warn me. So damn glad you came to find me again."

"I am, too," she whispered before her mouth met his again and he was lost to her.

That steady passion that never managed to burn out between them flared hot as a Nevada August. Jake kept his mouth on hers as he quickly stripped her of the T-shirt and yoga pants all while she managed the same with his jeans and work shirt.

He molded his hands to her body as he slipped her bra off, teasing the tight points of her nipples. He was rewarded with a low moan when he bent and took one into his mouth, her reactions to him hotter and so much better than the fantasies he'd allowed himself this past year.

To have her in his arms again was everything.

To feel her respond was electric.

Jake wanted to take this slow—there was so damn much missed time they needed to make up for—but the sheer power of touching her again made him weak.

And needy.

And oh so greedy.

Without taking his mouth off her skin, he laid her back onto the bed. With a very clear destination in mind, he began a journey of exploration, tracing a path from one breast to the other, taking her other nipple deeply into his mouth.

Her hands fisted in the sheets as he moved lower, flicking his tongue over her belly button before he moved on even lower, his tongue dampening her skin just to the edge of her panties. That tiny silk barrier was soft against his face and he rested his chin just there, giving himself an opportunity to look up the long length of her.

Her skin was a beautiful pink, flushed with pleasure, and Jake gave himself a moment to simply take her in.

Beautiful.

Perfect.

His.

All the reasons he'd run felt so far away, and Jake vowed to himself to leave them behind.

He'd been given a second chance, no matter how little he actually deserved it.

With great care he slipped a finger under her panties and tugged them down, reveling in the slow slide of silk against her legs.

And then there were no barriers.

Nothing between them.

Jake kissed his way back up the side of her calf, on to

the inside of her thigh and stopped just before he reached that small triangle of curls. He held himself there, looking once again up the length of her body, and met that glorious crystal-blue gaze.

Her Mona Lisa smile was sexy as hell as she stared back at him.

Never breaking eye contact, he bent forward and pressed his lips to that most intimate part of her. And made the fantasies he'd lived with for the past year the most perfect reality.

Pleasure tore through her body in great, magnificent waves and Caroline could do nothing but ride each swell and dip. Breath clogged in her chest as his tongue did the most wicked, perfect things to her. And each time she thought he couldn't do better, couldn't love her hotter or sweeter or more completely, he angled his mouth and took her higher.

The need for release grew with each stroke of his tongue, her body spiraling higher and higher as Jake ruthlessly drove her on.

And then he added the stroke of two fingers and she was flying, her body disintegrating with pleasure only to be rebuilt again.

It was heavenly and if she never took another breath she'd die complete. And thoroughly replete from the pleasure of his mouth.

But she was very much alive and with a mindless sort of fervor, Caroline could only tug at his shoulders to pull him back up the length of her body.

"Now, Jake."

"I—" The sexy, supremely confident smile vanished as he let out a groan.

"What?"

He dropped his forehead on her stomach. "I don't have any condoms."

"I—" Caroline stilled, her hand already fumbling with the drawer of his nightstand. "Oh, well, I assumed. Because, before—" She broke off, the tips of her fingers brushing against a box as she was trying to pull her hand out of the drawer. "Are you sure you don't have any?"

"Yeah, I'm sure. I mean, I haven't needed them and well, I wasn't thinking about it and…"

His voice faded out as she bonked him on the head with the box. "What are these?"

Jake looked up, his expression of shock comical. "Not mine."

"They're in your drawer."

"Caroline, I didn't buy those."

Caroline held up the box, turning it over in the glow of the bedside lamp. "There's a note on it."

Jake looked suspicious, but hardly upset as he tugged the box out of her hands. "For interesting pursuits."

A hard laugh filled her chest. It sort of stuck there based on the weight of the man currently sprawled over her, but she hardly cared. "I love this house."

"Who left us condoms?"

"The amazing, wonderful, kindly grandmother figure who cooks like an angel."

Jake was still dazed but not enough to miss her point. "Bernice stuck condoms in my drawer?"

"She most certainly did. I may buy her a car."

"Not if I beat you to it."

In unison, they both realized the treasure Jake still held in his hand. And with it, the scorching heat returned.

Caroline snatched the package back from him, tearing

at the box until a sleeve of condoms fell out. He reached them first, tearing one off and tossing the rest on the floor.

It was clumsy and silly and wild and perfect and there was a part of her that didn't want it to end.

But the other part of her—the part that wanted all of that great, glorious *and* he'd talked about this morning—sighed in pleasure as he positioned himself between her thighs, poised at the entrance to her body.

"I want you, Jake."

"I love you, Caroline."

And before she could say a word, he slid into her in one long, breathtaking stroke.

Her second orgasm shouldn't have come on her so fast, but the blend of his words and his body and those long, perfect strokes took her over.

And as Jake followed, Caroline was lost to everything but what was between them.

She'd loved him from the first.

And by some miracle, he loved her, too.

"Do you think anyone missed us at dinner?"

It was an abstract thought that floated into Caroline's mind and it seemed like a good question to ask.

Of course, it led to the next idea, which was wondering if the entire kitchen knew what they'd gotten up to in Jake's bedroom.

Jake hadn't moved at her question—his head still lay pillowed on her stomach—but she did feel his breath feather against her skin when he spoke.

"They all think I'm up here grieving."

"Grieving people have sex. They're not mutually exclusive conditions."

"Have you made a study of it?"

She swatted him on the shoulder. "No, but the human condition is such that people seek hopeful, happy experiences whenever they can."

"Woo hoo, let's go, human condition."

It was silly conversation, but wrapped up in Jake it *felt* important. Because they could share it together.

And talking about it had delayed the inevitable.

"I love you, too, you know."

He never lifted his head. "I was wondering when you were going to get around to it. Figured you heard me."

"Of course I heard you. You said it while looking deeply into my eyes."

"What took you so long?"

"You sort of *and*-ed my brains out."

Jake lifted up onto his forearms and faced her, his grin sexy and thoroughly unrepentant. "I most certainly did."

"And it was only ten minutes ago."

"Yes, and you've had at least five since your vision cleared to say it back."

"I love you."

"Then what are we going to do about it?"

Nothing about their conversation should have surprised her, but something about that question did.

"What do you want to do about it?"

"I asked you first."

"But clearly you've got some idea in your mind."

Caroline recognized the prevarication. Even more, she recognized her need to protect herself.

"This isn't a stable and barn argument. One of us isn't right and one of us isn't wrong." Jake rolled to the side and moved so that he was ultimately next to her in the bed. He pulled her close, pressing a kiss to her head.

"What if we want different things?"

"What if we want each other enough to figure it out?"

For far too long, Caroline had kept her feelings to herself. She'd done it with Jake, but it had started long before that.

All those conversations with her sisters.

The men she'd dated in college.

Even her boss when she'd been overlooked for the Stilton case.

She took the answers she was given and overlooked her own needs.

And she didn't want to do that any longer.

Caroline turned so that she could look up at him. "I think I'd like to live here."

"I really think I'd like you to live here." He tightened his hold, pulling her against his chest for a hug.

"It's settled. We catch my lying brother, we move in together and we watch the sparks fly."

"You think we're still going to fight?"

"Oh, baby, I'm counting on it."

Funny enough, Caroline realized as she sank into another mind-altering kiss, she couldn't imagine it any other way.

Chapter 16

Caroline smoothed her hands over her pressed slacks and wondered if she'd ever felt so uncomfortable in her life. And that included the time a pair of underwear had stuck to her pantyhose and fallen out from beneath her skirt while in court.

She and Jake had arrived at his mother's an hour ago and they were still sitting in the living room, looking at photos of coffins and discussing the funeral arrangements.

Details Jake had already gone over with her several times on the phone.

"I wish we could have an open casket."

"It's not appropriate, Mother. He was hurt too badly for it to make sense."

"People need to see what was done to him," Beverly had cried before grabbing a tissue to dab at her eyes.

She'd dabbed a lot, Caroline had observed, but the tissues never seemed to get all that wet.

It was unkind in the extreme—the woman *had* lost her husband—but Caroline was struggling to find her sympathy chip in all of this.

This was the woman who had stood by and allowed Jake's father to ruin his childhood.

It pissed her off.

But it also added to the lingering anxiety that there was something important they were missing.

She, Jake and Hogan had driven back to Las Vegas, getting in late the night before. The trip had proven uneventful, but the constant watch to make sure they weren't followed had made for an exhausting drive. Trace and Nic had caravanned behind while the rest of the crew had stayed in Liar's Gulch to work on preparations for what Trace kept calling a Peach Street Parade.

"Not an Omaha Hustle," Trace had informed her, "but the discussion over Olivia's help the other day gave me an idea."

"That might work," Nic said, warming to her husband's idea.

"But what is it?" Caroline persisted, suddenly out of her depth as she realized just how skilled Jake and his friends really were.

"In its simplest sense, think of it as lots going on and too many places to look at once," Trace said.

"We use confusion as a strategy," Nic added, her excitement growing as she grabbed a legal pad off Mia's stack in the dining room.

"But what if Zack isn't confused?" Caroline asked.

"Oh, he will be."

Trace's ominous words had lingered in her mind ever since, but she wasn't entirely convinced.

Too much had happened for her to believe Zack and whomever he was working with didn't have a few tricks up their sleeves. But she also trusted that they knew what they were doing.

And just like how she'd felt the day she had her play session with Jordan, Caroline was forced to sit with another uncomfortable truth.

She wasn't in control and she had to find a way to accept that.

She also had to accept that until they worked out a plan to capture Jake's brother and actually understand the depths of his crimes, they had to play nice and pretend everything was okay.

Hence the dinner with Jake's family.

Beverly took a sip of her chardonnay, the discussion of her husband obviously over for the moment. "Caroline, dear. What type of law do you practice?"

"I'm a public defender."

"Why ever would you want to do that? Defending criminals." Beverly shuddered before waving a hand. "You're a beautiful woman. I'm sure you'd have great success in corporate law."

"I studied it, of course, as part of my course work for my law degree. But I've always felt called to the DA's office."

"Just like Jake and his police crusade." Beverly reached for another tissue. "His father always said Jake wasted his potential."

"Jake's right here."

The ringing of the doorbell had kept his mother from saying anything further and when she came back she announced the dinner order she'd called in had arrived.

"Mrs. Stilton, you didn't need to do this. We'd be happy to take you to dinner."

"Oh, I can't do that. Too many people are watching. It would look crass to be out so soon after Al's death."

Caroline saw her opportunity and took it, silently hoping Jake wouldn't be mad. "You've shared what a generous man the senator was. I can't believe he'd want you sitting home. You're quite successful in social circles and your volunteer work is well-known. Surely, you will keep up your commitments."

"Again, dear, I don't wish to be crass."

"But it's valuable work. The senator would have wanted that." Caroline kept her voice level, pushing as much sympathy into it as she could. "Jake's quite proud of the fact you didn't allow the senator's trial to interfere with your public life. He said that you still visit Washington, DC, regularly."

The DC photos and his mother's absences on major dates in Jake's father's trial was still another loose end. The coincidence bothered her and Caroline had continued to question it during each pass through the minimal data they had.

Which made Beverly's response a surprise.

"I've gone a few times to see friends and fulfill the last of my commitments. I didn't care to be there. Frankly, I've never cared to be there."

"You don't like Washington?"

Jake's question was careful, his tone casual as he helped himself to one of the small puff pastries she'd set out for their cocktails.

"I've never liked that place. I played my part as the dutiful senator's wife but the city doesn't interest me."

"But, Mom, you're good at it."

Beverly's eyes—the same shade as Jake's—had widened then. "What does that have to do with anything? Your father and I had a good marriage before that place ruined him. I'd be fine if I never went back."

His mother's complaints were…a revelation.

One Jake was still puzzling through as they walked into the kitchen a little while later.

She hated Washington?

How had he never known?

Dinner was Italian from one of his favorite places and he helped his mother plate it all while Caroline offered to set the dining room table.

"I'm sorry I didn't know."

Beverly stilled from where she pulled a platter off a high shelf and turned to face him. "Know what, darling?"

The past week flashed through his mind, the emotions he'd worked through over his feelings for Caroline suddenly making sense in the broader context of his life.

He'd wrapped himself up so tightly in all the things he hadn't wanted to be for his family—all the expectations he *didn't* want to meet or take on—that his anger had become his own personal echo chamber.

And as a result, he knew nothing about them.

With Zack it was the horror of realizing his brother had made a terrible series of choices.

But with his mother it was something different. The understanding that he'd underestimated her in every way.

"I haven't given you very much credit and I'm sorry for it."

"It's fine."

"No, Mom, it's not."

He took the platter from her hands and set it on the counter before pulling her close. "It's really not."

She went into his arms and for the first time in far too long, he gave his mother a real hug. Not a perfunctory greeting or something done out of duty for a photo op, but genuine contact given out of real care and concern.

Her arms came tight around him. "Thank you."

They stood there for quite a while, neither of them moving or saying anything. But when she finally spoke, it was with a layer of sadness he'd never imagined.

"They took him away, you know."

"Who did?"

"The kingmakers. The ones who decided Al was a star and could serve them well."

"I thought the people decided that."

His mom's smile was small and sad. "Who do you think gives them their choices?" She reached up and straightened his collar. "He always saw the same in you."

"I didn't want any of it. And because of it, I didn't have a relationship with him, either."

"He always said you had *it*. The qualities that people wanted. The strength and honor that people rally behind." She laid her hands on his chest, the sadness fading a bit. "But you did know what you wanted instead and you deserved to have it."

"I thought you hated my job?"

"I hated the danger of your job. That doesn't mean I'm not proud you did it."

One more revelation in a series of them that stunned and stumped and left Jake feeling both buoyed and surprisingly empty.

How had they gotten this far? Him leaving, his father dead, his brother…lost to them.

Trace had spent the week talking about their plans to cause confusion in order to generate answers, but Jake had never expected some of the answers would hurt so much.

And in ways he hadn't imagined.

"Come on, let's go eat. I owe Caroline an apology for my public defender comments, though she probably would make an outstanding corporate lawyer." Beverly picked up one of the serving platters before turning toward him once more. "I was never fair to you, letting my fear of your career choices color how I spoke of them. I did the same to that lovely young woman you can't stop looking at."

"She's amazing." Jake warmed to the subject, picking up the other platter and a basket of rolls. "And I love her."

His mother's smile was radiant as they headed for the dining room. "That makes me happier than you can ever know. And it's all I want for you."

She pushed through the swinging door into the dining room, that smile never wavering in her voice as she called out.

"Zack! I can see you've met Caroline."

Jake followed directly on his mother's heels, his gaze going unerringly to his brother.

Zack stood a bit too still and far too close—a predator waiting to strike—beside Caroline at the table.

But in the gaze that swung around to meet him, Jake recognized one final truth.

He might have underestimated his mother, but he'd sorely miscalculated his brother.

And it put them all in peril.

Jake was quiet as they drove back to her apartment. Caroline wanted to give him the space to process the evening but grew increasingly concerned when quiet reflection turned to raw anger.

He still hadn't said a word, but she saw it stamped clearly in the set of his shoulders and his tight grip on the steering wheel.

And in the lethal cold that had settled in his eyes.

He did his standard check around the entrance to her apartment, searching for any surprises before opening the door. Only when he was confident Hogan was in place and unharmed did he allow her to enter.

They'd done this each time they'd come home and she hadn't gotten used to it. Even knowing their large, furry protector was on the other side hadn't added much in the way of comfort.

Because the fact they needed to do any of this in the first place was the real problem.

Jake didn't even bother to change, just leashed Hogan up to take him outside. He gave his usual instruction to lock up behind him and to wait for his signal and left.

The heavy thud of the door felt absurdly loud as it closed and Caroline stood there staring at it, wondering how to help Jake.

How to take some of this burden.

Since telling each other they loved one another, she and Jake had been inseparable. They talked as easily as they fell into bed and Caroline would almost have called it halcyon.

Except when it came to his family.

Jake refused to speak about them or even admit how he felt. And every comment she made around Al Stilton's death was met with dismissal. It concerned her, but more than that, she knew the sad reality.

Grief was an ugly taskmaster and it was going to have its way.

His continued claims that it didn't hurt as bad because he and his father weren't close was nothing more than an excuse.

Would tonight change that? She'd heard him and his mother through the door—not eavesdropping because she couldn't hear what they said—but more how they spoke to one another.

It had been warm.

Genuine.

And she'd felt a lightening that they might find a way forward.

Then Zack had arrived and all the air had been sucked from the dining room.

She'd summoned up every ounce of her legal training on courtroom etiquette and theatrics and remained warm and polite, never once allowing the crawling shudders through that threatened to roll down her spine.

But they were there.

Jake did their preplanned knock on the door, pulling her from the memory and allowing one of those shudders to sneak through—and she responded with their pre-agreed signal.

Hogan entered first, followed by Jake, who still wore that surly, frustrated expression.

It pulled at her and without checking the impulse, she walked to him, putting her arms around him. "Why don't we talk."

"I don't want to talk. I don't want to analyze. I sure as hell don't want to plan." That cold fire she'd observed when they got out of the car was no longer banked in his eyes.

Instead, it flared high and bright and obviously needed someplace to land.

"Then I have an idea better than all of those things."

Without breaking stride or dropping her arms, she whispered some of the coarsest sex language she'd ever spoken in her life, right into his ear.

And was rewarded with a harsh expletive as he dragged himself from her arms and stalked toward the kitchen.

Oh, yes, she thought as she slipped out of her heels and kicked them next to the couch. Grief was a harsh taskmaster indeed.

A bottle of vodka was on the counter, the seal cracked as he searched for a glass.

"Far right cabinet."

"Leave me alone."

"So you can get drunk?"

"So I can think about what a fouled-up mess of a family I have. A dead father. A mother I haven't actually looked at or listened to in more than two decades. And a brother who's got fantasies of killing me and everything I hold dear."

"Why bother with the glass, then? Just take the bottle."

"Damn it!"

The bottle in his hand slammed into the sink, a heavy shattering as the thick crystal hit stainless steel.

Before he could reach for it, she grabbed at his sleeve. "Leave it. You're likely to cut yourself to ribbons in this state. It's all contained. We'll get it later."

Feral with his anger, he pushed off the edge of the sink and stalked past her, back toward the living room. He'd nearly made it when he seemingly thought better of it.

Caroline had already started out of the room, intending to grab her heels and head to bed, when she heard it.

That low, keening moan that came out just before he dragged her into his arms and pressed her back against the doorway to the kitchen.

One hand gently stroked her face while the other gripped her hips, fisting in the thin material of her blouse.

"He touched you. Had his hands on you and his eyes on you and his attention on you. He was there and all I could do was look at him watching you and pretend I didn't know what he'd done."

The words were laced with so much anguish Caroline's heart broke with it.

"I'm fine, Jake." She pressed a kiss to where his open collar made a V at his throat. "I'm here with you and I'm fine."

She continued kissing him, chest, throat, jaw. Anywhere she could reach with her hands still at her sides and his body caging her against the doorway.

His head dropped beside hers and she pressed her lips to his cheek, continuing to whisper against his ear. "I'm fine."

And then there were no whispers.

No shouts.

No words.

The large body that covered hers moved, his hands rough on her clothing as he sought her skin. Buttons flew and she heard the distinct rip of her blouse as his fingers traced her skin before moving on to decimate her bra.

Unwilling to be left behind, she matched his speed with her own, dragging his shirt off before moving on to his slacks. His belt gave her the slightest trouble as she had to work through the mind-numbing pleasure of his hands on her skin, but she finally got it undone, sliding one hand beneath the waistband to grip him fully while her other loosened the closure and undid the zipper.

He moaned in her mouth, his tongue doing wicked, carnal things against her own, mimicking what she knew he'd do with his body.

What he'd do to her and with her and for her.

He pressed himself into her palm as she continued the long, sure strokes, his own hands plying her skin with pleasure.

It might have been seconds or it could have been hours; Caroline was far from knowing. From caring.

She only needed him.

Everything else faded away when they were together and she allowed the mindless oblivion to push out all the clamoring.

All the sadness.

All the danger.

Here she was safe. With Jake.

Always Jake.

With their clothes in disarray, some hanging from body parts, others around their ankles, he finally found her center.

Found his way in as he pressed her more firmly against the doorway.

And as she moved with him, her body surrounding him in welcome, Caroline let herself fall.

And forget about what waited beyond the door.

Caroline zipped up the demure black dress and considered the day ahead. The former senator was being buried and all they'd planned for over the past week was coming to fruition.

It scared the hell out of her.

Even as she continued to reassure herself that all their planning and preparation couldn't fail.

They knew their enemy. There was actual proof Zack was behind her attack as well as the bomb at the ranch and they'd constructed a rock-solid case against him. Trace and Nic had worked with some locals they both knew from their days in the CIA, and Dawson had called in a favor with someone he went through the academy with.

They'd deliberately avoided having Jake reach out to any former colleagues, not knowing if Zack's tentacles had reached the police department, but not willing to risk it.

It was the same reason she'd maintained her workload, keeping her head down and her questions minimal in the office.

No one needed to know about her quick trip to Wyoming on her days off. She hadn't told anyone where she was going so it was easy enough to lie and say she'd enjoyed a few days of staycation to rest and recharge her batteries.

She hadn't quit yet, not wanting to lose access to her

files, but as soon as they made a convincing arrest on Zack, she was getting out.

She had a future to plan for and couldn't wait to get to it.

Everything was in place.

It had all come down to the execution.

"You look like you're going to a funeral."

Jake had made a variation on the same joke all morning, his gallows humor a counterpoint to his continued concerns something was going to go wrong.

"We just need to get through today. Trace and Nic are set with the details to trap your brother. Everything's in place for the pickup right after the funeral finishes." She crossed over to him where he tied the gray tie that matched his black suit. "I'm more worried about you."

"You don't need to be."

"Today's a hard day."

"Nothing can change that."

That ever-present need to poke and spar with him vanished as she considered it from his side.

All she saw was what waited for them on the other side. But for Jake?

Until they caught Zack and made him pay for his crimes, his focus needed to be on getting *through* it all.

She could only hope that the tentative shoots of understanding between him and his mother would aid in reducing some of the burden.

Which brought her right back around to Zack.

They'd been careful and with work as her excuse, they'd removed any chance of her seeing him again as Jake finalized the funeral details with his family.

Did Zack sense anything was happening in the background? Or was his own mask so firmly in place he wasn't aware his brother had figured him out?

It was only a few more hours. They just had to get through the funeral.

That had been her steady litany to herself since they woke up. Everything was in place and they'd collected all the evidence they needed, between the attack at her home and the footage from the ranch cameras.

She could only hope Trace's *Peach Street Parade* was as effective as he claimed.

"I'm going to take Hogan out one more time." Jake pressed a kiss to her cheek, lingering there. "I wish I could bring him."

He'd discussed it with her mother and gotten an absolute no on that front. Jake had nearly overridden her and then seemed to relent, their new understanding enough to respect her wishes.

"It will be over soon. All of it."

"I know."

He headed out and she quickly finished up with applications of lipstick and hairspray.

And then headed for the living room to wait for Jake's signal.

It came quickly enough and she rapped back her own.

It took Jake an extra moment with the return signal for all-clear and it should have been her clue.

Because they'd practiced it.

And she knew the risks if she ignored it.

But that clamoring awareness that something was off didn't hit until she'd fully opened the door.

Her instincts went into fight mode and she was already trying to slam it home when Zack pushed his way in, Jake or Hogan nowhere in sight.

Chapter 17

Jake lay in a black haze, his head throbbing as he lifted a hand to block the unrelenting sun that pierced his eyelids.

What happened?

What—

He struggled to sit up, only to realize that he was trussed up behind what looked like a maintenance shed, his wrists in zip ties behind his back. Hogan lay a few feet away, his body prone and his tongue lolling out.

How the hell had someone gotten the jump on him?

Caroline!

Panic swelled in his chest and he fought around the breath clogging in his lungs. Forcing deep breaths in and out, he tried to calm his mind along with his breathing. And realized the details were slowly coming back when he looked over at Hogan. A small dart stuck up from the dog's back left hindquarters and a few more impressions of their earlier walk slid into place in Jake's mind.

The dart in his leg must have been what caused Hogan to stumble, and Jake had been so focused on seeing what was wrong with his partner he never registered the person at his back who'd cold-cocked him on the head.

Zack.

They'd been so focused on their plans it never occurred

to any of them that his brother might have been making several of his own.

Jake struggled against the ties once more before falling back. Struggling wasn't going to do him any good. He'd be far better off wiggling his way away from the shed out into the grounds that surrounded the apartment where someone would see him.

Where he had a shot at getting someone to help them, even if it was just to call the police and help create a commotion on the lawn.

Because there was no way he'd be fast enough to get to Caroline trussed up like this.

He could only hope she followed their agreed-to process.

The careful way they'd practiced coming in and out of the apartment.

And the agreed-to signals for an all-clear.

Zack was *here*.

That thought filled her as he pushed his way into the apartment, kicking the door closed at his back, a gun held firmly in his hand.

Caroline backed up, not wanting to be anywhere near him. And not wanting to be a barrier if Jake and Hogan came rushing into the apartment.

If they were even able to.

"Where's Jake?"

"Gone, like he always is. Figured you'd get the gesture."

"He was here five minutes ago."

"He was standing upright, too."

Zack laughed at his own joke, the discordant sounds at odds with the man who stood before her.

He was attractive, with a similar build to Jake's and the same blue eyes as both Jake and his mother. He cut a similar figure to his older brother as well, with broad shoulders and a slim waist.

So much was similar, anyone would make them for brothers.

Yet, as Caroline looked at the man standing before her, she saw none of the things that drew her to Jake.

The large, fit body was strong, but she didn't see someone capable of uplifting others.

The smile was cunning and calculating instead of inviting.

And those blue eyes didn't carry an ounce of warmth. Or, she was increasingly coming to realize, sanity.

Whatever this man had once been—whatever hope and promise there'd been for him—was gone.

In its place was a monster.

Despite the throbbing in his head, Jake found a way to scoot himself over to the maintenance shed. Once there, he used his feet, pushing off the ground and the building for maximum effect.

The movements were far slower than he'd have liked, but he managed to clear the edge of the small building and could see the apartment grounds spread out before him.

Several two-story buildings rimmed the broad courtyard space, with another set of structures farther off in the distance. He calculated how far he was from Caroline's apartment and, with startling clarity, realized it wasn't far.

Which meant Zack's plan was to subdue him and then quickly get her out of there.

His brother didn't have any time to waste, especially with the funeral in an hour, which meant Jake didn't, either.

Hogan whimpered and he glanced over to where the dog struggled to sit up, his eyes glassy with the drug Zack had used to take him down. He wanted to call him over but figured it would be easier to let him rest until more of the drug wore off.

Frustrated at his absolute uselessness with his hands tied behind his back—and aware the mid-morning hour meant the courtyard was rather empty of people—he needed to *move*. If he got lucky and someone showed up, he could approach them then.

Right now, he needed to get to Caroline.

Curling over to his side, Jake pulled up his knees and worked his weight onto his shoulder until he had enough distance to further lift himself up onto his elbow. It was awkward but effective and gave him enough leverage to get to his feet.

And nearly tripped for attempting to move too quickly with the zip ties around his ankles.

Forcing himself to slow down, Jake began the painstaking walk toward the apartment.

And hoped like hell he wasn't too late.

Caroline mentally calculated how long Jake had been gone as she continued to stare Zack down.

He hadn't argued when she said five minutes, but how long had it really been since he'd left to walk Hogan?

She'd abstractly glanced at the clock when he walked out of the bedroom, thinking they had to leave in about ten minutes for the funeral. And had looked at the small clock she kept on a nearby end table when she'd reached the door at Zack's knock, the ten minutes nearly up.

"You work fast," she said, her only goal to suss out if Zack was working alone. "But I'm not sure what you hope to gain doing this an hour before the funeral."

"Which makes this the perfect time. No one would ever

assume I'm here. Especially once everyone, including all that press, sees me at the funeral."

"You've got it all figured out."

"I don't like to waste time. I'm strong and efficient and I get things done. It's why I'm going to be so effective in Washington."

"That's the end game? Your dad's seat in the senate?"

"For starters."

Good God, he was delusional. "You think you've got what it takes?"

"I know I do."

"Then why are you so busy putting out attacks on women and bombing out your brother's home? He's washed his hands of this place. I'd have thought you would be happy. Instead, you're dragging him back here. Putting the focus on him."

"Putting the focus on me!" Zack screamed it and Caroline took another few steps back. She knew she needed to get to the door—backing up toward the kitchen only put her farther away from it—but something about staring at the man who looked so much like Jake but was so very far from the man she loved disgusted her.

She only wanted to get away.

"And when he's gone, all anyone will see is the grieving brother. The grieving son."

Caroline backed up a few more paces, only to hit the door frame. Something deeply sad filled her at the memory of what she and Jake had shared here. Their incendiary coming together, in desperate need for what they gave to each other.

And now she stood in the same place and questioned if she'd ever walk back out of this apartment, let alone see Jake again.

The thoughts nearly consumed her when something in Zack's words penetrated through.

"Grieving son?"

"You don't actually think that was an accident, do you? Some random prison yard violence?" He did laugh at that, more of those big belly laughs that crawled over her skin like acid.

Zack killed his father?

Or arranged for it, based on the fact that he hadn't actually worked the shiv that had killed the senator.

Caroline calculated the distance between herself and the door, frustrated she'd come this way.

Angry she'd given in to the fear.

Zack stalked another step closer and her gaze swung in an arc, taking in the space around her.

And there, just at the edge of the counter, was a piece of the bottle Jake had smashed the other night. How they'd both missed it for two days she had no idea, but it glittered there, waiting for her.

Without checking the impulse, her only goal getting out, Caroline leaped for the broken glass, whipping it around to slash at him as soon as she had it firmly in hand.

Zack screamed as the bottle shard ran the length of his face, narrowly missing his eye in the process. The gun fell to the floor, firing as it dropped.

The errant shot went wide, ending up somewhere toward her bedroom, but Zack seemed oblivious as he continued to scream, clutching his face, blood pouring out over his fingers.

"You bitch!"

But it was the voice behind him that broke through the noise.

"Shh. Quiet now, Zack."

He turned, his mouth dropping as he took in his mother.

Caroline could only watch as Beverly bent and picked up the gun, then tilted her head toward the couch.

"Go sit over there."

* * *

"Jake!"

Trace hollered his name as he raced toward him, Nic keeping pace right alongside. His painfully slow walk across the grounds had felt endless and he hadn't even seen them drive up as he worked to navigate the wide expanses of stone and desert plant life.

Nic reached him first, a knife already in hand. She dropped to the ground and cut the zips while Trace moved around his back and cut the ties on his wrists.

Shaking to get the feeling back, Jake didn't wait. "Her apartment's over there. He's got her."

Neither Trace nor Nic questioned whom he referred to; they just followed him as he hightailed it to Caroline's apartment.

The biggest part of him desperately hoped she hadn't opened the door.

That she'd recognized any signal given wasn't *their* signal and had barred the door.

But as he, Trace and Nic closed the distance to the apartment, he saw the open door and heard the shot.

Jake came up short at the sound of the shot, his knees nearly buckling in fear of what they would find.

But there was no time to wait.

He had to get to her.

And as he raced the last ten yards to her door, the loud bark behind him confirmed his partner was up and moving.

And going through the door with him.

Beverly held the gun, her gaze roaming over it before she turned to look at her son. Zack had listened to her, taking a seat on the couch as he held his face in his hands.

Caroline simply stood there and watched her, the piece of glass still gripped firmly between her fingers.

"Why are you doing this?"

"Because my son needs to pay for his crimes."

Which son?

Zack's blood still dripped over her hand where she'd slashed at him and she stared down at it now, all the implications of Beverly's words sinking in.

Was she with Jake?

Or against him?

Even as Caroline didn't dare give herself too much room for hope, something quiet unfurled in her chest all the same.

Beverly specifically said *pay for his crimes.*

And Jake had committed none.

Beverly looked at the shard of glass but made no move to ask her to put it down.

"I've known Zack's ambitions were a problem for far too long. I erroneously believed he'd heal. I'd put too much hope that once Jake was gone these things I kept seeing in him would go away."

"You knew?"

Beverly's quiet smile never reached her eyes. "I'm his mother. I know my boys. And I thought that once the brother Zack resented was out of the picture and far away, that it would get better."

And then her face crumpled, tears filling those eyes so like Jake's before they spilled over.

"I thought he'd be okay."

Caroline leaped forward just before Beverly dropped the gun, wanting to offer comfort but unwilling to give Zack a moment to get the upper hand.

Once she knew she had the gun secure in her own grip, she pulled Beverly close with her free arm.

"It's okay. And it's going to be okay."

"I don't know that it will be."

The woman's tears were a hot brand against Caroline's shoulder, a mother's love running through every bit of it.

Her love and her regret, braided in equal measure.

Zack had quieted, but he started screaming again from the couch as Hogan raced into the room, growling and barking at him.

Jake raced in right behind, Trace and Nic on his heels.

Confusion warred with relief, both emotions stamped clearly on that beautiful face as he took in his brother and his mother before his gaze landed firmly on her.

"Are you okay?"

"I'm fine." Caroline smiled, feeling the way it trembled on her lips. "You?"

"Been better."

"Yeah. Me, too."

With Nic and Trace and Hogan standing guard over Zack, Jake crossed to where she still stood with her arm around his mother. He gently took the gun from her hand, setting the safety and putting it on the counter.

With that done, Jake moved back to them, pulling her and his mother into his arms.

"We're going to be okay. I promise."

And as Caroline stood in the circle of his arms, she closed her eyes and hung on.

Jake Stilton was a man of his word.

And he loved her.

And if Bernice was right, if more than half of love was about showing up, then they all were going to be okay.

Epilogue

"No, no, dear. Liquid eyeliner takes a more delicate hand. Like this."

Jake eyed Trace from the other side of the kitchen table as his mother continued her makeup tutorial with Olivia. The two of them sat side by side, staring into a lighted makeup mirror that was large enough to be visible from space.

It had been four months since his father's funeral.

Since the depravity of his brother's crimes had come to light and Zack had earned himself a lifetime stay in a maximum security prison.

Since they'd made it to *the after*, as Caroline called it.

And in that time, Jake had recognized they were healing. He hadn't quite convinced his mother to move to Wyoming, but she was currently on week three of her most recent visit and didn't show any signs of leaving.

She and Bernice had become quite the talk of Liar's Gulch, their ladies-who-lunch gatherings at the diner garnering quite a bit of interest. They'd also become the local instigators of a social hour, two nights a week in the hotel bar downtown, and were credited with bringing in more than a few of the local over-sixty-five crowd.

His mother was even dating a man from town—Grizzly Bob as Olivia had dubbed him—and the name had stuck.

Even by his mother.

It was a significant departure from her old life but just as he had, she seemed to find the western wilderness more of a fit than anyone would have thought possible.

"Trace. Jake." His mother looked up from the tutorial. "Tell us what you think."

Trace was blunt. As expected.

"I think it's too much black stuff on her eyes."

"Dad!"

His mother was already waving a hand and proclaiming, "That was nonsense," when Jake figured he'd hightail it out to the barn and do some chores.

"Coward," Trace hissed as he walked out of the kitchen.

"You know it," Jake agreed, unfazed by the insult.

He made it as far as the paddock when he caught sight of Caroline, high atop Orlando, moving into a steady canter around the ring.

They'd been working with the horse for four solid months and she was the only one he allowed on his back.

But that was healing, too.

She expertly maneuvered Orlando around the ring and Jake gave himself the pleasure of simply watching the woman he loved, her cheeks reddened by the brisk air, doing something she loved.

He'd almost lost this.

And not only because of the pain his brother caused, but also because he'd been too afraid to reach out and take what she offered.

Friendship.

Honesty.

And love.

Caroline dismounted, giving Orlando a chance to rest and walk about at his leisure. Satisfied he was good on his own, she walked over and stepped up on the first rung of the paddock, planting a kiss on him before hopping back off the bottom rail. Her smile was as wide and bright as the vivid blue above them.

"Hey there."

"Hey yourself. He's looking good."

"He's coming along. Every day he gets a little more comfortable. A little less scared."

"Sort of like me?"

She cocked her head at that, considering. "You've made up for lost time."

"It's all that *and*," he couldn't resist teasing her. "It's very therapeutic."

"Oh, is it now?"

"He still won't let me ride him."

She glanced back at the horse, letting out a low whistle. Orlando came straight over, never hesitating.

"Why don't you give it a try now?"

Jake wasn't nearly as sure as she was, but he climbed over the paddock rails anyway, figuring Orlando would let him know pretty quickly if he didn't want him there.

The winter wind blew against them as he placed his foot in the stirrups. Caroline held Orlando's lead in place, but she didn't need to. The horse stayed still and allowed him to mount.

And that, Jake realized, was trust in a nutshell.

You found your people and believed they'd stick with you and that they'd always treat you with understanding.

He'd certainly found his.

And when Caroline climbed up behind him, wrapping her arms around his waist, Jake twisted his head to kiss her.

And knew he'd always find the warmest welcome in her arms.

* * * * *

Get up to 4 Free Books!

We'll send you 2 free books from each series you try
PLUS a free Mystery Gift.

Both the **Harlequin Intrigue**® and **Harlequin**® Romantic Suspense series feature compelling novels filled with heart-racing action-packed romance that will keep you on the edge of your seat.

YES! Please send me 2 FREE novels from the Harlequin Intrigue or Harlequin Romantic Suspense series and my FREE gift (gift is worth about $10 retail). I may cancel anytime by emailing ReaderServiceInfo@Harlequin.com or by calling 1-800-873-8635. If I don't cancel, I will receive 6 brand-new Harlequin Intrigue Larger-Print books every month and be billed just $7.19 each in the U.S. or $7.99 each in Canada, or 4 brand-new Harlequin Romantic Suspense books every month and be billed just $6.39 each in the U.S. or $7.19 each in Canada, a savings of 20% off the cover price. It's quite a bargain! Shipping and handling is just 75¢ per book in the U.S. and $1.75 per book in Canada.* I understand that accepting the free books and gift places me under no obligation to buy anything—they are mine to keep for free no matter what I decide.

Choose one:
- ☐ **Harlequin Intrigue Larger-Print** (199/399 BPA G3CD)
- ☐ **Harlequin Romantic Suspense** (240/340 BPA G3CD)
- ☐ **Or Try Both!** (199/399 & 240/340 BPA G3CE)

Name (please print)

Address   Apt. #

City   State/Province   Zip/Postal Code

Email: Please check this box ☐ if you would like to receive newsletters and promotional emails from Harlequin Enterprises ULC and its affiliates. You can unsubscribe anytime.

Mail to the **Harlequin Reader Service:**
IN U.S.A.: P.O. Box 1341, Buffalo, NY 14240-8531
IN CANADA: P.O. Box 603, Fort Erie, Ontario L2A 5X3

Want to explore our other series or interested in ebooks? Visit www.ReaderService.com or call 1-800-873-8635.

HIHRS2603